Gone
with the
Woof

Center Point
Large Print

Also by Laurien Berenson and available from
Center Point Large Print:

Doggie Day Care Murder
Unleashed
Hush Puppy
Dog Eat Dog

**This Large Print Book carries the
Seal of Approval of N.A.V.H.**

A Melanie Travis Mystery

Gone with the Woof

Laurien Berenson

CENTER POINT LARGE PRINT
THORNDIKE, MAINE

This Center Point Large Print edition is published
in the year 2013 by arrangement with
Kensington Publishing Corp.

Copyright © 2013 by Laurien Berenson.

The text of this Large Print edition is unabridged.
In other aspects, this book may vary
from the original edition.
Printed in the United States of America
on permanent paper.
Set in 16-point Times New Roman type.

ISBN: 978-1-61173-890-2

Library of Congress Cataloging-in-Publication Data

Berenson, Laurien.
Gone With the Woof : A Melanie Travis Canine Mystery /
    Laurien Berenson. — Center Point Large Print edition.
pages cm
ISBN 978-1-61173-890-2 (Library binding : alk. paper)
1. Dogs—Fiction. 2. Large type books. I. Title.
PS3552.E6963G66 2013
813′.54—dc23
                                                    2013028199

Gone
with the
Woof

Chapter 1

Life is made up of small moments, most passing by in the blink of an eye, unremarked and unremarkable. But every so often one of those small moments expands and time seems to stop. We're faced with an occurrence so intense, so monumental, that the rest of life's cluttered minutiae simply slip away like a passing wisp of breeze.

What remains is a haze of shock and emptiness, a void that we must somehow learn to negotiate. There's an elemental shift in worldview and a lesson never forgotten: that nothing in life is as permanent as we once believed.

That was how I felt when a murderer whom I'd been chasing stood two feet away from me and looked me in the eye, then lifted a gun to his temple and blew his brains out.

It was an instant when everything changed.

Maybe clarity of vision is a sign of maturity. If so, I earned mine the hard way. But in that fleeting speck of time when I put my own life at risk and watched another life end, I knew with absolute certainty what was important to me and what was not.

I had a new baby, an almost new husband, and a nine-year-old son, whom I loved more than anything. I also had a houseful of dogs and an extended family whose only goal seemed to be to drive me crazy. The thought that I might never have seen any of them again was beyond unbearable.

And yet in that single moment I had put all of that on the line. What was I thinking? I didn't know.

One thing I did know. I needed a break.

"I just want to say that you've become rather dull."

"Really?" My tone might have been a bit dry.

I was sitting across the kitchen table from my Aunt Peg, a woman who in her first sixty-five years has stirred up more excitement and controversy than many South American dictators. Come to think of it, she also runs the members of her family like a small, somewhat unruly, junta. Peg stands six feet tall and has iron-gray hair and sharp brown eyes. Should a brawl erupt anywhere in the vicinity, my money's on her.

"Yes, really. Don't make me say it twice. I shouldn't have to say it at all. You used to be interesting. Now . . ." Aunt Peg stood up, walked over to the counter, and poured herself a second cup of Earl Grey tea. Her gaze slid pointedly to the window over the sink.

It was New Year's Day, and we'd had six inches of fresh snow overnight. Eighteen months had passed since I'd made the decision to try to realign the balance in my life. I'd wanted to attain some sense of normalcy, and I liked to think that I'd achieved that goal.

What Aunt Peg saw in the backyard was my husband, Sam, and our older son, Davey, shoveling the new snow off the deck. From the way the pile was shaping up, I suspected there might be a snowman in the offing.

Younger son, Kevin, twenty-two months old and all but swallowed up by a snowsuit, boots, and mittens, was toddling unsteadily around the yard, accompanied by several big black Standard Poodles. That was what passed for normal at my house.

"Now I'm happy," I said.

"So you think," Aunt Peg sniffed. "You're what? Thirty-five years old?"

I nodded warily. Not because her assessment of my age was wrong, but because Aunt Peg never begins a lecture without a purpose in mind, usually one that involves work for me.

"You need to get back in the game."

"Excuse me?"

"For one thing, you need to figure out what you're going to do with the rest of your life now that you no longer have a job."

Aunt Peg was referring to the fact that after

Kevin was born, I had taken a leave of absence from my position as special needs tutor at a private school in Greenwich, Connecticut. A single semester away had now stretched to three.

When Davey was little, I'd been a single mother. I'd had to work. This time around I had a choice. And the thought of leaving Kevin with a nanny or an au pair didn't appeal at all. Even if my son's current favorite word—from an admittedly limited vocabulary—was an emphatic and defiant *no.*

"I have a job," I said calmly. "I'm a mother."

"Oh, please. Hillary Clinton is a mother. It didn't stop her from becoming secretary of state."

"You want me to go into politics?"

Okay, that was immature. The verbal equivalent of sticking out my tongue. But give Aunt Peg the slightest bit of encouragement, and she tends to run roughshod over anyone in the vicinity. Speaking as the person most likely to be trampled, what can I say? Sometimes I sink to my kids' level.

"Don't be ridiculous. I want you to use your brain. I want you to think. I have an idea."

"Wonderful," I muttered.

The back door came flying inward, bringing with it a blast of cold air, five scrambling, sodden Standard Poodles, and three rosy-cheeked, snow-covered men of varying sizes. Davey had his gloved hands cupped together. He was holding a snowball the size of a small globe.

Sam was just behind him, carrying Kevin. Even in chunky boots and a puffy down jacket, with a red nose and snow-tipped eyelashes, Sam looked like the kind of man most women would want to take straight to bed. Even after six years together, I'm no exception.

Sam lowered the toddler into my arms and, having heard my last pronouncement, said, "What's the matter?"

"Aunt Peg has an idea."

"Good day for it," Sam said mildly. He and Aunt Peg are the best of friends. Sometimes that irks me, but mostly I try to rise above it. "New Year's resolutions and all."

Davey, who had pulled open a low cabinet and was rummaging around inside, stood up and spun around. "Are we going to make resolutions?"

"Sure, if you want to. Put that snowball in the sink, okay?"

"I can't. I'm going to report on it for science class."

Davey's tall for his age. He takes after his father, my ex-husband, Bob. They're both long limbed and graceful. But my son's personality is all me. He could argue the spots off a Dalmatian.

Davey turned back to the cabinet and withdrew a large mixing bowl. "How long do you think it will take to melt?"

"It's started already," I mentioned. Between the five Poodles, the three sets of boots, and the water dripping from his hands, the floor was awash with melted snow.

Sam reached over, plucked the snowball out of Davey's hands, and plopped it in the bowl on the counter. Aunt Peg grabbed a towel from the stack near the back door and went to work drying Poodle legs. That left me to get Kevin undressed.

"Who wants hot chocolate?" I asked.

"No!" cried Kevin. I'd unzipped the front of his snowsuit and peeled the top off his shoulders. He yanked his arms free and waved his small hands in the air.

"Gotta love a kid who knows what he wants," Sam said.

"I think he takes after Aunt Peg." I lifted Kevin up and freed his legs. He kicked off his red rubber boots and they landed in a puddle on the floor beneath my chair.

"And isn't it nice that someone finally does," said Peg.

It took another twenty minutes to get everyone warm, dry, and organized. Amazingly, the floor even got mopped. Once it was dry, the Poodles lay down around us, forming a canine obstacle course for unwary walkers or—if you were Kevin's size—a fluffy stool on which to perch.

The five of them were Sam's and my blended

canine family. Faith and Eve were a mother-and-daughter duo, originally Davey's and mine. Faith had been bred by Aunt Peg and gifted to me six years earlier, either as a reward or an assignment. I'd never been entirely sure which. Raven and Casey were two champion Poodles from Sam's breeding program that he'd brought with him when he moved east from Michigan to Connecticut.

The remaining Poodle was Tar, the only male in the group. Also bred by Aunt Peg, he had been Sam's special dog: a champion whom Sam had campaigned to numerous Group and Best in Show wins at venues up and down the East Coast. Now retired, he, like the others, wore the close-cropped, easy-to-care-for sporting trim. With two children keeping us busy, both Sam and I were happy to be taking a break from having to "do hair."

"Finally," said Aunt Peg when we were seated around the table once more. "Can we now get back to the business at hand?"

"Certainly," said Sam. "Who wants to begin?"

"Me," cried Davey.

"Excellent. Someone with initiative." Aunt Peg stared at me pointedly over the top of her mug. Peg's sweet tooth is legendary, and her hot chocolate was coated with a layer of mini-marshmallows. "Unlike certain of my other relatives."

"I resolve to eat fewer lima beans," Davey said firmly. "And not to lose my homework. And not to call Kimberly Winterbottom stupid, even when she is."

"Good job," I said. "I don't like lima beans, either."

"Kimberly Winterbottom?" asked Sam.

"She thinks she knows everything." In sixth grade now, Davey was in his first year at Hart Middle School in North Stamford. The move from elementary school made him feel very grown up. "And she doesn't. Not even close."

"Fair enough," said Peg. "Sam, would you like to go next?"

"Not me," Sam said, demurring. He knew better than to get in Peg's way. "I'm not ready yet. Why don't you take my turn?"

"I'll be happy to."

No surprise there. Aunt Peg had been waiting for this opening since she'd arrived an hour earlier. Now she swiveled her seat around to face me.

"You've become boring," she said.

You know, just in case I'd missed that insult the first time.

"There you go," I replied cheerfully. "That can be my resolution. Be less boring."

New Year's resolutions have never been my thing. I just don't see the point of vowing on the first day of the year to read more books, lose ten pounds, or run a marathon. Because if I didn't want to do that stuff before, what are the chances that a change of date is going to make me want to do it now?

"You're stuck in a rut," Aunt Peg persisted. My easy acquiescence didn't even slow her down. "I can help with that."

"Don't tell me," I said. "Here comes the idea."

"As well it should. Somebody has to shake things up around here."

Kevin punctuated that thought with a loud bang. Settled on the floor, next to the cabinet Davey had opened earlier, he was engaged in one of his favorite occupations, stacking pots and pans. The leaning tower he'd been erecting had just lost its battle with gravity. Judging by the building skills he'd displayed thus far, Sam and I were guessing that a career in architecture was not in his future.

Aunt Peg didn't even lose a beat. "Edward March," she said.

Sam looked up. "What about him?"

"He's turning in his judge's license."

"Wow," said Sam. "I wouldn't have thought he'd ever retire. March seems like the type of judge who'd hope to croak in the Best in Show ring at Westminster, as he pointed out the winning dog."

"Don't we all," Aunt Peg remarked. "And Edward does like his dramatic moments. Nevertheless, I believe health issues have gotten in the way. He's taken very few assignments in the last several years, and now he seems to think that it's time to bow out gracefully and on his own terms."

"Who is Edward March?" I asked.

Aunt Peg and Sam have both been a part of the dog show world for so long that occasionally they forget that I don't have their wealth of experience and insider information to draw upon. Aunt Peg's Cedar Crest Kennel, founded decades earlier with her late husband, Max, had produced some of the top winning Standard Poodles in dog show history. Once a successful owner-handler who'd competed in dozens of shows a year, Aunt Peg still kept up the same hectic schedule, now serving as a much-in-demand dog show judge.

Sam's tenure in the dog show world was shorter in duration than Aunt Peg's, but he had been no less devoted. His Shadowrun Kennel was a small but select operation. Like my aunt, Sam had spent countless hours studying pedigrees, genetics, and the best available bloodlines. He was also a talented and enthusiastic dog show exhibitor.

Basically, in this group I was the redheaded stepchild.

"Don't worry, Mom," said Davey. "I don't know, either."

I reached over and plopped a few more marshmallows in his mug to thank him for the support.

"You don't need to know." Aunt Peg slanted her nephew a fond glance. "Whereas you"—her gaze shifted in my direction—"could be better informed."

Nothing new there.

I sipped my cocoa and leaned back in my seat. "Why don't you tell me what I'm missing?"

"Edward March is nothing less than dog show royalty."

"Like Prince William?" asked Davey. He had watched the royal wedding on television, fascinated less by the ceremony than by the vintage cars that transported the royal family.

"Not exactly," Sam explained. "Prince William has a hereditary position. Edward March earned his acclaim. His Russet Kennel was started in the nineteen sixties and soon became the driving force in Irish Setters. He was single-handedly responsible for dozens of champions in that breed throughout the second half of the last century. If there was an Irish Setter in the Group or Best in Show ring anywhere on the East Coast, chances are it was a Russet dog."

"Bob and Janie Forsyth handled all his dogs for many years," said Aunt Peg. "Surely, you know who they are."

Of course I did. The esteemed husband-and-wife team was dogdom's most famous couple. As handlers, they'd all but ruled the sporting dog and terrier rings for decades, before retiring to become

17

highly respected judges. I had shown Eve under Janie Forsyth and had picked up two points toward her championship.

"So he's a man who used to have good dogs," I said. So far, this all sounded like old news.

"Not just good," Aunt Peg corrected. "Some of the very best in his breed. And like his handlers, he followed up by becoming a very good judge. His opinion really meant something, and that's a rare gift. If Edward March put up your dog, you knew you had a good one."

That was high praise coming from Aunt Peg. She didn't hand out accolades lightly.

"And?" I asked.

"And what? Isn't that enough?"

"It's plenty. But what does it have to do with me?"

"Oh, that." Aunt Peg sniffed, as if the change in topic from dog show royalty to her wayward niece was distinctly uninteresting.

"Now you've got me curious, too," said Sam. "So March is turning in his judge's license. Where does Melanie fit in?"

"Apparently, in celebration of his fifty-some years in the dog show world, Edward intends to write his memoirs. Anyone who's ever seen his desk could tell you that organization isn't his strong suit. He's looking to find a coauthor to help him do the job properly. I told him I knew just the right person."

Chapter 2

I sat up straight in my chair. "Me?"

"Of course, you. You'd be perfect for the job."

"But I'm not an author. I don't have the slightest idea about what goes into writing a book."

"You used to be a teacher. You tutored children who were behind in English class. It's all the same thing, isn't it? Just grammar and stringing sentences together in a way that makes sense. How hard can that be?"

That was the sort of question Aunt Peg always asked when she wanted to involve me in a project that I knew better than to attempt. The problem is that my aunt has never run from a challenge in her life. So it's never crossed her mind that her relatives don't feel equally invincible.

"It sounds like an interesting idea," said Sam. "From what I know about Edward March, he's quite a character. I'm sure he has some fascinating stories to tell. His life was pretty much dog show history in the making. You could end up writing the definitive record of our sport over the last half century."

It's not as if *that* lowered the intimidation factor any.

"Will there be pictures in your book?" asked Davey.

"I should think so," Aunt Peg told him. "What good is history without illustrations?"

Sam nodded in agreement.

Did you hear that? "*My* book," Davey had said. And nobody had argued with him. Not even me.

That thought was enough to goad me back into the conversation.

"Wait a minute," I said. "I'm not even sure there's going to be a book."

"Of course there's going to be a book," Aunt Peg informed me. "That's already a given. With or without your help, Edward plans to write his memoirs. All we're discussing now is your participation . . . or lack thereof."

"Something like that would be pretty time consuming," I mentioned. Was I grasping at straws, or did it just feel that way?

"I'm sure it will be. I'd imagine that Edward would require a proper commitment from you. But since you currently have neither a job nor even a single dog in hair . . ." Aunt Peg swept an eloquent gaze around the room. "Really, Melanie, what do you do with yourself all day?"

Sam, that traitor, was laughing quietly. He'd angled his body away, but I could see his shoulders shaking.

"If I agree to do this, it means that you're going

to be spending more time taking care of Kevin," I said to his back.

The threat of extra baby duty wasn't nearly enough to sway him back to my side. Sam just shrugged. "Fine by me."

"Good," said Aunt Peg. "Then it's settled."

"Yay, Mom's going to write a book!" cried Davey.

On the floor, several of the Poodles lifted their heads and cocked an ear, wondering what all the excitement was about.

Nobody seemed to want to hear my vote.

"I guess that means I'm in," I said.

It all sounded so simple in theory.

Unfortunately, it wasn't long before reality reasserted itself. Less than three days actually, starting when Monday arrived and Davey's school reopened for the new semester. And we got four more inches of fresh snow.

Aunt Peg's call came just minutes after Davey's bus picked him up at the end of the driveway. I hadn't even had time to pour a second cup of coffee. Sometimes I think she must have our house bugged.

"You're all set," she said. "I told Edward to expect you at nine thirty."

"This morning?"

I knew Aunt Peg worked fast, but even for her, this was warp speed. And would it have been too much to ask for her to have checked with me first?

"Of course this morning. Edward's eager to get started. I assumed you would be, too."

Peg tends to be enamored with her own version of the truth. I bet she even said that with a straight face.

"Kevin has Gymboree this morning. We go every Monday."

"He's a baby, Melanie. I'm sure he doesn't know what day of the week it is. You can take him tomorrow instead. He'll never know the difference."

"*I'll* know the difference, and so will the teacher. Our class is today, not tomorrow."

"Really." Peg exhaled in a huff. "As if a baby should even have a schedule."

Yet another reminder that Aunt Peg had never been a mother.

"Gymboree?" Sam stuck his head out of his office door.

He designs computer software and works for himself. Most days that's a blessing. Today, not so much.

Frantically, I waved him off. Blithely, he ignored me. "I can take him."

"That man is an angel," said Aunt Peg. "You don't deserve him."

There were moments when I was quite sure that I didn't deserve either one of them.

. . .

Edward March lived in Westport, a cosmopolitan Connecticut town about fifteen miles up the coast from Stamford. Financially speaking, Westport has the same kind of profile as Greenwich, but the money there is quieter. Celebrities move to Greenwich when they want to be seen. They move to Westport when they want to enjoy the pastoral peace and privacy.

March's estate was on the north side of town. I took the Merritt Parkway and followed Aunt Peg's directions from the exit. Luckily, the trip took less than half an hour, because I'd gotten off to a late start.

Trust Aunt Peg to think that in a house with a husband, two children, and five big dogs, a half hour's notice would be enough time for me to get everything squared away before heading out for the morning. I used up ten minutes just folding laundry and emptying the dishwasher.

At least the tight schedule didn't leave me much time to worry about the fact that I was on my way to a new assignment for which I felt conspicuously underqualified, and which also involved working for an eminent person whom I'd never even met.

Sure. No butterflies there.

I navigated the last mile of the trip with care. March's quiet country road hadn't been plowed since the overnight addition of new snow, and a thin sheet of ice coated the shallow ruts left by previous travelers. My Volvo handles adverse conditions like a champ, but having lived in Connecticut my whole life, I've learned to give ice and snow the respect they deserve.

There was a tall wrought-iron gate at the end of March's driveway, but the intent seemed to be more decorative than functional, since it was sitting open. From the road, all I could see of the house were two brick chimneys, visible in the distance, above the treetops. Acres of rolling meadowland, snow covered and glistening with the soft sheen of the morning sun, extended outward on either side of the driveway and ended at a distant tree line.

The house was a traditional Colonial, two stories tall and built symmetrically square, painted white, with black shutters. It wasn't as large as I might have expected from the grand approach; most likely, it had been built before land values in Fairfield County had soared into the stratosphere.

The driveway circled around in front of the door, and there was a parking area off to one side. I pulled over there, turned off the car, and gathered up my purse and notebook. Really, an actual notebook. The kind with pages.

Running out the door that morning, I'd had no idea what sort of writing tools a potential coauthor might be expected to supply. I hadn't wanted to arrive empty-handed, but I didn't want to appear overeager, either. Just because Aunt Peg had nominated me for this position didn't mean that Edward March was going to agree with her choice.

The deep, sonorous tone of the doorbell had barely finished echoing before the front door drew open. A young woman, dressed in a chunky turtleneck sweater and faded blue jeans, greeted me with a smile.

"Good. You're here. Mr. March appreciates punctuality. Please come in."

After the cold outside, the house felt wonderfully warm.

"I'm Melanie," I said as she shut the door. I was already unbuttoning my coat and unwinding my scarf.

"And I'm Charlotte," the young woman replied. Her handshake was as firm as my own. She hung my coat and scarf on a rack tucked in a corner behind the door. "I'm Mr. March's assistant. He's waiting for you in the library. If you'd please follow me this way."

Charlotte's formal way of speaking was at odds with her college coed looks. Blond hair, straight and shiny, swung around her shoulders as she proceeded down the wide center hallway. Dangly earrings, one to each ear, swayed in time. Her makeup had been applied with a light hand, and her unpolished nails were bitten short.

"I know Mr. March is looking forward to meeting you," she said, stopping in front of a dark wooden door. "This project is dear to his heart, and he's been very anxious to get started."

"I hope I'll be able to help."

"Oh, I'm sure you will. Mr. March can be a little, um . . . disorganized. But he has so many wonderful stories to tell. All he needs is someone who's willing to listen and then figure out how to make order out of chaos. I'm sure you'll do just fine."

Her belief in my abilities was quite touching, I thought. Especially considering the fact that we'd just met.

"Besides . . . ," Charlotte confided in a low voice as she drew the door open. Her hand at my back ushered me forward into the room. "You look like you're made of much stronger stuff than the last two candidates."

Last two candidates? I spun around in surprise, only to find the door closing in my face. Having delivered that unexpected news, Charlotte was gone.

Briefly, I closed my eyes and wondered if Aunt Peg had been aware that her friend had already attempted—and failed—to begin writing his book with two previous applicants. Knowing my aunt, that was just the sort of incendiary information she'd have been tempted to keep to herself.

"Don't just stand there." Edward March's voice was an imperious growl. "Come over by the light so I can get a look at you."

Once I'd turned and had my first look around, it was easy to see why March had summoned me to join him by the window. The room was only dimly lit, and there wasn't anywhere else to sit down. The expanse of the library between us was impossibly cluttered.

A suite of overstuffed leather furniture was covered with cartons, books, and periodicals. Two file cabinets, a world globe on a massive frame, and a glass-fronted cherrywood cupboard all vied for floor space. I was pretty sure I even saw a wooden rocking horse tucked away behind a couch.

March himself, standing just in front of his expansive desk, was a large man with a stern look that matched the growl he'd just uttered. He had a full head of white hair and broad shoulders that stooped forward, causing his frame to look as though it was collapsing inward. The effect made him no less intimidating. March's left hand, fingers gnarled with age, grasped the top of a wooden cane.

No wonder the previous two candidates hadn't lasted long, I thought. I was half tempted to make a run for it myself. Then my gaze slid back up, and I saw the calculating look in March's eyes and realized that was exactly what he was expecting.

"Well?" he demanded. "How long are you going to keep me standing here? Do I look like I have all day?"

Begin as you mean to go on, I thought and walked with a determined stride across the room.

It was like navigating my way around an obstacle course. I didn't give March the satisfaction of looking down to see where I was going. And I didn't so much as wince when I stubbed my toe on the damn globe.

"My name is Melanie Travis," I said.

"I know that. Margaret called and told me to expect you."

Margaret? I'd never heard anyone call Aunt Peg by her full name before. Intrigued, I filed that tidbit away for further consideration.

He peered at me closely. "You don't look like a teacher."

"Really? What do teachers look like?"

"Skinny. Buttoned up. Like fun is out of the question."

"You don't look like too much fun yourself," I told him.

"You should have known me when I was younger." His laugh was a dry, wheezing cackle. He patted a nearby chair that was angled toward his desk. "Come over here and take a seat. Tell me how someone as pretty as you got to be a teacher."

Wonderful. A man who was twice my age was flirting with me. I wondered if this was why his assistant, Charlotte, had been in such a hurry to leave the room.

"I thought we were going to talk about you," I said. "My Aunt Peg tells me that you want to write a book."

"Indeed I do."

When March moved around behind his desk and sat down, I stepped forward and took the chair he'd pointed out. I folded my hands primly on the edge of the desk and settled down to listen.

"I've lived a long life. I have a lot to say. I need a good scribe, someone with a decent head on her shoulders to write things down for me. Do you think you could manage to do that?"

"Quite possibly," I said. "What happened to the last two people who tried?"

"They were idiots." His hand waved away the question.

"If I don't know what they did wrong, how do I know if I can do better?"

"That's not up to you to decide."

Maybe, maybe not. As far as I could tell, the jury was still out on whether or not March and I were going to be able to forge a decent working relationship. I sat and waited.

March frowned. Then he scowled. He seemed to have an entire arsenal of fierce expressions at his command. Idly, I wondered if he practiced in the mirror.

Finally, he said, "The first one . . . It turned out that she didn't like dogs. Now, how was I supposed to work with that?"

"Probably not very easily," I admitted. Considering the book's subject matter, it seemed like a valid objection.

"You like dogs, don't you?"

"Of course I do."

"You see? I knew any relative of Margaret's would have to be a dog person."

Luckily, March hasn't met my brother.

"And the second candidate?"

"That was a problem right from the beginning. When he took notes, he wrote things down in that horrid shorthand that passes for conversation nowadays. What's it called? Textspeak?"

"Oh my." My inner teacher cringed in sympathy.

"You see? Like I said, idiots. But I can already tell that this is going to work." March leaned toward me across his desk. His hand slid along the polished surface, grasped my fingers in his, and gave them a squeeze. "You and I are going to get along famously."

Gently, I disentangled my hand and put it down in my lap, out of reach.

That remained to be seen, I thought.

Chapter 3

There was a soft knock at the door, and Charlotte let herself in. She was carrying a tray with two cups of coffee, milk and sweetener, and a plate of sugar cookies. Even so encumbered, she maneuvered her way through the crowded room with ease.

Charlotte eased the tray down onto the desk, between March and me, then leaned across and whispered something in his ear.

"Tell him not now," March said shortly.

"But he said—"

"I don't care. He'll have to wait."

Charlotte glanced my way. I did my best to look as though I wasn't listening. I probably wasn't very convincing.

"Please help yourself," she said. "The cookies are Mr. March's favorite."

They looked good, but the coffee smelled heavenly. I picked up one of the cups and topped it off with a dollop of milk. March followed suit, then added sweetener as Charlotte let herself out.

I waited until the door had closed behind her, then asked, "Is everything all right?"

"Of course. That was nothing, just family

business. Let's get back to my book." March looked up from stirring his coffee. "What do you know about Irish Setters?"

I said the first thing that popped into my head. *"Big Red."*

I had discovered the classic book in grade school and had read it numerous times. In my dog-deprived childhood, it had shared a place of honor on my bookshelf, along with *White Fang* and *Lassie Come Home.*

"And, of course, I see them at the shows," I said. "They're gorgeous dogs."

March nodded. "It's that external beauty that has been the breed's glory, but also its undoing. Irish Setters are sporting dogs first and foremost. The first ones imported into this country were valued above all for their ability to work in the field."

March had slipped into lecture mode, and his enthusiasm for his breed was infectious. I was happy to sit back and be educated.

"As bird dogs, they're bold and tenacious, and they can work all day. But, of course, their appeal doesn't stop there. They're also charming, and happy-go-lucky, gentle, and loyal to a fault. Quintessentially Irish, you might say. Those traits, coupled with their good looks, have positioned them as the ideal show and companion dog."

"They sound wonderful," I said.

"They are." March was firm in his opinion. "There's not a better dog to be had."

I bit back a smile. Everyone feels that way about his own breed. Which isn't surprising, because every breed of dog has its charms. Let's face it. They're all pretty terrific.

"Speaking of Irish Setters," I said, "do you still have any of the dogs that you used to show? I've been told that your Russet setters were famous, and justifiably so."

"Indeed, they were." He sounded pleased with himself. Clearly, getting March to open up and talk about his achievements was not going to be a problem. "But I haven't been in the show ring except as a judge in more than twenty-five years. Now the Russet name lives on solely as a foundation bloodline for other breeders who were fortunate enough to appreciate its merits and put them to good use. I have just one dog left, Russet Red Robin. She's with Charlotte. I asked my assistant to keep her out of the way this morning so that we could meet without distraction."

Most dog people I know love to be distracted by their pets. That's the whole point. But as I was quickly learning, Edward March made up his own rules. Maybe that was why he and Aunt Peg got along; they both believed in bending the world to their will, rather than the other way around.

"So your book will be mostly about Irish Setters," I said.

"Certainly not." March selected a sugar cookie from the plate, dunked it into his coffee, then popped it in his mouth whole. "Whatever gave you that idea?"

"I thought that was what we were talking about."

"Oh, no, indeed. We're just getting better acquainted. Discussing a mutual interest, you might say."

If the interest was supposed to be mutual, we ought to be talking about Poodles, too, I thought. Yet another subversive notion best left unspoken.

"Are you thinking about something with a broader focus, then? Maybe a definitive history of dog showing in America?"

March propped his elbows on the desk and steepled his fingers beneath his nose. He stared at me thoughtfully. "I suppose if anyone is eminently qualified to attempt such a tome, it would be me. But no, that isn't what I have in mind, either."

"I should stop guessing and let you tell me." I pulled a pen out of my purse and opened my notebook to the first page. Hand poised above the empty space, I looked at March expectantly.

"*Puppy Love*," he announced.

"Excuse me?"

"That's going to be the title. What do you think?"

"It's cute." I thought for a moment. "Possibly a little light on dignity."

"My memoirs," March said firmly. "My choice."

"You asked for my opinion. If we're going to

work together, I assume you want to hear the truth."

March's wiry brows drew together as his eyes narrowed. "Perhaps you've misunderstood how things are going to proceed. I'm the one with the expertise. You're merely the scribe. I do the talking. You write down what I say."

I closed my notebook with a sharp slap. "If that's the kind of help you're looking for, you don't need a live person. All you need is a tape recorder."

"Now, that's where you're wrong. Writing a book is a lonely endeavor, and solitude is not my style. What keeps me interested is interaction. I need someone who can appreciate my stories, someone I can bounce things off of."

"Like a book title?"

March pushed himself to his feet. "I didn't say I wanted an argument. Just an opinion."

"One that agrees with yours, obviously."

"When I'm right!"

"Are you ever wrong?"

March considered. "I suppose it's been known to happen." He snorted under his breath. "On occasion."

I stood up, as well. "This won't work if you think I'm simply going to sit here and nod at everything you say."

"Are you going to argue with everything?"

"I don't know yet. It depends."

We glared at each other across the desk.

"At least you're honest," March said finally. "I suppose that ought to count for something. And you like dogs."

"And I hate textspeak."

That coaxed a small smile from him. March came around to where I stood. He escorted me to the library door. "So will we make a good team or not? It seems that we both have something to consider."

"I'm not sure I'll make your life any easier," I told him.

"I have no doubt that I will complicate yours. Nevertheless . . . I think we may have potential." He grasped the knob and drew the door open. "Let's talk again in a day or two. Charlotte?"

"Here, Mr. March."

The blonde came striding down the hallway. Following just behind was a man about my own age. Dressed in jeans, a flannel shirt, and heavy work boots, he had the physique of someone who enjoyed working outdoors. His expression was thunderous. I was just as happy that he didn't even glance in my direction.

"It's about time," the man snapped. "I thought you were going to keep me waiting here all morning." He pushed past me and entered the library. March paused in the doorway before following.

"Charlotte, please show Ms. Travis out."

"Of course, Mr. March."

Together, we retrieved my coat and scarf. "Who was that?" I asked when both men had disappeared.

"Andrew." Charlotte's low tone matched my own. "Mr. March's son. He lives in a house on the other side of the estate. Maybe you saw the other driveway when you came in?"

I shook my head. I'd been too busy watching out for ice to worry about a second entrance.

"Andrew runs the company now. The two of them don't always get along."

I could see that much for myself.

"What company?" I asked.

"March Homes. You know, the builders?"

I nodded. They advertised on local TV all the time. I just hadn't realized there was a connection. Typical of Aunt Peg to tell me all about Edward March's dogs and not a thing about what he did for a living.

"So are you going to do it?" Charlotte asked.

"I don't know yet."

She brushed aside my indecision. "You will."

"What makes you so sure?"

"The other two didn't last five minutes in there with him. You managed almost an hour. Trust me, the first time you meet him is the worst. He likes to act all surly and impossible, but if you don't let him walk all over you, things generally improve from there."

"Good to know," I said.

Charlotte stood on the top step and waved as I walked to my car. "See you soon!"

I wasn't at all sure I shared her confidence.

I arrived home to a house that was empty of humans but filled with kindred spirits. I entered the kitchen from the garage to find five pairs of dark eyes trained expectantly on the door. Living with Standard Poodles keeps you on your toes. They're always one step ahead.

As always, Faith was the first to greet me. I'm a mother, so I know I shouldn't play favorites. But Faith had been my first Poodle, the one who had introduced me to the wonders of dog ownership. Before she came into my life, I would never have imagined that we would share a bond that was so all encompassing. Faith understood my unspoken thoughts; she knew my every mood. I only hoped that I was half as good at reading her feelings as she was mine.

Standards are the biggest of the three varieties of Poodles. Faith's head was even with my hip, so I didn't have far to reach when I slipped a hand under her chin and scratched beneath her ears. Poodles in show coat have hair that must be protected at all costs; their owners quickly learn to stroke only those areas that are clipped short. It had been several years since Faith had been inside a show ring, but old habits died hard.

Eve came next, elbowing her dam to one side and pushing her nose into my cupped hand. *My turn,* she announced as clearly as if the words had been spoken aloud. Raven, Casey, and Tar were right behind her, bodies wriggling in delight as they pressed against my legs, tails beating a tattoo against my thighs.

"I know," I said softly. "I missed you guys, too."

I tossed my purse on the counter and sat down on the floor. Holding my arms open, I tried to gather them all in at once. Predictably, Tar was the first to wiggle free from my embrace. He dashed across the room, dove under the table, and came up with a tennis ball for me to throw.

"Not in the house," I told him. "You know that."

Actually, he probably didn't, but he was supposed to. The other four Poodles certainly did. Raven and Casey, like Faith and Eve, were typical Standard Poodles: highly intelligent, with an innate desire to please and an infectious sense of humor.

Tar was beautiful. He was funny. He was kind. But smart? Not so much. None of us had ever seen a dumb Poodle before, but there he was. The most well-meaning dog in the world, Tar could barely think his way down a flight of steps.

Lack of brainpower had never interfered with the big dog's total enjoyment of life, however. Pomponned tail whipping back and forth, Tar trotted back over and dropped the ball in my lap.

Then he backed away and waited happily for me to comply.

Faith and Eve watched to see what I was going to do next. Before Kevin was born, when I had more time to spend with them, I would take the Poodles for a run in the park. Now I was planning to make a shopping list and put in another load of laundry.

That thought brought a sigh. Maybe Aunt Peg was right. Maybe I had become dull.

Faith and Eve had adapted to all the changes I'd thrown their way. They'd thrived in our new, bigger family. But even so, I knew that sometimes they missed the easy intimacy of our prior relationship. And so did I.

I reached back and levered myself up off the floor. Housework could wait.

"Come on, guys," I said. "Let's go outside and play ball."

It turned out that the shopping list was unnecessary. On the way home from Gymboree, Sam and Kevin had stopped at the supermarket.

"You just like the fact that women fawn all over you because you have a baby," I said as we put away the groceries.

Kevin has his father's blond hair and blue eyes. Together, the two of them make an arresting pair, a fact that Sam is not above using to his advantage on occasion.

"What can I say? The kid's a chick magnet. If I could bottle his appeal, we'd be millionaires."

The chick magnet in question had already finished the peanut butter and jelly sandwich I'd had ready for him when he got home, and now was meandering unsteadily across the kitchen floor in the direction of the dogs' water bowl. I'd seen this trick before: Kevin liked to tip the bowl over and watch the water slosh across the polished hardwood. If he managed to place himself in a position to get soaked, too, that was an added bonus.

I swooped down and picked him up just in time. "No," Kevin said firmly. "Down."

"It's time for your nap," I told him. Despite his protests, my son's eyelids were already drooping.

Kevin had spent the first year of his life thinking that sleep was the enemy. Now he napped and slept through the night like a champ. I liked to take credit for the turnaround, but in reality I didn't have the slightest idea what had caused it.

Sometimes I think that motherhood is just one surprise after another. Luckily, most of them turn out to be good.

After the eventful morning he'd had, it took only ten minutes to get Kevin changed and down for his nap. When I got back to the kitchen, Sam was putting the finishing touches on a couple of chicken salad sandwiches.

"So tell me about your meeting with Edward

March," he said after we'd poured drinks and sat down to lunch.

The Poodles spread themselves out on the floor around the table. They're more likely to get lucky when Davey's home, but they like to keep their options open.

"It was interesting, certainly. And maybe a little odd. If that's what dog show royalty is like, I can't say I'm too impressed."

"How come?"

I shrugged. "March himself is a bit of a curmudgeon. No, more than that, a bully. And I think he'd be quite happy to hear himself described in those terms. He seems to enjoy browbeating people."

"He was known for running a strict ring, but that's not unexpected. The best judges have high standards. They know what they like, and they don't settle for less. It wouldn't surprise me to hear that he's a tough old bird." Sam slanted me a look. "I take it, he didn't succeed in browbeating you."

"He certainly tried. I ended up arguing with him, and judging by his response, that doesn't happen often. It turns out that I never did hear what his book is going to be about."

"I thought we already knew that."

"Apparently not. He was starting to tell me when I insulted his title."

"Way to go, Mel."

"It wasn't my fault. Listen to this. March plans to call the book *Puppy Love*."

"Seriously?" Sam grinned. He lifted a hand and cupped his fingers around his ear. "What's that I hear? Is it the sound of a sixties pop star crooning . . . ?"

I reached over and slapped his hand down. "Cut it out. I mean it."

"I'm not doubting you." He was laughing now. "I'm just setting the mood. So now what? Do you think you'll be going back?"

"I guess we'll have to see. The decision isn't entirely up to me. First, March has to decide whether he wants to work with me or not. Although, his assistant told me that two previous candidates for the job didn't even last ten minutes, so maybe he doesn't have a lot of choice."

"It sounds like you're a shoo-in," said Sam.

Chapter 4

I might have agreed, except that two whole days passed without any word from Edward March. Maybe he wasn't in a hurry to get started on his book. Or maybe he'd found a better candidate for the job. Either way, I had plenty of other things to keep me busy; I had no need to go chasing after him.

On the third day, there was a knock on my front door.

Sam and I live in a residential neighborhood in North Stamford. There are wide streets, large wooded lots, and spacious houses set well back from the road. Unlike at my former address—a tight-knit block in a fifties-era subdivision where there was always someone playing in a front yard and you could smell what your neighbors were cooking for dinner—we don't get drop-in visitors here.

Even cookie-selling Girl Scouts pass us by.

So someone showing up unexpectedly was cause for surprise, if not a small twinge of alarm. The Poodles agreed with me. They came running from all corners of the house and reached the door before I did.

Sam was out for the afternoon, seeing a client. Davey was at school. Kevin was in the family room, watching *Sesame Street* on TV. It was left to me to see what was up.

The booming sound of Poodles' deep-throated barking would stop most prudent visitors in their tracks. But when I opened the door, my uninvited guest didn't look alarmed. Instead, as the pack of Poodles spilled out to join him on the front step, his expression was merely one of annoyance.

"You're Andrew March," I said, surprised.

Luckily, I stopped before blurting out the rest of my thought. *What are you doing here?*

"Yes, I am. May I come in?"

Maybe March and his son didn't get along because they both shared the same imperious attitude. Without waiting for a response, Andrew simply walked past me and into the house.

Today he was wearing a suit, English cut with narrow lapels. His shirt was open at the throat. Though the temperature was in the thirties, his only concession to the weather was a cashmere muffler he'd wound around his neck. As I called the Poodles back inside and shut the door, I saw that he'd left a shiny black Escalade parked in the driveway.

"Nice house," he said, looking around with a practiced eye. "How old is it?"

"Ten years, give or take. We didn't buy it new."

He walked across the hall to the arched entryway that led to the living room. There was nothing I could do but follow along behind.

"It looks like it's in pretty good shape."

"It is," I said. "We take good care of it. Did you come here to discuss my house?"

"No, just force of habit. Professional interest."

Now Andrew was taking a peek at the dining room. This was truly bizarre. If he started to head upstairs, I decided I was going to call 911.

"Listen," he said, finally turning back to me.

"We need to talk. Is there somewhere we can sit down?"

Like he hadn't noticed during his nosy inspection that we had chairs?

"Living room. Dining room." I waved my arm from one side of the house to the other. "Take your pick."

It didn't matter to me which room he chose. If Kevin needed something, I could hear his call from anywhere on the first floor.

"This'll do," he said. Living room it was.

All five Poodles had been milling around our legs while we talked, but now Eve separated herself out and headed toward the back of the house. Having appointed herself his canine guardian, she took her job very seriously, and I knew that I'd find her later curled up by Kevin's side. *Good dog.* Under these decidedly odd circumstances, that gave me one less thing to worry about.

The remaining four Poodles jostled each other playfully as we moved toward the living room. Each jockeyed for position nearest to our visitor. It didn't take a genius to see that they were wondering what was going on. Funny thing about that, so was I.

Andrew dropped down a hand and brushed away an inquisitive nose. "Can't they go outside or something?"

"No."

Andrew frowned.

I shrugged. My house, my rules.

He glanced at the oversize couch, with its padded arms and plump pillows, and must have realized that if he sat there, the Poodles would join him. Wisely, he opted for the matching chair instead.

I settled on the couch. Now we were sitting facing one another. I folded my hands in my lap and waited. I had no idea what might come next. Nor did I intend to initiate the proceedings.

"We need to talk about my father," Andrew said.

"I can't imagine why. I barely know your father. We met for the first time at the beginning of the week."

"Nevertheless, I'm sure you're aware that he's hatched some crazy scheme to write a book. I understand that's what your meeting was about."

"Mr. March is looking for a coauthor," I replied mildly. "It remains to be seen whether or not that person will be me."

"It will not."

To tell the truth, I'd had my doubts, too. But the fact that Andrew March seemed to think that he could come into my house uninvited, and tell me what I could or could not do, got my hackles up.

"I believe that's for your father to decide."

"Listen, that came out wrong." He reached up and raked his fingers through his hair. Like his father's, it was thick and bushy. Tendrils spilled forward over his forehead.

"I'm sure you're qualified to"—Andrew paused and blew out an agitated breath—"do whatever it is that he thinks he wants done. But there isn't going to be a book."

"Because you object?"

"Hell, yes, I object. I'll get a restraining order if I have to."

This was getting interesting. "Against your father?"

"And you, too, if I have to."

Law was not my strong suit, but I was pretty sure he was confused about what a restraining order could or could not accomplish. I didn't think it could stop someone from writing a book about his own life.

"Why are you so opposed to the idea?"

"That's none of your business."

"Fine." I crossed my arms over my chest. "Then why are you here?"

"To tell you to back off. You need to leave my father alone."

"I met with your father once," I said. "I was there at *his* invitation."

Andrew looked annoyed. Obviously, he was no more accustomed to being argued with than Edward March was.

"I'm not telling you what my father wants. I'm telling you what *I* want," he snapped. "And how things are going to be. You need to listen to what I'm saying. There's no point in your getting any further involved with my family, because there isn't going to be any book."

"Mr. March thinks there is."

"He's mistaken. And trust me, it isn't the first time. There's no way I intend to sit by while my father pontificates about his own importance to anyone who will listen. We will not be airing our family's dirty linen in public. I have a business to protect, and I won't stand for it."

"Wait a minute," I said. One of us was clearly confused. I really hoped it wasn't me. "This book that you're so upset about, it isn't about your business. It's about dogs and dog shows."

Andrew's eyes narrowed. "Did he tell you that?"

"Well . . . no. Not in so many words. But the whole point is, what I know about is dogs. That's why my aunt recommended me for the job. Mr. March and I spent most of our time together talking about Irish Setters."

"Dogs." Andrew spat out the word. "That's all he ever talks about."

"That's what I'm trying to tell you. You don't have anything to worry about. The book is going to be called *Puppy Love*."

"Oh, hell no!" Andrew leapt to his feet. The Poodles, who had settled around us on the floor, jumped up and scattered.

"Okay, maybe it isn't the best title. But at least it describes the subject matter. Nobody could confuse *that* with a book about your company."

I'd thought the title might placate him. Instead, it was having the opposite effect. He leaned down and shook his finger in my face.

"This isn't over," he snarled.

I pushed his hand away and stood up. "I think you'd better leave."

Andrew rewrapped his scarf—like that was going to ward off the cold—strode over to the door, and let himself out. As the door slammed shut behind him, Faith whined softly under her breath.

"I know." I reached down to tangle my fingers in her topknot. "I feel the same way."

How very, very strange.

Cell phones are the bane of my existence.

At the risk of sounding like a Luddite, I have to admit that I was much happier before so many different ways existed for me to reach out and touch someone. Or vice versa, as is usually the case. I've simply never understood the appeal of being readily available to the world 24-7.

I carry a cell phone with me, but it's there for emergencies or in case a close friend or family member needs to get hold of me. Since I don't give the number to anyone else, I don't get a lot of calls. And that's just the way I like it.

So when my cell phone rang the next morning and an unfamiliar number appeared on the screen, I was already frowning when I pressed the phone to my ear.

"Melanie? Edward March here. Are you ready to get started?"

Good question. And now that I'd spent three days pondering it, I knew what my answer was going to be.

Andrew's visit the previous afternoon—meant to warn me away—had instead succeeded in whetting my curiosity. Not only that, but while my family life was wonderful, lately the opportunities for intellectual stimulation had been few and far between. That one interview with Edward March had been enough to remind me that I *liked* having a job, that I enjoyed feeling useful in some capacity outside the home.

I'd missed that. And it was time to get my brain back in gear again.

"I'm ready," I said. "Just one thing, Mr. March—"

"Edward. If we're going to be working together, you must call me Edward."

He couldn't see me, but I shook my head, anyway. I had no desire to call March by his first name. That small barrier of formality between us was just fine by me.

"Where did you get this phone number from?"

"Margaret gave it to me."

Of course, I thought with a sigh. I should have guessed.

March and I made arrangements to meet after lunch. I picked up Kevin, who was on the floor at my feet, and went off in search of Sam. I found him in the family room, unpacking a fresh load of firewood from a canvas log carrier.

Most of the logs were already in the wrought-iron rack. Sam was using the last few to lay a new fire. As he knelt on the floor and leaned forward to pile them directly onto the andirons, I took a moment to admire the view. Really, it never got old.

"Time for you to make good on your promise," I said as he finished what he was doing and turned.

Kevin wiggled in my arms. He wanted down. As I lowered him to the floor, Sam swiveled around and sat down on the rug in front of the fireplace. Kevin trotted across the room and into his father's outstretched arms.

"March just called. I'm going back to Westport after lunch. He wants me to help him with his book."

"Did you tell him that Andrew was here yesterday?"

"No, but I will when I get there." Sam and I had discussed Andrew's visit the previous evening, and Sam had been just as baffled as I was. "Can you watch Kevin this afternoon?"

"Sure." Sam cupped his hands around his son's, and the two of them clapped in the air happily. "Take all the time you need."

Once again Charlotte met me at the front door, and once again she escorted me to the library entrance. Since it was a straight shot down the wide center hall, then a left-hand turn into the room, I was pretty sure I could have found my own way, but March's assistant accompanied me, anyway.

"I'm glad you decided to come back," she said. "He's been in a good mood all day."

"I hope I don't do anything to ruin it," I said.

"Oh, I'm sure you won't. Now that he's going to be getting started on his book, I'm sure things will settle down around here."

I would have asked what she meant by that, but we'd already reached the library. March was waiting just inside the doorway, his body tipped forward as he leaned heavily on his cane. If he was happy to see me, it wasn't evident by his disgruntled expression.

"Shut the door behind you," he said to Charlotte, dismissing her with barely a glance. "Melanie and I have work to do."

As she complied, March began the slow walk toward his desk. "We've done a little rearranging since you were here last. Come along and find yourself a seat."

The room did look as though someone had done

some straightening. There was marginally less clutter, and a bit more open space had been carved out around the furniture. Several tabletops were cleared, and rather than just one empty chair, I had my choice of places to sit. I wondered why whoever had done the neatening hadn't thought to put higher-wattage lightbulbs in the lamps—or, failing that, to push back the heavy drapes that covered much of the large window behind the desk.

I'm a teacher. I like a cheerful workplace. And the thought of spending weeks confined to this somber, dimly lit library was mildly depressing. Surely, I couldn't be the only person who felt like I was entering a tomb each time I walked inside.

I sat down in a wingback chair not far from March's desk. "Before we get started," I said, "I have something to tell you."

"Well?" He reached his seat, a cordovan leather chair on rollers, and sank into it heavily.

"Your son came to visit me yesterday."

"Andrew?" He said the name with a scowl. So much for my not wrecking March's good mood. "Whatever for?"

"He warned me to stay away from you. He told me that there wasn't going to be a book."

"That's not up to him."

"That's not what he thinks."

"What Andrew thinks on this topic is immaterial. My son has always been under the impression that if he wants something, that's reason enough for it to be his. He has thwarted me in the past, but I assure you that despite what he might have told you, he won't succeed this time. Feel free to put him out of your mind."

I'd be delighted to, I thought, as long as Andrew was willing to do the same for me.

March opened a folder on his desktop and withdrew several sheets of paper. He lifted them up and stared at the top sheet thoughtfully, rubbing it back and forth between his forefinger and thumb.

"I've taken the liberty of drawing up a contract that outlines the details of our arrangement. Considering that this is my story, it seems to me that a ninety-ten split of any potential profits is more than equitable."

Up until that moment, I hadn't given any thought to the financial aspects of our collaboration. The project had simply come along at the right time, piqued my curiosity, and offered to satisfy my need for adult interaction. But now I stopped and thought about the fact that once I signed that contract, I'd be agreeing to work hard. There was no way I was going to sell my services that cheaply.

"No," I said.

"No?" He sounded incredulous.

"Ninety-ten?" I made sure I sounded equally dubious. "I don't think so."

March opened his fingers and let the papers drop. "All right, then, what sounds fair to you?"

I considered for a minute before answering. Even on our short acquaintance, March struck me as the kind of man who would take advantage of a situation if he could. I, however, spent my days dealing with a two-year-old. Which meant that I knew all about setting proper boundaries right from the beginning.

March was right about the fact that this was his book. But without my input, it wouldn't be written at all.

"Twenty-five percent for me, seventy-five to you," I said.

"Fifteen, eighty-five," he shot back.

"I'm not negotiating, Mr. March. You asked what split sounded fair to me, and I told you. If you don't agree, you may feel free to find another partner."

His eyes narrowed, his bushy brows lowering in a ferocious scowl. March gathered up the papers and shoved them back into the folder.

"I'll have the contracts redrawn. You can sign them the next time you're here."

"It's a deal."

March wasn't about to let me have the last word.

"Now, if you're finished taking advantage of an old man," he grumbled, "let's get down to work."

Chapter 5

On my first visit to March's house, I'd brought a notebook. This time I'd traded up and come equipped with a laptop. The only problem with that, I realized now, was that I'd left the computer sitting on the passenger seat of the Volvo.

"I'm ready to get started," I said, hopping up out of my chair. "I just have to run out to my car for a second. I'll be right back."

"Wait!" March cried.

I was already halfway to the door. When I paused and glanced back, the expression on the older man's face surprised me. He looked more than a little alarmed.

"I'm just going outside," I told him. "I brought a laptop to take notes on. It'll only take me a moment to get it."

"Stay right there. I'll call Charlotte."

"There's no need." I reached the door and pulled it open. "I know the way."

"Please . . ."

It sounded like a word he didn't use often. That, more than anything else, stopped me where I stood. As I hesitated in the doorway, Charlotte came running from the back of the house. She skidded to a halt in front of me.

"What's the matter?" she asked breathlessly.

"Nothing." Was it just me, or was the weird vibe definitely back? "I was just on my way outside to get my laptop so we can get started. I left it in my car."

"Oh." Charlotte blew out a breath. It almost sounded like a sigh of relief. "That's fine. Go right ahead."

I intended to. And I did. As I'd told March, it took me only a minute. Charlotte waited in the hall until I'd returned.

"How about some coffee for the two of you?" she asked brightly. "I was just brewing a fresh pot."

"That would be very nice," March replied. "Thank you, Charlotte."

Very nice? Really? The two of them sounded like they were reciting lines from a play. If this was an attempt to restore a sense of normalcy to what seemed to me like a very odd situation, I wasn't sure it was working.

Back inside the library, I dragged my chair closer to March's desk and looked for a place to set the laptop down. Obviously, the recent effort to reduce clutter had not extended to March's work space.

The desk itself was a massive piece of furniture, but nearly every inch of its polished surface was covered with . . . stuff. Aside from a leather-bound blotter, an ornate lamp, and a phone, there were also stacks of books and files, numerous pictures, and even old magazines, all vying for the same space.

I'm not a neat freak, by any means. But this place was a mess, even by my admittedly low standards. I had no idea how March was able to get anything done surrounded by so much disarray.

"Just push something aside," he said when I hesitated. "Make yourself comfortable."

I moved a towering pile of *Kennel Reviews* to one side. It merged with a nearby stack of *Gun Dog* magazines. I opened the computer up and turned it on. As I waited for it to warm up, I noticed that the periodical on top of the pile I'd just formed was dated March 2008.

"If you want, before we start, I can do a little cleaning up," I said. "It might be easier to work in here if we got things organized first."

"What do you mean?"

"Well, for one thing, these magazines . . . they're old."

In human terms, they were merely old. In dog years they were truly ancient—at least a generation, if not two, from containing current news.

"Those magazines contain valuable information. I like to refer back to the articles. That's why I saved them."

"Yes, but do they have to sit right here?"

March gazed around the room, perplexed. "Where else would they go?"

"How about over there?"

The longest wall in the room had been lined with floor-to-ceiling bookshelves. Unfortunately, they were also already crammed full. The contents had probably started as a display, but now books, figurines, framed photographs, and a collection of old dog show trophies, which were sadly in need of polishing, were all jumbled together in a haphazard fashion.

"That won't work," March said irritably. "I like to keep things handy for easy reference. You let them out of your sight and next thing you know, they start getting lost on you."

"Right." Considering how much junk there was in the library, losing some of it didn't sound like a bad thing to me.

Not my call, I reminded myself firmly. I turned back to my computer and opened up a new file on the screen. "Puppy Love," I wrote at the top of the empty page.

"Here's how it's going to work," said March. "I'll talk, and you take notes. Doesn't have to be word for word. It's the stories, the content, that's the important part. After we get a bunch of pages done, you can print them up and we'll go over them together."

"Okay," I said. "Shoot."

"We'll start with Caroline." March leaned back

in his chair and closed his eyes. A small smile played around his lips.

"Caroline," I typed.

"Was she your first dog?"

His eyes snapped open. "Certainly not. She was the first girl I . . ." He stopped and cleared his throat. "Let's just say, the first girl I ever loved. I was fourteen, and she was sixteen. An older woman."

"Older woman," I wrote down. I stared briefly at the description, then added a question mark.

"She had soft blond hair and big blue eyes . . ." March dragged out the words lovingly. He seemed to be enjoying his own descriptive prowess. "And a tiny little freckle at the base of her throat."

My fingers hovered above the keys. I was waiting for him to say something worth recording.

March glanced my way. "Write that down."

"Why?"

"So it will go in the book." As if *that* was obvious.

"A tiny freckle at the base of her throat?"

"It's description," March said curtly. "It's important."

"Maybe if you were describing your first Best in Show winner. Your readers will be interested to know what he looked like. Sixteen-year-old Caroline? I don't think so."

"I didn't ask you to think. I asked you to type."

"I am typing. Or I was a minute ago. And as

soon as you say something interesting, I'll start again."

March shoved back his chair and pushed himself to his feet. "You know nothing about the publishing business!"

"Maybe not," I agreed. "But I'm a voracious reader. And if a dog person of your stature wrote a book, I'd be first in line to buy it. I'd love to read about the shows you've participated in and all the great dogs you've had your hands on over the years."

"Rubbish. That's not what sells books."

"It would to me."

March glared in my direction. "I'm aiming for a bigger audience."

"Well, sure, but—"

"People want salacious details, the more the better. They want to hear secrets and feel like they're reading the inside scoop. Reality TV on the written page, that's what makes people buy books. And that's what I intend to give them."

"Excuse me?"

"Of course, there will be dogs in the book, plenty of them. It's not like we can put my stories in context without setting the stage. The dogs will make wonderful window dressing. But it's the people I've known and the relationships I've shared that will form the basis for the book."

"Window dressing . . . ?" I echoed faintly.

"I cut quite a dashing figure in my younger

days, and the ladies of the dog show community were more than eager to show their appreciation. Think Don Juan. His stories made him famous." March nodded with satisfaction. "And now it's finally time for me to tell all."

Puppy Love? No wonder he'd chosen that title. What had I gotten myself into?

"Coffee's here!" Charlotte sang out cheerfully. She shouldered the door open and carried the tray into the room. "Let me just set this down and get out of your way. It looks like everything's going splendidly!"

"Splendidly, my foot," I said to Aunt Peg.

We were sitting in her kitchen, eating cake. Aunt Peg has a voracious sweet tooth. She thinks that a good dose of sugar can cure most of the world's ills, and unfortunately for the sake of my waistline, when I'm with her, I find it hard to argue.

March and I had gone on to spend a second hour working together earlier that afternoon. It was all time wasted, from my point of view. We had moved from the chronicles of Caroline to a narrative about Nancy, and had finished up with what I was pretty sure was a total fairy tale concerning a woman named Rosemary. At least Nancy had been a fellow judge. Which kept things slightly on topic, from my perspective.

By the time I left March's house, it was mid-afternoon. I decided to do what I've always done in times of inner turmoil and intellectual confusion: visit Aunt Peg and see what she had to say. Peg loves meddling in other people's problems, even ones of her own making. She has plenty of opinions, and she's never been shy about sharing any of them.

On my way to her house, I'd swung by Davey's school and picked him up before he could get on the bus. In earlier years, the three of us had spent countless hours together. But now with Davey in middle school, Kevin taking up so much of my time, and Aunt Peg's busy judging schedule, it seemed as though our lives were constantly spinning in different directions. Pulling into Aunt Peg's driveway with Davey sitting in the backseat, something I'd done so many times in the past, made me feel a brief twinge of nostalgia for those simpler days.

Then Aunt Peg opened her front door, and I quickly snapped back to the present. Like Sam and me, Peg lives with a herd of Standard Poodles, and I needed to watch what I was doing as the rambunctious horde came spilling down off the porch to circle the car and offer a canine chorus of greeting.

Already laughing, Davey jumped out to join them. Within seconds, he was down on the ground, surrounded by sniffing noses and wagging tails. It was no wonder that he felt right at home, as the group included Tar's dam and both Faith's and Eve's littermates. Our canine families were every bit as intertwined as our human ones.

"There's something wonderfully heartwarming about the sight of a boy and a dog together," Aunt Peg said happily as she watched the proceedings from the porch.

"Or six dogs," I pointed out.

My son was barely even visible in the midst of the eddying throng. I wondered if he'd noticed yet that he was sitting in snow.

"Really, Melanie, there's no need to be literal."

She waved her hand, and the Poodles immediately stopped playing and ran back up the steps. Even Davey leapt to comply. Aunt Peg just has that kind of effect on people. It's a gift. One that I don't share, unfortunately.

"Have you grown another inch since last week?" she asked Davey as we all trooped inside. The top of his head now approached her shoulder; considering that Aunt Peg stands six feet tall, that was no small accomplishment.

"Could be." My son grinned. He likes to think of himself as a budding basketball star.

"And how is school?"

"Fine."

"Sports?"

"Fine."

"How's your little brother doing?"

"Fine."

My son, the king of the one-word answer.

"Davey," I said in my best mother's voice, "a little elaboration please."

He looked up at Peg. "He's fine. Thank you."

Aunt Peg hooted with laughter. She held up a hand, and the two of them slapped their palms together.

"You know you're only encouraging him," I told her.

"Of course I'm encouraging him. That's what aunts are for. It's parents who have to worry about things like teaching good manners." She slipped Davey a wink. "I've got cake."

Of course she had cake. Aunt Peg always had cake. And so here we were. Davey had already scarfed down two pieces, drunk a tall glass of milk, and regaled his aunt with numerous intricate details about the geography paper he was doing on Lithuania. Then he'd excused himself and gone off to play with the Poodles while Peg and I talked.

"I'm guessing you stopped by to talk about Edward March," Aunt Peg began. "I'd imagine he's getting on your nerves."

"Good guess."

She nodded. "He gets on everyone's nerves."

"And it didn't occur to you to tell me that *before* I volunteered to work with him?"

"Why would I have wanted to do that? For all I knew, you might have been different."

At moments like this I can't help but think what a wonderful con artist my aunt would have made. She certainly had the look of injured innocence down pat.

"Well, I'm not," I grumbled.

"So I see. Pardon me for having higher expectations of my relatives than I do for the general public. I've seen you in action, Melanie. It never for a moment occurred to me that you wouldn't be able to handle Edward."

"Handling him isn't the problem."

"Oh?" Aunt Peg deftly slid a third piece of cake onto her empty plate. Good thing Davey wasn't there to see it. "Then what is?"

"It's his book. The one that you and Sam thought would be a historical overview of his decades in the dog show world? Well, it's nothing like that. March intends to write a kiss-and-tell book about his amorous exploits in the dog community. He's calling it *Puppy Love*."

"Really, Melanie." Aunt Peg sputtered out a laugh. "I don't think so. The man is pulling your leg."

"No, he's not. He's serious. We started working on it this morning. I heard all about his first love, the beautiful Caroline, with the alluring freckle at the base of her throat. . . ."

Aunt Peg set down her fork. "Not Caroline Trendle?"

Caroline Trendle was a Doberman breeder and,

like my aunt, a highly respected judge. She was every bit as steadfast and muscular as her favorite breed. It would take a brave man to kiss that Caroline, and an even braver one to gossip about it afterward.

"I doubt it," I replied. "March's Caroline was sixteen years old."

"Well, that's a relief."

"For you maybe. But it doesn't help me. And here's something else that's strange. Have you ever been to March's house?"

"Several times." Aunt Peg thought back. "When his wife was still alive, there were parties. None recently, though. I'd imagine it's been almost two decades."

"Did it seem normal to you?"

"As far as I remember. Why? What's the problem?"

"For some reason, I'm not allowed to go anywhere in March's house unescorted. Not even just from the library to the front door."

I explained what had happened earlier, when I'd left my laptop in the car. But rather than focusing on my concerns, it turned out that Aunt Peg was intrigued by Charlotte's timely and breathless arrival.

"How do you suppose Edward managed that?" she mused.

"I actually know how because I asked Charlotte about that when I was leaving. She said there's a buzzer hidden under March's desk. He presses it with his foot when he wants to summon her. Usually, she just hears a little ring, but the way he was pounding on the button earlier, she thought the house must be on fire. That was why she came running."

"A buzzer to summon the servants. How positively feudal."

"March walks with a cane now. It's not that easy for him to get around."

"Even so."

Peg enjoys oddities, and I could tell that she was pondering the possibility of installing a buzzer of her own. I had no idea whom she'd use it to call. Maybe she'd taught her Poodles to make tea.

"It all seems very strange," I said. "Where do they think I'm going to go? What don't they want me to see?"

"Perhaps it's like Jane Eyre. Maybe there's a crazy relative locked away in the attic and they're afraid you'll find her."

"I don't see why they would be. March seems pretty loony himself, and he's right there, front and center."

"Well, I certainly can't help you with that," said Peg. "And as for Edward's book . . ."

"Yes?" I leaned forward eagerly.

"You'll simply have to steer Edward back onto the right path. Don't let him get sidetracked.

Amorous adventures, indeed." She sniffed. "Who would want to read about that?"

Here's the thing: going to Aunt Peg for advice is like playing with a wheel of chance. You never know whether she will solve your problems or magnify them tenfold. This time, however, she'd done neither. Instead, she'd simply lobbed the hot potato back into my lap.

"In case you haven't noticed," I said drily, "March is not the most malleable man."

"Perhaps not. But he isn't a totally unreasonable one, either. Keep reminding him of all the wonderful dogs he's known over the years. Make him tell you those stories, and it will all work out in the end."

Aunt Peg always made things sound so easy. Too bad that they never seemed to work out that way.

Chapter 6

Somebody has to be the first to admit it. Winter dog shows in the Northeast aren't really that much fun.

For three seasons of the year exhibitors travel to wide open spaces. They show their dogs beneath gaily striped tents, in spacious rings spread out over freshly mowed meadows. But during the cold, dark months of a New England winter, all that changes.

Kennel clubs that host cold weather shows have had an increasingly hard time finding venues to accommodate their needs. They often have to settle for whatever they can get. Exhibitors find themselves in downtown civic centers or conference halls or, if they're really unlucky, high school gymnasiums. Parking is at a premium, as is interior space.

At indoor shows the rings are small and the floors, even where matted, are slippery. The light in the grooming areas is often inadequate. And yet we continue to come back anyway.

There are a number of reasons for that. Some exhibitors are chasing points, whether to finish a championship or with an eye toward year-end awards. Others can't bear to pass up a good judge who's been hired for their breed. And all of us enjoy the opportunity to spend a day hanging out with friends and fellow competitors.

That weekend, as Sam and I have done many times before, we packed up the boys and headed off to a dog show. This one was up the Connecticut coast, in New Haven. We weren't exhibiting, as none of our Poodles were currently in hair. But Aunt Peg was judging, and that was always fun to watch. Plus, we hadn't been to a dog show since before Christmas, and both of us were ready for a fix.

Over the years since she was first approved to judge, Aunt Peg's repertoire of breeds has expanded exponentially. She began her judging career with Poodles, but their three varieties—Standard, Miniature, and Toy—gave her entrée into two different groups. Now she's approved to judge all the breeds in both Toy and Non-Sporting.

The New Haven Kennel Club had hired her to judge most of the individual toy breeds plus the group, and she had repaid their confidence in her abilities by drawing an entry large enough to keep her busy all day. Aunt Peg had handled her own Standard Poodles in the show ring for decades. Known as a dedicated owner-breeder, she drew entries from amateur and professional handlers alike. She was fair and conscientious, and everyone who exhibited under her knew that she would do her utmost to uncover their dogs' better qualities.

Between the crate, the grooming table, and individual grooming supplies, I used to think that it took a lot of equipment to show a Poodle, but traveling with a two-year-old child is almost as bad. Sam carried the diaper bag. I had the pre-packed lunch and a satchel filled with toys.

Davey was holding his brother's hand and steering him in the right direction. Kevin's walking skills are a work in progress, and he tends to get distracted easily. The two boys' movement across the exhibition floor wasn't fast, but at least it was steady.

Sam and I were heading toward the grooming area on the far side of the exhibition hall. Poodles weren't due to be judged until after lunch, but they'd already be out on their grooming tables. Handlers would be busy brushing, scissoring, and putting up topknots. The preparations would have started several days earlier with bathing and clipping, and now would continue right up until the moment the dogs entered the ring.

Sam strode past the already full rings like a man on a mission. It was left to me to notice that Davey and Kevin had fallen behind. When I stopped and looked back, I saw that Davey had paused beside a ring where a Junior Showmanship class was in progress.

Two summers earlier, he'd given the competition a try himself. Coached by Aunt Peg, he'd been moderately successful before deciding when school started again in the fall that he preferred to devote his time to team sports. I fell back and went to stand beside him.

Kevin's eyes were wide open. His head swiveled back and forth in fascination as he watched the activity in the ring. A teenage girl gaited past us with a blue merle Collie. The toddler leaned forward over the low barrier, reached out a hand, and tried to touch the dog's bushy tail.

"Oh no you don't!" I caught Kevin's hand just in time. As a further precaution, I scooped him up and placed him on my hip. "You can look, but no touching."

"Want," Kevin said firmly. Like Aunt Peg, he's a great believer in his own opinions.

Davey laughed. "He wants everything he sees."

"So did you when you were his age." I nodded toward the ring. "Do you miss it?"

"No," he replied, then quickly looked up to gauge my reaction to his honest answer. "Is that okay?"

"Of course it is. You shouldn't have to do something you don't enjoy just because your relatives think it's fun."

"I guess . . ."

"But?"

"Aunt Peg is disappointed, isn't she?"

"Aunt Peg has high expectations, and she isn't satisfied unless people live up to them. That kind of attitude can lead to disappointment. But that's her problem, not yours. Just between you and me . . ." I juggled Kevin to one side, leaned down, and whispered in Davey's ear, "Aunt Peg can also be a little pushy when it comes to telling people what she thinks they ought to do."

I'd expected Davey to laugh. Instead, he still looked uncertain. "She told me I had the makings of a great handler."

"You do," I agreed. "But do you want to be a great handler?"

"Not particularly."

"Then there's your answer. Aunt Peg might have been disappointed briefly, but trust me, she'll get over it."

"I guess she knows how." Davey glanced up at me with a teasing smile. "She's disappointed in you all the time."

Sad to say, there was no point in arguing with the truth. Contrary to Aunt Peg's opinion, it wasn't my fault that her goals for me and my goals for myself sometimes failed to coincide.

"There you guys are," said Sam. He came up behind us and found a spot ringside. "I didn't even notice I'd lost you until I reached Bertie's setup and you were gone."

"We just stopped for a minute to watch Junior Show."

Sam glanced at the ring, then at Davey. Then he looked at me and raised a brow. I knew he was wondering the same thing I had about Davey's previous involvement. Silently, I shook my head.

"We're ready to move on," I told him. "Here, take this guy. He's too heavy for me."

Sam took Kevin out of my arms, swung him up, and settled him on his shoulders. Kevin laughed with delight at his new vantage point. He tangled his chubby fingers through Sam's hair and wrapped his short legs around Sam's neck.

The best thing about that was that it meant I could relax. Riding up above the crowd, Kevin was too high to reach out and create havoc with anyone's carefully coiffed entry. For the moment my family was actually under control—at least as much as they ever would be. With that happy thought in mind, I led the way across the room.

Bertie Kennedy is my best friend, a professional handler, the mother of three-year-old Maggie, and married to my brother, Frank. As you can probably guess, she's a very busy woman. Her setup was on the near edge of the grooming area, just beyond the toy ring where Aunt Peg was judging. I spared Aunt Peg only a brief glance— she would *not* have appreciated an interruption— on my way to giving the tall redhead a hug.

"It's about time you arrived," she said, her hands holding scissors and comb carefully angled out and away as she hugged me back. "Is it noon yet?"

It was barely 10:00 a.m. Since dog shows run on a tight schedule, I was assuming Bertie knew that.

"You try getting out of the house early with two kids," said Sam.

"Bite your tongue. One is hard enough." Bertie chuckled. "Maggie's barely out of diapers, and she already has to change her outfit three times before she decides she's ready to go."

"And what's wrong with that?"

The voice, floating over from the next setup,

belonged to Terry Denunzio, assistant and partner to Crawford Langley, the top Poodle handler in the Northeast. Terry was young and gorgeous and knew how to play to an audience. He also knew how to keep one thoroughly entertained.

Both his wardrobe and his manicure are better than mine, and Terry is constantly threatening to take me shopping. The implied insult might have annoyed me if I didn't enjoy his company so much. I wasn't surprised that Terry had been eavesdropping on our conversation. He has big ears, and he puts them to good use. It's no wonder that he knows everyone's secrets.

Crawford, who is closer in age to Aunt Peg, is in many ways Terry's opposite. Dignified, professional, and known for his discretion, he's been in the game longer than any of us. Crawford is often dismayed by his partner's nosiness. I thought it added enormously to Terry's appeal.

"And yet you were probably here at dawn," I said to him.

A professional handler's day is long, and it starts early. It wasn't unusual for Crawford to bring several dozen dogs of various different breeds to a single show. Their schedule was hectic, to say the least. Even now, Crawford was nowhere to be seen. Most likely, he was up at the rings, showing a dog, while Terry stayed behind at the setup to do prep work on the others.

"Before dawn," Terry corrected. "You know

Crawford. He likes to crack the whip." His eyebrows waggled comically. "Lucky for me, I like that."

"Do you mind?" I squeaked. "There are children present!" I reached up and covered Kevin's ears.

Thinking it was a game, Kevin responded with a toothy grin. He clapped his hands enthusiastically and just missed boxing Sam's ears. Davey only laughed. He has known Terry for most of his life and doesn't take anything he says too seriously.

"I don't mind a bit," Terry replied. His eyebrows were still dancing. Any moment now, his body would join in. "That's the whole point."

"No, the whole point is that you're supposed to be brushing dogs."

Crawford, back from the ring with a Chow Chow on a slender leash and a purple ribbon tucked in his pocket, leveled me a look. He thinks I'm a bad influence on his partner, probably with good reason. "Melanie, if you don't have enough to do, I can put you to work."

"No, thank you. I'm here to watch Aunt Peg judge."

"Is that so? Her ring is over there." Crawford squinted toward ring three. "It looks to me like she's doing Yorkies."

"Well . . . maybe I need to ask a few questions, too."

Crawford muttered something I couldn't quite hear. I suspected that was just as well.

"It's not like you didn't see that coming," Terry told him. He turned back to me. "So, who are we dishing about this week?"

Bertie snorted a laugh under her breath. She swept a Bichon off a tabletop, tucked it under her arm, and left for the ring.

"That's my cue to bow out, too," said Sam. "The kids and I are going to go see the sights." Holding Kevin carefully in place, he dropped a quick kiss on my lips. "Try not to annoy Crawford too much, okay?"

"You should listen to that man," Crawford told me as my family left, heading toward ring three. "He knows what he's talking about."

He slipped the Chow into an open crate, then tucked the ribbon into his tack box. At shows, Crawford's almost always on the run. Now I waited for him to grab another dog off a table and head out. Pumping Terry for information is much easier when Crawford isn't in the background, grumbling about our conversation.

Now, however, he shrugged out of his sports coat and hung it on a hanger attached to a stack of crates. Then he pulled out an apron and slipped it on over his head. A white Standard Poodle was lying on its side on a grooming table next to him. Crawford picked up a pin brush and spray bottle.

I must have looked surprised, because he glanced my way and said, "What? You don't think I can brush out a dog?"

"Of course you *can*. You just never seem to have time to."

He pointed to a schedule taped to the inside lid of the tack box. "Next up, Standards at one o'clock."

Since I obviously hadn't already figured it out for myself, Terry leaned over and whispered, "Crawford has fewer dogs today because he isn't showing under Peg."

Of course. I should have realized. Crawford and Aunt Peg were old friends, and both would want to avoid any appearance of favoritism or impropriety in the judging. The fact that Aunt Peg was doing all the toy breeds meant that half his string must have stayed home.

Crawford pulled a pair of reading glasses out of his apron pocket and perched them on his nose. Then he misted the dog on the table and went to work. Expertly.

Geez, I thought, even his line brushing was perfect.

"So," he said. "Ask."

Crawford giving me an opening? That was a first. And I certainly wasn't about to squander the opportunity.

"Edward March is writing a book."

"Oh, goody," cried Terry.

"Not really," I said. "It's going to be a kiss-and-tell memoir filled with juicy details about his amorous adventures in the dog show world. March thinks it will be a best-seller."

Crawford lifted his head and gazed at me over the rims of his glasses. "And we care about this, why?"

"I'm his coauthor," I admitted.

I thought he might snort or grumble. A discreet swear word wasn't out of the question. But once again, Crawford surprised me. Instead, he began to laugh.

"I'll give you this, Melanie," he said. "You're a constant source of entertainment. How in hell did that happen?"

"Aunt Peg."

The two words alone were explanation enough. Both men nodded.

"I'd read that," said Terry. "Seriously. It's not like Edward March would lack for content."

"Apparently not," I agreed unhappily. "The only reason I got involved with the project in the first place is because I thought he meant to write a history of dog shows and great dogs. Instead, it seems that March thinks of himself as the Don Juan of the dog show world."

"Understatement has never been one of his problems." Crawford's hands continued to fly through the Standard Poodle's hair. "Especially when it came to promoting his own dogs."

Crawford was modest to a fault. At the very top of his game, he was the least self-aggrandizing person I knew. I could see how March's attitude might have gotten on his nerves.

"Were March's Irish Setters as good as I've heard?" I asked.

"Sure. Over the years, they were some of the best. I don't know how many he has left anymore."

"Only one," I said. "I've been to his house twice, but I've never seen her."

"That's not surprising. Irish Setters are big, active dogs. Last time I saw Edward before he retired, he was looking pretty fragile. I think his health was worse than he wanted to let on."

"No wonder he wants to relive his glory days," said Terry. "Last hurrah and all that. Is he actually going to name names?"

"So he says. Though I can't imagine that the women he was involved with are going to be happy about it."

Terry shrugged. "There aren't that many secrets in the dog world, hon. We probably already have a fair idea of who'll be popping up."

"Like who?" I asked. "Anyone I know?"

Crawford sent us both a stern look. "Facts are one thing. We don't deal in gossip."

"Speak for yourself." Before Crawford could stop him, Terry gestured toward a nearby ring where half a dozen Vizslas were gaiting around the perimeter mats. "Maribeth Chandler, for one."

I squinted in that direction. "Which one is she?"

"Frosted blonde." Terry sniffed. "Like that's not a giveaway she's gone gray. Front of the line. Looks like she's about to win Best of Breed."

"I thought the Poodles moved fast," I said. The Vizslas were racing around the ring at the speed of light.

"High-energy breed," Crawford commented, trying to steer the conversation back to neutral ground.

Blithely, Terry ignored him. "Maribeth's a high-energy woman. Good thing the judge has her at the head of the line, otherwise she might run someone over. I wouldn't want to be the one to get in her way."

As we watched, the judge lifted his hand and pointed at Maribeth's Vizsla. She gave a happy little jump, swooped down and patted her dog, then ran to stand beside the BOB marker.

"Okay, that's one person," I said. "Who else? Tell me someone I know."

Crawford and Terry exchanged a meaningful look. Then they both lowered their heads and studiously went back to work.

That couldn't be good.

"Terry?"

"Hon, you don't want to know."

Perhaps not, but the way things were shaping up, I could hazard a guess.

Aunt Peg. Edward's Margaret. It had to be.

Chapter 7

"When?" I asked

Fingers still moving through the hair, Crawford glanced up innocently. "What are we talking about?"

"Aunt Peg, apparently."

"This is your fault," he said to Terry.

"Me? I didn't say a thing."

"Last hurrah? Naming names?"

"All right, maybe I said that." Caught red-handed, Terry still looked unrepentant. "But I never mentioned Peg."

"You didn't have to," I said with a sigh. "Whenever anything exciting is happening, it's a safe bet that Aunt Peg will be right in the middle of it. I wondered why March called her Margaret. Nobody ever calls her Margaret."

"Edward would have," said Terry.

Crawford shook his head. "You're really going there, aren't you?"

Ignoring him, I asked, "Why?"

"Edward always called the women he was involved with by their full names. That was his shtick, his own little secret touch. He thought it made them feel special."

"It doesn't sound like much of a secret to me," I grumbled.

"There's a reason for that," Crawford said shortly. "Edward has never been able to resist talking about himself. That's probably why he decided to write a book. Now, between the two of you, I think you've pretty much pushed my patience to its limit. It's time to talk about something else."

I nodded in acquiescence. Crawford had already opened up far more than I'd expected him to. As for Aunt Peg, who was currently in the middle of her assignment, I'd deal with her later.

"Who's going to win Best in Show?" I asked.

It was a mystery to me, but somehow Aunt Peg always knew these things ahead of time. She said it was a combination of knowing the dogs' records, the judges' preferences, and a little bit of a tingle in the air on show day. However she managed it, most of the other ardent exhibitors always seemed to be similarly clued in.

"The Peke," said Terry. "Anyone who doesn't know *that* hasn't been paying attention."

See what I mean?

"Is he a good one?"

"Oh, honey." Terry laughed. "You really have had your head under a rock."

"Ling was number one all systems last year. He'll retire next month, after Westminster."

Crawford nodded in the direction of the rings. "Go take a look for yourself. Peg'll be judging him in half an hour or so."

I couldn't tell whether Crawford was hoping to educate me or just get rid of me. Nevertheless, it seemed like a good time to move on. I found Sam and the boys sitting ringside, watching Aunt Peg judge.

Pomeranians were in the ring. To the inexpert eye—that would be mine—the animated balls of fur looked more like plush toys than real dogs. Kevin must have agreed, because he was bouncing up and down on Sam's lap, both hands outstretched in the direction of the ring. Luckily, his desire exceeded his grasp.

Davey was watching Aunt Peg's judging technique intently. There was an empty seat between them, and I slipped into it.

"Did you find out everything you needed?" asked Sam.

"And more," I replied ruefully.

Sam pulled his gaze away from the ring and stared at me for a long moment.

"What?" I asked him.

"I know I was originally in favor of your working with March, but I had a whole different project in mind. There's no reason to continue if you don't really want to. Just call him on Monday and tell him you're bowing out."

Now we had Davey's attention, too. He leaned

around me and inserted himself into the conversation. "You mean, like, *quit in the middle of an assignment?*"

"Now look what you've done," I said to Sam.

Parenthood. It's a veritable minefield of good intentions.

As I'd arranged with March at the end of the previous week, on Monday morning I headed back to Westport. I hadn't yet decided what I was going to do when I got there: did I want to follow Aunt Peg's advice or Sam's? At the moment my only plan was to show up as promised and wing it. Believe it or not, that's a strategy that has worked well for me in the past.

The weather was crisp and dry; the temperature was in the thirties. Though it had been overcast all weekend, now that it was time to go back to work, the sun was shining brightly. The glare off the drifts that lined either side of March's narrow country road was almost blinding.

It hadn't snowed in several days, and the road itself was mostly dry. But mindful of the winding turns and the ice that still lingered in shaded areas, I wasn't going very fast. Even so, when I rounded the last curve before March's driveway and came unexpectedly upon a brace of police cruisers parked by the side of the road, I had to slam on my brakes.

Immediately, I felt like an idiot. I've been

driving in snow since I was sixteen. I ought to know better.

The Volvo skidded only briefly. Thanks to gifted Swedish engineering, I quickly regained control. Pumping now instead, I slowed down beside the first police car.

There were three officers at the scene. Two were unspooling a long skein of yellow tape. It looped around two trees and ran along a low stone wall that bordered the road. Cones marked off another restricted area on the road itself. The entire right-hand lane was blocked off.

The third officer lifted his hand to wave me past. Instead, I stopped beside him and rolled down my window. March's driveway was still a hundred yards away, but now that I was stopped, I noticed a narrow break in the stone wall and a small lane that meandered back onto the estate. Charlotte had mentioned that Andrew lived on the property and had his own entrance. I wondered if that was it.

The officer leaned down and looked in my window. His mirrored sunglasses covered half his face and removed any vestige of an expression.

"What happened?" I asked.

"There was an accident here earlier. I'm going to have to ask you to move along."

"Was someone hurt?"

"Ma'am, is that your driveway?"

"No."

"Then I need you to keep moving and not block the road." The officer straightened and stepped away from the car.

Right. As intended, that told me exactly . . . nothing.

My past experiences with the police have been a varied lot, ranging from cooperative to contentious. Occasionally, they take me seriously. Most times—like now—I think they just wish I would go away.

So I did.

Driving well within the speed limit and making judicious use of my blinker, in case anybody with a badge happened to be watching, I eased down the road and turned into March's driveway. Maybe he and Charlotte would know what was going on.

I parked in my usual spot, gathered up my purse and laptop, and was on my way across the driveway when an Irish Setter came bounding around the side of the house. Ears flapping, feathers floating, she gamboled gracefully through the knee-deep snow. Then, abruptly, she stopped, and her head came up. She caught sight of me and changed direction.

The red setter woofed softly. It sounded more like a greeting than a watchdog's warning bark. She trotted toward me, hopping easily over the small drifts of plowed snow that bordered the pavement.

There are those who say that Irish Setters are the most beautiful breed of dog, and looking at the one before me, I certainly couldn't argue. With her mahogany red coat, long-limbed elegance, and dark, soulful eyes, she was the picture of canine glamour. She approached with her tail up in the air and waving slowly back and forth. The fringe of hair beneath it rippled with the languid movement.

"Aren't you pretty?" I crooned. "You must be Robin, right? Is that who you are?"

The setter's tail began to wag faster. Whether it was because I had guessed correctly or because she was simply an agreeable dog, it was hard to tell. I held out my hand and was politely sniffed. Now we were friends.

As she stepped in closer and investigated the length of my pants—no doubt gathering information about the Poodles at home—I ran my hands over her long, sleek body. Her hair was soft and fine, and she was shivering slightly in the cold.

"Come on, girl," I said. "Let's get you inside."

Robin followed me up the front steps to the house and waited at my side as I rang the doorbell. Once, then again. Then I tried knocking. Still there was no response.

Odd, I thought. Maybe this was Charlotte's day off.

I pulled out my cell phone and dialed March's number. He didn't pick up. I snapped the phone shut and looked at my watch. It was still Monday, now shortly after 11:00 a.m. March should have been expecting me.

I looked down at Robin. "Now what?" I asked.

That was reflex. I've been known to hold entire conversations with my Poodles. Not only that, but they're better at communicating their wishes than many people I know.

Not unexpectedly, the setter didn't answer. She was shivering harder now, though. I could see the small tremors rippling the length of her body. And yet she continued to wait patiently beside me, certain that I would figure something out.

If I'd been the only one standing outside the house, I probably would have given up and gone home. I was already conflicted about the project. If March couldn't even be bothered to keep our appointment, I would have figured that I had my answer.

But there was no way I could leave Robin outside by herself in the cold. And I couldn't very well take her home with me, either. As if sensing my internal debate, the setter gazed up at me trustingly.

Damn. I've always been a sucker for a dog with big, soft eyes.

"Back door," I said aloud.

There had to be one. Most likely, that was how Robin had come out. Maybe it was unlocked.

I threw my stuff back in the car, gave silent

thanks that I was wearing boots, and stepped into the snow beside the driveway. Now that we were moving again, Robin wanted to lead the way. She ran on ahead, leaping and bounding through the low drifts. The setter disappeared around the side of the house, then doubled back a moment later to see if I was still following.

"I'm coming," I said, laughing at her antics.

Robin lowered her front end and raised her hindquarters. Her tail was wagging madly now, high in the air above her body. Her hind feet danced in anticipation. Clearly, I was being invited to race.

"Really?" I asked. I leaned down, scooped up some snow, rounded it into a ball, and tossed it to her. "You want a piece of this?"

Robin opened her mouth and snagged the snowball out of the air. When she snapped her jaw shut and the snowball disintegrated on her tongue, the expression on her face was truly comical. She bounced up, sent me a fleeting glance, then ran around the back of the house again.

By the time I rounded the corner, Robin was already standing at the back door. She hopped impatiently from paw to paw on the stoop. I stepped up beside her, shaded my eyes against the glare, and looked through the window that formed the door's upper half. Just inside was a mudroom; the kitchen lay beyond.

Nobody was visible. I gave a hearty knock on the door, anyway. Still no answer.

So I took off my glove and tried the knob. It turned easily. So easily, in fact, that standing as I was, with my weight braced forward, the door pushed open before I even had a chance to think about whether or not I really wanted to go in. Immediately, Robin slithered through the narrow opening and dashed inside.

So now I was standing on the stoop by myself. You know, doing the breaking-and-entering thing.

I opened the door wider and stuck my head in. "Hello? Anybody home? Charlotte?"

I know. It sounds stupid. If they hadn't answered the doorbell or the knocking or the telephone, what was I expecting would happen? And, of course, there was only silence.

So I paused for a moment and thought about what to do. I'd already accomplished my original mission. Robin was now safe inside the house. I could return to my car and leave, guilt-free.

Like that was ever going to happen.

Instead, I let myself in and closed the door behind me. The house was utterly quiet. I had no idea where Robin had disappeared to. I couldn't even hear the sound of her nails clicking on the floor.

Carefully, I wiped the snow off my boots on the mat inside the door. It was bad enough that I'd let myself in. I wasn't about to leave a trail of cold water across the floor.

The kitchen was spacious and looked too

modern to have been original to the house. There was a Sub-Zero refrigerator and a restaurant-quality stove. The granite countertops, empty save for a bowl of fruit and a small television set, were gleaming.

I guessed that this was Charlotte's domain, and a desk tucked away in one corner confirmed that thought. A laptop sat open there, along with a purse and a pile of library books. A quick peek inside the wallet revealed Charlotte's ID.

Curiouser and curiouser, I thought.

So I kept going. I could see through an open doorway on the far side of the room that it led to the front hall. I'd been there before. Nearer to where I stood was a set of closed double doors. Dining room, most likely.

I grasped the nearest knob and pulled the door open. Then gasped softly. The room was large and semi-dark, the curtains drawn against the sunlight outside. It was also filled with junk.

Really, there was no other way to describe it. Everywhere I looked was a jumble of miscellaneous debris. The only thing that belonged was the dining-room furniture, but even that was barely visible due to the sheer multitude of things piled haphazardly around and on top of it.

I saw bedding and clothing and toys, all pushed up against several tall stacks of newspaper. There were shopping bags stuffed with a random assortment of items and two dog crates, one of which was missing its top. A pair of skis leaned against the wall. A giant candelabra balanced precariously on top of a crumbling cardboard box. Listing drunkenly to one side, it was a wonder that it didn't fall.

"Wow," I said aloud. Too bad Robin wasn't there to comment.

The look of the room was bad enough. The smell was worse. I didn't even want to stop and consider what was causing that. Instead, I drew the door shut and moved on.

I passed through the kitchen and out into the center hallway, which led from the front of the house to the back. The staircase leading up to the second floor was on my left. Other than that, I could see three closed doors. One, I knew, led to the library. Another appeared to be a second access to the dining room. The third, across the hall from the other two, I was guessing led to the living room.

Just to make myself feel better, I stood at the foot of the stairs and tried announcing my presence again. Like that was going to excuse my behavior. By this point, I'd moved well beyond doing a good deed; now I was trespassing. All the calling around in the world wasn't about to mitigate that.

The living-room door stuck, but when I put my shoulder against it and pushed hard, it gave way grudgingly. As soon as I stuck my head through the opening, I could see the problem. Just as in the dining room, this room's contents resembled those of a flea market gone berserk.

Where had this incredible accumulation of junk come from? I wondered. And why would anyone have ever wanted to save it?

Slowly, I withdrew my head and closed the door behind me. It seemed that I had my answer as to why no one had wanted me to go walking around the house by myself. There wasn't a crazy relative hidden in the attic. Instead, the lunacy was taking place right inside the front door.

It was definitely time for me to leave.

I turned to retrace my steps to the kitchen, then jumped and gave a small squeak of surprise. My breath caught as I inhaled sharply. Charlotte was standing three feet away at the foot of the stairs. She'd appeared so silently that I hadn't even heard her descent.

Her eyes looked huge and dark against the pallor of her face. Charlotte's hands were clasped in front of her, fingers twisting together in agitation.

"I see you've discovered our little secret," she said.

Chapter 8

"I'm sorry," I sputtered, feeling every bit the interloper I was. "I rang the doorbell. I knocked. . . ."

The excuses sounded weak, even to me.

"What are you *doing* here?"

"I . . . we . . . Mr. March and I had an appointment for this morning. Eleven o'clock?" I pushed back the sleeve of my jacket and showed her my watch. Like that was going to help. "But nobody answered the door. And then Robin was outside, and she was cold, so I thought I should let her back in. . . ."

Charlotte nodded. Whether it was because the explanation made sense or because she appreciated the effort, I wasn't quite sure.

"Eleven o'clock," she repeated. "I totally forgot. You're right. We should have been expecting you. I'm sorry. I should have called and told you that there won't be any work today. Mr. March is indisposed."

Somehow in the span of only a few seconds I'd gone from being the person in the wrong to being the one wronged. I had no idea how that had happened. But no one looking at Charlotte would presume that she was thinking clearly.

She was there beside me, and yet not there. She formed the words and spoke them, but looked as though they had no meaning for her. Her gaze remained vague and unfocused.

I thought of the policemen outside on the road, erecting their barriers. There'd been an accident that morning, they'd said.

"Is everything all right?" I asked.

"No." Charlotte's voice was small. "No, it isn't."

I reached out and took her hand. Her fingers were like ice. "Let's go sit down."

The library was March's domain, and the other downstairs rooms were unusable, so we headed back to the kitchen. Bright sunlight slanted in through the tall windows. It gave the room a warm, cheery glow.

Charlotte didn't seem to notice. She simply walked over to the butcher-block table, pulled out a chair, and sank down into it, as if her body was a burden and she was relieved not to have to support it anymore.

"Tell me what happened," I said.

"Andrew . . . Mr. March's son . . . he's dead."

The words hit me like a blow. All at once I could picture Andrew clearly: striding around my house and poking his nose into everything with his "professional curiosity." I hadn't liked March's son, but I certainly hadn't wished him this. I walked across the kitchen and sat down beside Charlotte.

"There was an accident on the road out front," she said softly. "Andrew was jogging. He does two miles every morning, even in the winter. A car hit him from behind and didn't stop."

"How awful," I said.

"There's more. It's worse." Charlotte's fingers tangled into a knot in her lap. "The police think maybe it wasn't an accident. They said that there were no tire marks on the road. Whoever hit him never even tried to stop."

"Maybe the driver skidded on the ice," I said.

"The officers who were here earlier didn't think so. There wasn't any ice near where they found him. I guess they can reconstruct the scene and figure out what happened?"

She looked at me for confirmation, so I nodded. I watch as much TV as the next person.

"Another driver saw him lying there and stopped. This isn't a busy road. . . . He may have been there for some time. That driver called the police. They brought an ambulance, but it was too late." Charlotte's eyes looked haunted. "Andrew was out there in the snow beside the road, and we didn't even know it."

"I am so sorry," I said, the most inadequate words in the English language.

Charlotte just nodded.

"How did you find out what happened?"

"The police came. They didn't know who Andrew was. He wasn't carrying any ID. I mean, why would he? He thought he'd be back home in twenty minutes, just like every other morning. Our driveway was the closest, so an officer came in and asked if we knew who he might be."

I swallowed heavily. It was all too easy to picture that terrible scene. "How is Mr. March holding up?"

"Not well. He's resting upstairs. He didn't want to lie down, but I told him he had to. I couldn't think what else to do. Once the officers found out that Andrew was Mr. March's son, they asked us all kinds of questions. They said a detective would be back this afternoon to talk to us again."

Charlotte paused. Her lower lip began to quiver. She pinched it between her front teeth to hold it still.

"I don't even know how we're going to manage that," she said. "Mr. March doesn't deal with unexpected visitors. You saw . . ." Her hand waved vaguely in the direction of the dining room. "Well, I imagine you can guess why."

I could. This was a house where people were rigidly controlled and things were wildly out of control. That was a bad combination at any time. Now, under the worst of circumstances, it was just one more thing to worry about.

I leaned forward in my seat and waited until

Charlotte looked up. "Mr. March is a hoarder, isn't he?"

She nodded. "I guess that's what you'd call it. When I first started working here, I didn't even know there was a name for that kind of behavior. I just thought he was really messy and needed someone to help him get organized. You know, an older man living by himself? I figured he probably had no idea how to pick things up and put them away."

I could see that. I know plenty of younger men who have never mastered the skill of cleaning up after themselves.

"But it's more than that. Mr. March never throws anything away. Ever. And eventually, there's no place to put everything. So it just piles up all over."

"He hired you to help him," I said. "Maybe he was hoping that you'd take charge."

"I've thought about that. Officially, I'm supposed to pay Mr. March's bills and manage his appointments. I make sure that he gets two good meals a day and has clean sheets to sleep on. But aside from those things, I try to do whatever I can. You should have seen this place when I first got here. At least I managed to get the kitchen cleaned up right away. But then it took me another six months just to make the library mostly livable."

"You did a good job," I told her.

"Thanks." Charlotte looked pleased by the

compliment. I doubted that she'd heard many from her employer. "I work at it every day. But it's always a struggle. What am I supposed to do? It's not like I can force Mr. March to give up his memories, and it seems like he has a story to tell about every single piece of junk in here.

"That's why I was so happy when he said he wanted to write a book about his life. I thought if he wrote the stories down, maybe we'd be able to clean some of this stuff out. I was hoping things might become a little more normal around here. Now it looks like that's never going to happen."

I could understand her frustration. In this house, anything approaching normal seemed like a stretch.

"How long have you worked for Mr. March?" I asked.

"Almost two years. After college I didn't really know what I wanted to do, so I spent some time just bumming around, taking odd jobs. Then my mother told me about this. She and Mr. March are old friends."

"Does she know about his hoarding?" I asked curiously.

"No way."

"You've been working here for two years, and you haven't told her?"

"It would mean my job if I did. Mr. March says it's nobody else's business how he chooses to live his life."

102

"That may have been true yesterday," I told her. "But not necessarily anymore. Once the police start investigating Andrew's death, they're going to be asking lots and lots of questions."

"I should hope so," said Edward March.

Charlotte and I both spun around in our seats. March was standing in the kitchen doorway, leaning heavily on his cane. Robin was with him, her tall body pressed against his good leg, offering her support. Even with my back to the door, I should have heard the two of them coming.

"What are you doing here?" he asked me.

"Talking about you," I told him. There was no point in lying, especially since I had no idea how long he'd been standing there. "I'm very sorry about what happened to your son."

"Me too." He sighed deeply. "There were times I wanted to kill that boy myself, but I never imagined anything like this."

He walked slowly toward us. I started to get up and offer him a hand, but Charlotte kicked me under the table. She gave her head a slight shake.

"Don't," she said under her breath. "He won't like it."

March reached out and banged the back of my chair with his cane. "What are you two whispering about now? Me again, I suppose. Why isn't somebody offering to pour me a stiff drink? Do I have to think of everything myself?"

"I'm more likely to offer to escort you back

upstairs," Charlotte told him. Her employer's gruff incivility didn't faze her in the slightest. "You're supposed to be resting."

"I already did that. At my age too much lying down just reminds you that you don't have much time left. Now I'd rather be halfway to stinking drunk. There's a bottle of twenty-year-old scotch in the pantry." Leaning a hand on the tabletop, March lifted his cane and pointed it in my direction. "You'll join me in a glass, won't you?"

I started to decline. If I started drinking scotch before noon, I'd be asleep by 2:00 p.m. Then I considered the circumstances and changed my mind. March's son had just died. How could I refuse something that might make him feel better, even if it was only briefly?

"Just a sip," I said. "I have to drive home."

Charlotte got up to fetch the liquor. March sat down in her seat. Robin came over, touched her nose to my knee in greeting, then turned a small circle and lay down beneath the table, next to March's chair.

"I see you two have met," he said approvingly.

"Outside."

"Damn dog loves the snow. Her coat gets all balled up with it. Next thing you know, there are puddles all over the house."

"You wouldn't have it any other way." Charlotte delivered a bottle of Glenfiddich and three tumblers to the table. She reached down and gave

Robin's head a pat before taking a seat opposite us.

March unscrewed the cap and poured a generous amount of amber liquid into each glass. Then he set the bottle aside and nudged a tumbler toward each of us. Lifting his own, he held it aloft and said, "Here's to Andrew."

"To Andrew," Charlotte and I echoed.

The three glasses clinked together in the air.

I took a small sip. Charlotte did the same. March tipped back his head and downed the contents of his glass in one long swallow. He set his tumbler back down on the table with a firm thump and reached for the bottle again.

Charlotte leaned over, extended her hand, and gently wrapped her fingers around the neck of the bottle, on top of his. March paused to look at her before refilling his glass.

"The police are coming back," she said. "The officers who were here earlier said that a detective would want to talk to us."

"When?"

"Sometime this afternoon. They didn't say when."

March grunted derisively and pulled the bottle to him. Charlotte hesitated briefly, then let it go.

"I may be drunk when he gets here," he said.

I watched March down another finger of scotch without pausing for breath. The third time he filled the glass, his hand wasn't as steady as it had been. A bit of the liquor sloshed out over the rim.

March didn't seem to notice. He was staring off into the distance.

"I'll have to go back to work," he said. It wasn't clear whether he was speaking to us or to himself.

"You don't want to think about that now," Charlotte replied. She stood up, picked up the Glenfiddich bottle, recapped it, and put it away.

March continued to gaze thoughtfully out the window. "If not now, when? It's not like the company can run itself."

"March Homes," I said, remembering what Charlotte had told me. "That's you."

"It *was* me. I built that company from scratch." He swiveled around in his seat to face me. "We started with custom kennels. Can you imagine? For several years that was our first and only product. Now March Homes is the sixth largest home builder in the state. And I'm out."

"Andrew has been in charge for the past five years," Charlotte told me.

"Not by choice," March growled.

Charlotte quickly shot me a warning look, but I asked, anyway. "What do you mean?"

March raised his glass again. This time he was content to take a sip. "What do you know about families?"

"Mine is like a three-ring circus," I said

honestly. "Other people probably aren't so lucky."

March snorted. "Relatives. Half of mine are crazy. It's no wonder I like dogs better."

A dog person myself, I couldn't argue with that logic.

"Andrew is my only son. He grew up watching me run the business and knowing that one day it would be his. Problem was, he didn't want to wait for that day to come."

"Mr. March." Charlotte looked pointedly at the tumbler in his hand. "Are you sure you want to be talking about this?"

"You think the whiskey has gone to my head."

She gave a small nod.

"So what if it has? What does it matter now? Andrew's gone, and nothing I say or don't say is going to bring him back. Besides, Melanie and I are writing a book together. She's bound to learn my secrets one way or another."

"It's no secret that families don't always get along," I said. "Perhaps especially when they have to work together."

"Andrew and I worked together just fine for years," said March. "His mother died when he was in high school, and he was already working summers for me then. He started at the bottom. I made sure of that. But he was good at every job I gave him. Eventually, he worked his way up to second in command. That's when he began to think that he knew everything about the business, even more than his old man."

March shook his head. "Maybe it was my fault for trusting him with so much responsibility. But I was busy with my dogs. First, breeding and showing, and then later judging. Andrew grew up around the setters, but he never appreciated them for what they were. To him, they were just pretty pets. He didn't understand the importance of my involvement in the breed. I created a premier family of Irish Setters, bloodlines that will continue to impact the breed for generations to come."

"You did indeed," I agreed.

March accepted the compliment as his due. "Margaret Turnbull's niece would know a little something about that, I should think. You know what a judge's life is like. The more assignments you take, the more time you spend on the road. Next thing you know, everybody wants your opinion, and it's turned into a full-time job."

I was eons away from becoming a judge myself—if, indeed, it ever happened—but I was well aware of Aunt Peg's busy schedule. And hers was probably moderate compared to that of someone with the stature of Edward March.

"So I was away a lot," he said. "Looking back now, maybe I was naive. I didn't worry about things when I was gone. I didn't think I had to. I knew I was leaving the company in good hands. That was what I'd been grooming Andrew for, after all. To take over for me when I felt the time had come to step down."

"And then Andrew decided to hurry you along," I said.

"There was no big overt move on his part, just a succession of little things. He undermined my authority in a dozen different ways. He took over projects that maybe I should have overseen myself. While I thought I was trusting Andrew to take care of the details, he used the opportunity to launch himself right into the big picture."

"Even so," I said, "March Homes was your company. Presumably, you could have reasserted control."

"Sure, I could have. But the only way to do that would have been to throw my son out on his ear. You can't have two alpha dogs sharing the same space. Andrew was clever. I'll give him that. When I looked around, I saw how neatly he'd ingratiated himself with my best customers. Now when they needed something, they went straight to him. While I was busy elsewhere, I'd been shunted aside, marginalized, in my own company.

"My own son saw to it that I'd lost my customers' confidence. These were people I'd known and done business with for years. In the end, I knew I had to do what was best for both the company and for my family. So I stepped down."

The three of us sat in silence for several moments. I watched the play of sunbeams on the glass-fronted cabinets and wondered if March was in shock. It didn't sound that way. If anything, he seemed to be thinking very clearly. And his first thought—with his son dead for only a matter of hours—had been to take back control of the company he'd lost.

"Charlotte said the police don't think Andrew's death was an accident," I mentioned.

"The officer told us that this morning," said March. "They must be wrong."

"If they're not," I said slowly, "they'll look for someone who has a motive."

"Who?" March demanded. "Who would have wanted to harm my son?"

I gave him a moment to think about that.

Then I said, "Based on what you've just told me . . . you."

Chapter 9

"They wouldn't dare!" March thundered.

"Trust me, they would."

Charlotte's eyes widened in shock. "How do you know that?"

"Unfortunately, I've been involved in a couple of murder investigations."

All right, maybe it was more than a couple. But

this didn't seem the right time to be sharing details about my complicated past.

March's eyes narrowed. "Margaret told me you were a teacher."

"I am. I mean, I *was* a teacher. Now I'm a full-time mother."

"One who dabbles in police investigations?"

His skepticism was warranted. In March's place, I'd have probably felt the same way.

"Not on purpose," I said in my own defense. "I just seem to have a knack for being in the wrong place at the right time."

"You sound like a bad-luck penny." March drained his glass again. "Margaret should have warned me about you. Things were fine around here until you arrived."

I gave him the look that that comment deserved. Fine? Seriously? In what universe could this household, with March's dysfunctional family relationships, secret hoarding, and apparently out-of-control love life, be considered even remotely *fine?*

"Mr. March, you need to pay attention to what Melanie's telling you," Charlotte interjected. "A detective will be coming back to talk to us. So maybe you should be thinking about what you want to say."

"You think I ought to make something up?"

"No," I said quickly. "Don't do that. You should only tell the police the truth."

"You just told me I had a motive for killing my own son. Surely, you don't expect me to lead with that?"

"No, but I don't think you should hide it, either. The police are going to find out what happened. They'll investigate everybody around Andrew."

"Even me?" Charlotte gasped.

"Even you. But unless you had a reason for wanting to harm him—"

"Of course not!"

"Then you have nothing to worry about."

"If we have nothing to worry about," March said sharply, "why are you trying to scare us?"

"I'm not trying to scare you. I'm simply telling you what might happen. You think of yourselves as grieving friends and relatives. The police are more likely to see you as potential suspects. It's what they do. Those closest to the victim always undergo the most scrutiny."

Lying beneath the table, Robin lifted her head and pricked her ears. A moment later, the doorbell rang.

I stood up and pushed in my chair. "I should be going," I said.

"No, don't." March's brusque mask slipped. All at once he sounded tired and overwhelmed, and I could see the toll the day's events had taken on him. "Stay for just a few more minutes. If that's the detective, Charlotte and I could use the moral support."

While Charlotte went to answer the door, I called Sam and told him that I might be gone longer than expected. I forestalled his questions with a promise to tell him everything later.

As I clicked the phone shut, Charlotte returned. She was accompanied by a middle-aged man with fleshy features and a sharp gaze. Robin woofed softly and started to rise. March put a hand on her shoulder. The setter resisted for a moment, then lay back down at his feet.

"This is Detective Wygod," Charlotte announced to the room at large. Her voice sounded overly bright. "Detective, I hope you don't mind if we talk in the kitchen. Can I make you some coffee?"

"No thank you. I'm good."

Wygod looked first at March and the cane that leaned against the table. Then his gaze shifted to me and the empty tumblers. Last of all, he glanced at Robin. She stared back.

"I guess that one's not a watchdog," he said.

Way to get started on the wrong foot, I thought. Detectives were supposed to be observant, but Wygod had obviously missed the interplay between March and the setter. Maybe he'd been too busy considering our a.m. drinking habits?

"She is when she needs to be," March said mildly. He didn't rise, but he did hold out his hand. "I'm Edward March. This is my friend Melanie Travis. And you've met my assistant, Charlotte. Please, have a seat."

Wygod shook March's hand, then pulled out a chair and joined us at the table. He was wearing a wool suit, no tie. A cashmere sweater covered his open-neck shirt, causing the jacket to pull tight across his shoulders.

"I know this is a bad time," he said. "And I'm very sorry for your loss. Believe me, we'll do everything in our power to find out what happened."

"I appreciate that," March replied. "And please know that we'd like to assist your investigation in any way we can."

"Excellent. I have several questions I'd like to ask about this morning's events. Your son, Andrew, he lived here with you. Is that correct?"

"Not exactly. He lived on the property, but not in this house. His cottage is several hundred yards away. Now that it's winter, you can just about see the roof from the back terrace. He also has his own driveway."

"So then you wouldn't necessarily have been aware of his activities?"

"That was the point, Detective. Andrew is—was—thirty-six years old. A grown man. He wanted his privacy, as did I. He built that cottage himself ten years ago. The distance suited us both."

"Do you know how your son happened to be outside, on the road, by himself at seven o'clock this morning?"

"He was a runner," said Charlotte. "Andrew ran a couple of miles every morning before work. He's been doing it for years."

"How many people were aware of his schedule?"

March looked perplexed. He glanced at Charlotte. She shrugged.

"I would think there'd be any number of people," March said finally. "The neighbors, or anyone else who drives this road frequently at that time of day. Friends of his and other runners. He liked to compete in mini-marathons when he had the time. Andrew ran track in high school, so that's how many years he's been going out to run every morning."

I hadn't realized that the incident had taken place so early. "It would have just been getting light then," I said.

Wygod inclined his head in my direction.

"Maybe the driver never saw him. Maybe he was hit by accident."

"We don't believe that's the case."

"Why not?" asked March.

"There are several reasons. Aside from the fact that the driver left the scene, Andrew March was also wearing a reflective vest and shoes. So he should have been very visible even at that time of day. In addition, there are no skid marks or evasive tire tracks, nothing to indicate that the driver tried in any way to avoid hitting him. And on top of that . . ." Wygod paused.

"Go ahead," March said gruffly. "I want to hear all of it."

"He was wearing a runner's armband that was meant to hold a cell phone, but the phone itself was missing."

March closed his eyes briefly and drew in a breath. He sighed heavily. "Andrew always had his phone with him. Always. He wouldn't have left the house without it."

I'd been clinging to the hope that Andrew's death was nothing more than a tragic mistake.

But the implications of that piece of news were definitely damning.

"You think that someone ran him down, stopped the car, and went back to make sure that he was dead," I said quietly.

Wygod nodded. "Either that or they saw he was still breathing, and removed the phone so he couldn't call for help."

March had been sitting upright, elbows braced on the table. But now he leaned back in his chair, and his shoulders slumped. He seemed to crumple in upon himself.

"What kind of animal could do such a thing?" he asked.

"That's what we intend to find out." Wygod withdrew a small notebook and pen from an inner pocket. "If it's all right, I have a few more questions for you."

"Go ahead."

"Your son was president and COO of March Homes. Is that correct?"

"Yes."

"A company you started."

"Correct."

"And you are now retired?"

"Nominally, I'm the CEO. But Andrew has been running March Homes for several years."

"Is the company experiencing any problems . . . financial trouble, union issues, administrative difficulties . . . anything at all?"

"Not that I'm aware of."

Wygod made a small notation, then changed the subject. "Your son isn't married. Is that correct?"

"No. Never has been."

"Current girlfriend?"

"I'm sure there is one. I wouldn't know who she is. Like I said, Andrew and I both like our privacy."

Wygod looked around the table, including Charlotte and me in the question. I had no idea. I'd only just met Andrew, and I said so.

"There was Julia," Charlotte said hesitantly.

March looked at her and frowned. "They broke up."

"When was that?" asked Wygod.

"Before Christmas."

That sounded pretty current to me. The detective must have agreed.

"Last name?" he asked.

March only glowered.

After a moment, Charlotte answered again. "Davis. She lives in Norwalk."

Wygod made another note.

"What about the car?" I asked as an uncomfortable silence stretched between us. "The one that hit Andrew. Wouldn't it be likely to need a repair?"

"We would expect so," Wygod agreed. "But unfortunately, so far we've found nothing at the scene to indicate a make or model, or even the color of the vehicle. Between Fairfield, New Haven, and Westchester Counties you're talking about several hundred repair shops, all within easy driving distance. We might as well be searching for a needle in a haystack."

"Oh," I said, disappointed. That was no help.

The detective turned back to Mr. March. "We're going to need access to your son's house, as well as his computers both at home and at work."

"Of course," March replied. "I'll call the office. And Charlotte can let you into his cottage whenever you want."

"Thank you. I appreciate your cooperation. Before I go, I'd like each of you to consider carefully for a minute. Is there anything I haven't asked that you think I ought to know? Do any of you have any idea why someone would have wanted to harm Andrew March?"

I shook my head quickly. Edward and Charlotte

were slower to answer, but the end result was the same.

Wygod pushed back his chair and stood up. "Thank you for your time. There is just one more thing. Where were each of you between seven and seven thirty this morning?"

I'd expected him to ask the question. I knew it had to happen eventually. And even though I knew I'd had nothing to do with Andrew's death, when the detective's steel-gray eyes stared in my direction, I still flushed and felt guilty.

"At home," I said. "Getting an eleven-year-old ready for the school bus."

"And home is where?"

"Stamford."

You do the math, I thought. But I didn't say it out loud.

"Home as well," said Charlotte. "In Fairfield. I was just getting ready to leave. I start work here at eight. Your officers out on the road saw me arrive for the day."

"And you, sir?"

I'd felt guilty answering the question. March sounded annoyed. "Upstairs in bed. Right where I was supposed to be."

"Asleep?"

"Of course."

Charlotte walked Detective Wygod out. As the two of them left the room, I got up to follow.

"You'll come back," said March. It was a

statement, not a question. "Wednesday will do."

The schedule we'd agreed upon previously had called for us to work together three days a week. But considering the morning's events, everything was different now. It had to be. Surely, March didn't intend to go right back to work on his book.

"I don't get around like I used to," he continued. "I'm going to need someone to be my eyes and ears."

"Excuse me?"

"Oh, I know that the police will do their job. They'll go around and ask people where they live and what time they went to bed. Maybe they'll find the right answers, or maybe they won't. But either way, their salaries will still get paid. I'll tell you something I learned a long time ago. Never trust a civil servant to do something that you can do yourself.

"Andrew and I didn't always get along, but he was my son. I want to know what happened to him, dammit. Who did he get mixed up with that would do such a terrible thing? My brain is every bit as sharp as it ever was, and I refuse to just sit around and wait for somebody else to get to work figuring things out. All I need is a better pair of legs. That's where you come in."

"Me?" I said faintly.

"Think about it." March flapped his hand in the air, shooing me toward the door. "No need to give me an answer now. We'll talk on Wednesday."

• • •

When I got home, I found out that Sam had called in reinforcements. Aunt Peg was coming to dinner.

"How did that happen?" I asked.

"When you left this morning, I was half convinced you were only going to see March so that you could quit in person. Then I get a cryptic phone call telling me that instead of a quick visit, you're going to be in Westport half the day. So something must have gone wrong."

Sam paused and lifted a brow, waiting for me to fill in the blanks.

"March's son, Andrew, was killed this morning. He was jogging on the road and was hit by a car."

"Oh no."

"And March himself is a hoarder."

Sam stared. "Really? When did that happen?"

"Not recently, I can assure you. Plus, Andrew wrested control of March Homes away from his father five years ago. And now that he's dead, March gets the company back."

"Anything else?"

I got the sense that the question was a rhetorical one, but I answered, anyway. "March doesn't have a lot of faith in the police. He wants to do some asking around himself."

"Of course he does," Sam muttered darkly.

I shrugged. "You *asked.*"

"I guess I wasn't expecting quite so many answers."

Welcome to my world, I thought.

"Aunt Peg?" I tried again.

"Oh, right. She called earlier. I told her you were with March and that there might be some new developments. She invited herself over."

Under those circumstances, I was surprised Aunt Peg hadn't arrived already.

Sam went back to his office, the Poodles trailing along behind. I spent half an hour straightening up the house, and then Kevin and I went to the supermarket. On the way home, we picked Davey up from basketball practice.

By the time Aunt Peg arrived that evening, Kevin was fed and bathed and ready for bed, Davey was working on his homework, and there was a pot of chili simmering on the stove. I love it when a plan comes together—even if it's one I didn't make myself.

Davey kept us entertained throughout most of dinner. As always, he had plenty of news. His intramural basketball team was on a winning streak, he'd recently joined the ham radio club at his school, and his best friend, Joey Brickman, was getting braces on his teeth. At eleven and a half, these are major developments.

Aunt Peg asked probing questions, made all the right comments, and did her part to be an appreciative audience. Where her nephew is concerned, Peg is the best kind of cheerleader, and Sam and I were happy to let the two of them hold the floor.

Afterward, Davey went back to his homework, and Sam and Tar went upstairs to put Kevin to bed. I piled the dirty dishes in the sink; then Peg and I settled in the living room to talk. Faith and Eve lay down next to my chair. When Aunt Peg sat down on the couch, Raven and Casey immediately hopped up to join her.

I know I'm supposed to teach my dogs to stay off the furniture, but really, what's the point? If they were on the floor, I'd only have to reach farther to pat them.

"So?" Aunt Peg beckoned to Raven, and the big Poodle crawled across the cushion and into her lap. "I got the impression that there were things we didn't want to bring up in front of the children. Or is my imagination working overtime?"

"No, I'm afraid you're right."

It took ten minutes to bring her up to speed on the day's events. Peg listened in silence, but I could envision the wheels turning inside her head. By the time I finished talking, Sam and Tar had rejoined us.

"Poor Edward," she said softly. "What a blow that must have been."

"I didn't know Andrew," said Sam, finding a seat between us. "Did you?"

"Only in the very vaguest way. If I'm remembering correctly, the last time I saw him, he was a pimply-faced teenager."

"He was here last week," I told her.

"Here? Whatever for?"

"He warned me not to continue working with his father. He said there wasn't going to be any book, that he would block it by whatever means necessary in order to protect the family business. At the time I was baffled. I couldn't figure out what he was so upset about. But now that I know about March's affairs and his hoarding, I guess it makes more sense."

"It sounds like their relationship was pretty contentious," said Sam. "If Andrew was responsible for ousting his father from a company he'd built from scratch, I can see how that would cause plenty of family friction."

"Things were very different when Isabelle was still alive," Aunt Peg mused. "Although even then I remember her running interference between the two of them. But Edward was putty in her hands. He was absolutely devoted to her."

I snorted indelicately. Faith lifted her head and cocked an ear. It's a sad thing when your own dog feels a need to comment on your manners.

"March plans to write a kiss-and-tell book about his sexual exploits in the dog show world," I said. "That doesn't sound much like devotion to me."

"Yes, well . . ." Aunt Peg's gaze slipped away. She suddenly busied herself with teasing a mat out of Raven's ear.

I'd brushed that ear earlier, I thought with a frown as I watched her fingers work through the silky hair. There was no knot there. Then, abruptly, I remembered the gossip that Terry had let slip at the show.

"Although I guess maybe you would know all about that," I said. *"Margaret."*

Aunt Peg's gaze was still averted. Sam just looked confused.

"That's what March calls Aunt Peg," I told him.

"Aha." Sam's expression cleared. He might have been biting back a smile.

Aunt Peg's head snapped up. "Aha nothing!"

"You and Edward March?"

"It was a long time ago."

"I should hope so," I said. Aunt Peg had been married to my Uncle Max for several decades.

"We were barely more than teenagers."

Sam was grinning in earnest now.

"And it was the sixties. Things were different then."

Indeed.

"Sex, love, and rock and roll?" asked Sam. "Like that?"

"Oh, for pity's sake."

Then I was laughing, too. Usually, I'm the one

on the receiving end. I'd never seen my aunt blush before. So this was what it felt like to have the shoe on the other foot. I could definitely get used to that.

Chapter 10

"You realize that this changes everything," Aunt Peg said, deftly switching the subject. "I wonder what Edward will do now."

"He has several ideas," I told her. "One of which is to take back control of March Homes."

Tar, who had yet to find a spot to settle, decided instead to pick up a thick knotted rope from a pile of dog toys in the corner. He carried it over to Sam, who grasped the other end absently and began to pull. It's a family trait: we all seem to think better when we have a dog in our hands.

"He has to be thinking in terms of a temporary measure," said Sam. "Considering that health issues have forced him to retire from judging, I can't see him wanting to return to the workforce full-time, even in his own company."

"Quite right," Aunt Peg agreed. "So he'll be looking for a successor." She paused, then added, "Now, there's a dandy motive for you."

It was no surprise that she would be thinking

along those lines. Aunt Peg has a devious mind herself, so she tends to attribute that same quality to others.

"Here's another," said Sam. "If March does go back to work, that should sideline his plans for a book indefinitely. I wonder how many of the women he planned to write about knew about the project. And how many of them might have objected to being part of it?"

"I don't know the answer to your second question," said Peg. "But as for the first, I'm guessing that a good portion of them found out about it just recently."

That was unexpected. "How?" I asked.

"Though I would have credited Edward with better social skills, he sent out a mass e-mail—of all things—at the end of last week. It detailed his plans to write a memoir and said he hoped we'd all feel honored to be included."

"Honored?" I had to laugh. "Did he mention the capacity in which he meant to talk about you?"

"Not directly." Aunt Peg shifted her hand downward and began to scratch Raven's throat. The big Poodle leaned into the caress happily. "Nevertheless, I wouldn't be surprised if the e-mail didn't cause more than a few nervous flutters among the recipients. As you've already surmised, Edward didn't find marriage vows—his own or anyone else's—to be much of a hindrance when seeking out potential partners."

"What about you?" said Sam. "Weren't you worried about what he might say?"

"Oh, heavens, no." Aunt Peg smiled slyly. "What did I have to worry about? Melanie is to be the book's coauthor, after all. I was depending upon her to simply edit my segment out."

It's gratifying to know that every so often Aunt Peg thinks my skills are good for something.

Early Wednesday morning I got a call from Charlotte.

"I know you had an appointment with Mr. March today," she said. "But it's just too soon. He'd rather not see anyone."

"Of course. I understand completely."

"I also wanted to let you know that there's going to be a memorial service for Andrew on Monday at the Matthews Funeral Home in Westport," Charlotte continued. "I hope you'll come. Mr. March waited until after the weekend so he wouldn't interfere with anyone's plans, and I'm hoping there will be a big turnout. A gesture of support on the part of the dog community would really buoy his spirits."

Fervent dog show exhibitors hold their weekends sacrosanct. Since I started going to shows with Aunt Peg, I've come to think of midweek parties, weddings, and even funerals as normal.

"Certainly, I'll be there," I said. "And I don't think you'll have to worry about drawing a crowd. Mr. March has been a prominent member of the dog world for decades. I'm sure everyone will want to pay their respects."

Given what felt like a reprieve, I spent the rest of the week doing the Mom thing. I caught up on chores, took Kevin to Mommy-and-Me swim class at the Y, and baked three dozen cookies for a bake sale at Davey's school. Between that and bathing and blowing dry three Poodles, plus making plans to go to Westminster, then shoveling out from another six inches of snow, there should have been plenty to keep me busy.

So why did my thoughts keep wandering back to a crotchety old man I barely knew who needed someone to be his eyes and ears and thought that I was the right person for the job? By Sunday night I'd spent so much time thinking about Edward March and his problems that I'd begun to wonder why I'd ever even hesitated to say I would help. It was beginning to seem like a foregone conclusion.

When I called Aunt Peg and told her, she thought I was daft.

"Of course you're going to look into things," she said. "Did anybody ever doubt that?"

Only me, I guess.

"You'll start this evening, at the memorial service. Absolutely everyone will be there. What a perfect place to find guilty parties."

It looked like I had my first assignment.

Aunt Peg's assessment of March's drawing power was correct. When Sam and I arrived at the Matthews Funeral Home Monday evening, the parking lot was already full and cars lined the street for several blocks in both directions. The imposing redbrick building, situated on a knoll overlooking Route 1, was lit up like a candelabra. After climbing the wide steps leading up from the sidewalk, Sam and I had to join a line of mourners waiting to negotiate the entrance.

Once inside, I saw dozens of familiar faces. Some were friends; others I knew only by reputation. Aunt Peg was somewhere in the crowd, as were Crawford and Terry, and my sister-in-law, Bertie. Andrew's coworkers were easy to pick out. They stood huddled together in a tight group, looking thoroughly bemused by all the dog chatter eddying around them.

Sam and I entered the funeral home together, but the ebb and flow of conversation soon drew us in different directions. Edward March was seated at the front of the largest reception room, near a tiered bank of flower arrangements and a collection of photographs of Andrew, several of which were large enough to be propped up on easels. I kept trying to make my way in his direction to offer my condolences, but he was constantly surrounded by a large crowd of well-wishers.

As I paused mid-room, an arm slid around my

shoulders from behind and I smelled Bertie's perfume. Chanel No. 5. She's a traditionalist when it comes to scent. We hugged briefly, then stepped apart.

"Some crowd, huh?" she said. "I'm glad I found you. I was beginning to think I was going to have to spend the entire night listening to guys talk about field trials."

That's the thing about dog people. You can take us out of the show milieu, but we still just stand around and talk about our dogs.

"Is Frank here?"

Bertie shook her head. "Home with Maggie. You know Frank. Dogs aren't really his thing. He wouldn't have known anyone. What about Sam?"

I gestured toward a far corner. "He seems to have found the Non-Sporting side of the room."

"Who's got the kids?"

"We're trying out a new sitter," I said with a grimace. "Here's hoping she lives up to her references."

Bertie nodded sympathetically. She'd been there.

"We barely got a chance to talk at the show last weekend," she said. "Peg tells me you've gotten involved in some sort of book project with Edward March. Did you know Andrew, too?"

"Not really. We'd only just met, and I have to say, he certainly didn't make a great first impression."

"It sounds like he took after his father. Edward can be pretty prickly." Bertie spared a glance in his direction. "For all his standing in the dog community, I don't think he has a lot of close friends."

That didn't come as a surprise. I'd witnessed March's isolation for myself. But the realization that it extended beyond the older man's home and out into the real world came with an unexpected stab of pity.

"It seems like a shame," I said. "Especially considering how prominent a role the dog world has played in his life."

"I guess," said Bertie. "But you know what shows are like. People are traveling all the time, and they stay in the same hotels. They groom their dogs together in close quarters under the tents. Sometimes it feels like everyone is living on top of everybody else. And then the element of competition just complicates things further. Even when everyone tries to play nice, there can still be plenty of tension to go around. Edward was a good judge, but socially . . . well, he wasn't above causing problems."

"Because he liked chasing other men's wives?"

Bertie nodded. "And it's interesting that you would phrase it that way. Because that was my impression, too—that it wasn't the affair itself that Edward wanted so much as the pursuit and the conquest. It was all just another competition to him. The women themselves were almost incidental."

"I can see how that might have left a lot of women feeling used," I said.

"Maybe. But it's not like they weren't willing participants. And many of the women he was involved with maintained some sort of relationship with him afterward. Tonight's a good example. Look around the room."

We both did.

"See that woman there?" Bertie pointed discreetly toward a short brunette in a tight Chanel suit. "Sybil Forest. She's one of his exes. That's her husband beside her."

The husband was built like a linebacker. From the look of him, he could have torn March limb from limb, should he have chosen to do so.

"Bloodhounds," Bertie added. For a dog person, no description was complete without the addition of breed affiliation. "And over there?"

We both shifted slightly in the other direction.

"Black pantsuit, gray hair," Bertie stated.

"India Fleming," I said. I had shown under her.

"And the blonde next to her . . ."

That woman looked familiar. It took me a moment to remember why.

"Maribeth something," I said. "Terry pointed her out to me last weekend."

"Chandler," Bertie replied. "She has Vizslas."

133

Then the crowd between us shifted slightly, and I saw a swing of silky blond hair framing another familiar face. "That's Charlotte standing with them," I said.

"Who?" Now it was Bertie's turn to discreetly crane her neck to look.

"The young blonde is Charlotte, March's assistant." I paused and thought back. "She told me that her mother and March were old friends. That's how she got the job."

"Her mother didn't do her any favors, did she?" Bertie muttered.

I thought about March's squabbling family, his debris-filled house, and Charlotte's cheery attempts to make everything seem normal. Bertie didn't know the half of it, I thought.

"There are more," she said. "Should I keep going?"

"No, I get your point. But how do you know all this stuff? March must be at least seventy. A lot of it must have happened before you started showing dogs."

"*Everybody* knows this stuff." Bertie jabbed a finger into my shoulder. "Except maybe you. You know the dog show world. The good gossip never dies."

"Who died?" asked Aunt Peg, coming up to stand beside us. "We're already at a memorial service. Isn't that enough for one day?"

"We're talking about gossip," Bertie told her.

"Perish the thought."

Someone with less self-control might have rolled her eyes. I settled for a baleful look.

"What?" Aunt Peg asked innocently.

"I must have you confused with someone else," I said. "Because I could have sworn that you were the person who sent me to help March write a kiss-and-tell memoir."

"Kiss and tell?" Bertie quickly stifled a giggle. "Are you serious? Nobody told me that part."

"It's hardly my fault that Edward looked at the body of work his life encompasses and then chose to take the low road," Aunt Peg said with a sniff. "Truly, I would have expected better of him than that."

I leaned closer to Bertie and whispered, "And she should know. After all, Aunt Peg and Edward March are *old friends*."

"Oh, dear." Bertie tried biting her lip in an attempt to maintain decorum appropriate to the setting. Clearly, she was losing the battle. Her hand came up and covered her mouth. "I may have to step outside."

"And you thought you had all the good gossip."

"I'll never underestimate you again," she said.

"Look." Peg grasped my shoulders firmly and turned me so I was facing the front of the room. "It's time to pay attention. Somebody's about to speak."

The director of the funeral home had stepped up to a small podium situated on the dais next to the photographs. He waited until the room quieted, then thanked us all for coming to pay tribute to our dear departed friend Andrew. He assured us that Andrew's grieving family appreciated our presence, and announced that several of Andrew's friends would like to take this opportunity to say a few words.

First to speak was a man named Sherm Yablonsky. He introduced himself in a voice that quavered initially, then grew stronger as he recounted his favorite memories of March's son. "Andrew and I were college roommates at Columbia," he said. "Purely luck of the draw. Most freshmen end up hating the guy they're assigned to. We immediately became best friends instead."

When he finished speaking, he stepped off the dais and went and shook Edward March's hand. Another man came forward to take his place.

"I'm Walt McEvoy," he said. "Andrew was my boss. He told me what to do, and at least some of the time I did it." There was a small ripple of laughter from the peer group. "Seriously, I couldn't have chosen a better guy to work with these last ten years."

He, too, walked over and shook Edward March's hand when he was done. Watching as that interplay repeated, I noticed a dark-haired woman in a severely styled black dress who was standing just behind March's chair. Her eyes were large and luminous, and she appeared to be on the verge of tears. Her arms were crossed tightly over her chest, and it looked as though the secure hug was all that was holding her together.

Now that I stopped and thought about it, I realized that she'd been occupying that somewhat conspicuous spot for most of the evening. And yet neither March nor any of the other mourners had taken the time to speak to her. No one was paying any attention to her at all.

I elbowed Bertie. "Who is that?"

"No idea," she whispered back.

When someone else began to speak, I kept watching the woman as she stood and listened politely. She appeared to be about my age, more likely to have been a companion of Andrew's than his father's. Why, then, were his friends snubbing her? And what made her remain in place in the face of their obvious incivility?

"Well, that's that," said Aunt Peg.

I looked up and realized that the last speaker had finished. People were beginning to head toward the door. Sam was making his way through the thinning crowd in our direction.

"I haven't had a chance to speak to Mr. March yet," I said. Once again, he was surrounded.

"You came, and you offered your support," said Aunt Peg. "I'm sure that's enough."

"Ready?" asked Sam. He'd already been to the cloakroom.

I wound my scarf around my neck and slid my arms into the wool coat. Together, we headed out into the cold night.

Chapter 11

"You're going to want to see this," March said. He was seated behind the desk in his library, holding a sheet of paper, which he tilted in my direction. "I made a list."

I had just arrived and barely had my coat off. As usual, Aunt Peg's assumption had proven to be correct. Only two days after the memorial service, I'd been summoned back to Westport. Apparently, March and I were going to be working together, and he was eager to begin. He didn't even wait for Charlotte to close the door before starting to issue orders.

I probably should have been annoyed by his peremptory behavior. Instead, I found myself unexpectedly pleased to see that March was looking better than he had the last time I'd seen him. There was color back in his cheeks and a definite stiffening of his spine.

Before I even had time to react, he looked up at

me and flapped the paper impatiently. I crossed the room and took it from his hand.

"What kind of list is it?"

"Things for you to do. I've laid my son to rest. Now it's time to get to work."

I looked at the first item at the top of the page. *Talk to the neighbors and find out what they saw.*

"The police will have already done that," I said.

"And what did they tell me about what they've found out?" March demanded. "Not a single blessed thing. That detective hasn't even bothered to return my latest call."

I moved around the desk and stood by the window behind it. Now that I could actually see its dimensions, the window was surprisingly large. The drapes that framed it, however, were made of dark, bulky velour. Hanging partially closed—the only position I'd ever seen them in—they blocked out all but a small sliver of light.

"When did you call Detective Wygod?" I asked.

"At least twenty minutes ago," March said irritably. "Maybe more."

Those drapes were annoying me. I tried bundling up an armful of the heavy material and pushing it to one side. The curtain receded briefly, then slid slowly back into its accustomed place.

"Leave that." The elderly man craned his head around to see what I was doing. "Come and sit down."

I stepped back around in front of the desk,

where it was easier for March to see me. "We're going to make a deal," I told him.

"We already have a deal."

March's index finger tapped up and down on a folder beside his blotter. As I recalled, I'd never signed that contract. I'd never even seen the revised version he'd promised me—the one that was supposed to protect both our interests. The wily old businessman probably still thought that he was keeping his options open. If that was the case, he was about to find out that having me for a partner might not be as simple as he'd initially assumed.

I set the list down on his desktop. Given a small nudge, it went sailing across the polished surface.

"If you want me to do those things for you, you're going to have to do some things for me, too. For starters, it's too damn dark in here. It's a beautiful day outside. Why would you want to shut that out?"

March crossed his arms over his chest. His expression turned mulish. "I like it dark. And it's cold out there."

"Cold, but sunny," I pointed out. "Being in here is like sitting inside a cave. I don't know how you can work like this. I'm getting rid of those drapes."

"You're not getting rid of the drapes."

"Yes, I am." It was time March learned that he wasn't the only stubborn person in the room. "We need to get more light in here. What are you afraid of? That I'll see that your library is full of junk? Guess what? I already know. We still need to be able to see what we're doing."

Back around the desk I went. The drapes looked like they weighed twenty pounds or more. I might not be able to take them down off the rod, but with all the stuff scattered around the room, I was pretty sure I could find something with which to tie them back.

"I said leave it alone," March growled.

"The air in here is stale, too," I told him. "You're lucky I'm not opening the window while I'm at it. Why is the door always closed, anyway?"

"I like my privacy."

"There's nobody in the house but you and Charlotte. She doesn't strike me as a snoopy sort of person."

"Unlike you."

"Unlike me," I agreed. "Whose snooping talents you would apparently like to put to good use."

That shut him up. I continued to work on the drapes.

Poking into their depths, I'd discovered that a pair of bronze tiebacks was screwed into the window frame. Not only that, but there was a long decorative tassel hanging from one. Any minute now, I'd have all that heavy velour under control and out of the way.

"You ought to be listening to me," said March. "This is my house."

"I am listening," I told him. "Any minute now, you might say something I want to hear."

I bunched up half of the heavy material and shoved it hard to one side. Before it could rebound, I got it anchored behind the tieback. For good measure, I tied the drape in place with the tassel.

"Now that looks much better." I surveyed my work with satisfaction. One side done, I turned and attacked the other. "How long have these things been hanging here, anyway? They look like a holdover from the seventies."

"Could be they are. My wife picked them out." March waved a hand, dismissing the topic. "Who cares? They do the job."

"You're right. They do," I said. One last knot and the second side was trussed in place, too. "They keep the world out. I'm wondering why you want that."

"What? Are we going to analyze me now?"

March spun around in his seat to glare at me. Instead, he found himself blinking at the unaccustomed brightness. The snow outside sparkled beneath the sun's rays. The vista, looking out across the yard to a meadow beyond, was dazzling.

"I'm just trying to improve our working conditions," I said. "What a beautiful view you have from here."

"It's all just a lot of snow." March sounded

grumpy. "But if you think you need to be able to look at it, by all means, help yourself."

"Thank you," I said happily. "Even better, now we can see what we're doing."

I skirted back around the desk and went to take my usual seat. The chair was where I'd left it, but its cushion, empty on my previous visit, was now stacked high with a tilting pile of old leather-bound photo albums. Abruptly, I stopped in place, assailed by a sharp stab of guilt. In the wake of his son's death, March must have been doing some reminiscing. And I'd gotten so caught up in trying to assert myself that I'd almost forgotten the reason for my visit.

"I'll just leave these here," I said, backing away.

"Oh, for Pete's sake," March snapped. "What's the matter with you today?"

Just that quickly my contrition vanished. Feeling sorry for that old man was like showing weakness to a tiger—it only invited him to bite your head off.

"Put the damn things anywhere," he said. "Put them on the floor, if you have to. Just move them out of the way."

Easier said than done in this room.

"You know, we could do some straightening up in here," I mentioned.

"It doesn't need straightening. This is my stuff, and I like it where it is."

I hefted the stack of photo albums. "Maybe just a little reorganizing?"

March's cane had been leaning against his desk. Now he picked it up and shook it in my direction. "How about if you sit down and stop trying to run my life? Any minute now, you're going to make me regret hiring you."

"*Hiring* me?" Arms full, I turned around to face him. "Does that mean you're going to pay me?"

"Book royalties. Like we agreed upon before."

"Oh, right." I found a spot for the albums on a nearby crate beside a nest of pillows. "That assumes there *is* a book."

"Of course there's going to be a book," said March. "Why wouldn't there be?"

Finally I sat down. "I heard you say you were going back to work."

"So?"

I reached out and picked up the sheet of paper. "And now you've got a list of things for me. So who's going to be writing your memoirs?"

"Maybe the book gets delayed a little. It's still going to happen."

I sincerely hoped not. But I wasn't about to waste anybody's time debating the issue. Instead, I looked at March's list again.

"Number two," I read aloud. *"Come up with likely suspects."*

March nodded. "I read P. D. James and Elizabeth George. That's how it's done."

144

"Good to know," I said.

Before I could get to the next item, the library door opened behind me. As I turned to look, Robin came bounding into the room.

"I've got coffee," Charlotte said, entering behind the setter. "Sorry about Robin. She was supposed to wait in the kitchen. But like everyone else around here, she just does what she wants to do."

"Come here, pretty girl," I said to Robin, holding out a hand.

She was already on her way in our direction. Having seen March by the window, the setter snaked through the cluttered room handily. Her long feathered tail wagged back and forth, smacking into furniture and odds and ends.

Robin spared me a glance and sniffed my fingers politely, but it was March she wanted. She scooted around the desk and sat down happily beside him.

"This looks different." Charlotte stopped in the middle of the room.

"We're trying a new concept," I said. "Light instead of darkness. We might even do some straightening."

"Don't listen to her," March grumbled. His hand was stroking Robin's head. "She doesn't know what she's talking about."

"I like it." Charlotte continued on to the desk and set down the tray. Then she stepped over to the window and had a look at the arrangement for herself. "Maybe I should take these drapes down and have them cleaned."

"What is going on today?" March asked. "Why is everybody suddenly trying to run my life?"

"We're only trying to help," I said.

"Maybe I don't need your help!"

"All right." I stood up. "That makes my life easier."

March glared. "Now where are you going?"

"Home, I should think."

"Not before you've had a chance to finish reading my list. I expect you to get started right away."

"Mr. March, you and I seem to be talking at cross purposes."

I braced my hands on the edge of the desk and answered his glare with one of my own. Out of the corner of my eye, I saw Charlotte quietly withdraw. The door snicked shut behind her.

"Edward," he corrected firmly.

"*That's* the biggest problem you have with what I just said?"

"My name is Edward. I'd rather you use it."

I wanted to stay annoyed at him. Instead, I found myself sighing. For all his bluster, March suddenly looked like nothing more than a frail old man who'd gotten caught up in a whirlwind of events beyond his control. Sitting there with Robin's head cradled in his lap, his fingers scratching absently beneath her ear, he seemed like someone who really did need my help.

"Edward," I said.

"Better." He nodded. "Now sit."

So I did.

"I have a couple of questions to get started," I said.

"Shoot."

"You said you've been speaking to the police—"

"Not recently!"

"Okay, maybe not today, but since your son's death. Did they find anything incriminating on Andrew's computers? What about in his cottage?"

"Not a thing," said March. "I even asked Detective Wygod, 'What about forensics?' On TV that stuff works miracles."

"*If* they find something to work with."

"Well, they didn't."

That was too bad.

"It's been ten days," I said. "Other than that, what have the police been doing? Who have they spoken to?"

"Plenty of people, apparently. Employees at the company and some of Andrew's friends. The detective made it pretty clear that he knew Andrew and I were at loggerheads when he died."

"Because your son took March Homes away from you?"

March frowned. "There's a little more than that."

147

"Because of your book?"

He waved a hand impatiently. "The book was the least of it. Andrew and I would have gotten that sorted out."

"What, then?"

"Andrew had recently been looking to expand the company. He said he wanted to take the foundation I had created and build on it. What he really meant was that he was willing to take on debt in order to test out new markets. All so that he could feel like he was his own man, making his own decisions."

"I take it you didn't think that was a good idea."

"In this economy? He'd have to be crazy to make a move like that. And if he'd ever stopped and thought about it logically, he'd have known better. But instead, he was willing to let his childish need to feel important destroy everything I'd spent decades putting together. I told him in no uncertain terms that I wouldn't allow it."

"And what did Andrew say to that?"

"He called me a cowardly old man who didn't understand that risk taking was necessary to grow the business. Let me tell you something. I know all about growing a business. I was running March Homes when my son was in diapers—and I was doing a better job of it, too."

"Could you have prevented him from going forward with his plan?" I asked curiously.

"If it had come to that, yes. Where the big

decisions are involved, I still hold most of the financial reins. But Andrew had been busy marshaling support among the other company officers. A fight like that between the two of us would have torn the company apart. Instead, I was hoping I'd be able to make Andrew see sense. I wanted us to settle our differences amicably."

"And then he died," I said quietly.

"And somehow the police seem to think I got what I wanted." March shook his head incredulously. "As if my own son wasn't more important to me than any company could ever be."

Robin lifted her head and whined softly. I felt the same way myself.

"Here's the bad news," I said. "If the police have settled upon you as their chief suspect, they'll spend more time trying to build a case against you than they will looking at other possibilities."

"I already figured that out," said March. "That's why you and I need to get busy."

"That's what we're doing," I told him. "That's why I'm asking questions. Have you considered the possibility that someone might have been trying to strike at you through your son?"

"No." He looked up. "How? In what way?"

"Maybe there's someone you planned to write about in your book who didn't want you telling tales."

"There could be one or two like that," March allowed. "But I don't see how going after Andrew helps."

"Are you writing?"

"Well . . . no. Not right now."

"Probably not for the foreseeable future," I said.

"The delay can't be helped. March Homes is more important. I have to get the company back on an even keel first."

I let him think about that for a minute.

"Aunt Peg said you recently sent out an e-mail."

March must have heard the censure in my tone. "It would have taken too long to call everyone. That seemed like the easiest solution."

Plus, I thought, if he'd taken the time to actually speak to the women, he might have gotten an earful of antagonistic feedback.

"When did that e-mail go out?" I asked.

He thought back. "I sent it after the second time we met."

"Two weeks ago, then. Only a couple of days before Andrew was killed."

"No," March said firmly. "I refuse to believe that. *A woman?*"

"Don't be so old-fashioned," I scoffed. "Besides, it could have been a disgruntled husband. With your history, there was no shortage of options."

March frowned at that. He was ready to move

along. "What else do you want to know?" he asked.

"Who was the dark-haired woman standing next to you during the memorial service?"

"Nobody important."

"That's not how it looked to me."

"What do you mean?"

"Everyone seemed to be doing a good job of purposely ignoring her. Plus, I got the impression that she knew Andrew's friends."

"They weren't talking to her," said March.

"As far as I saw, no one was talking to her. Which made me wonder why that was."

"She shouldn't have been there, that's why."

It hadn't escaped my notice that March was still dodging my original question. "What was her relationship to your son?"

"Ex-girlfriend. Emphasis on ex."

"Julia Davis," I said.

Charlotte had mentioned her name to Detective Wygod. As I recalled, March had been similarly dismissive of the woman then. Now I waited for him to expand upon the subject. He didn't.

"I take it you were happy when she and Andrew broke up," I said after a minute.

"Andrew's love life was none of my business. Let's just say that my son got around some. He was popular with the ladies. Like father, like son." He had the nerve to sound proud of that, as if it were an accomplishment.

"But you must have known Julia," I said. "Or at least known something about her . . ." How else to explain the latent hostility?

"Oh, I knew her, all right. She'd been buzzing around Andrew for a year or more. Always flattering him, building him up, making him feel important. She tried that game on me, too, but I didn't fall for it. Julia wanted to be number one in Andrew's life. She wanted him to think that she was indispensable. A couple of months ago, she was looking to set up housekeeping with him in the cottage."

"Why was that a problem?"

"She was trying to tie my son down. She thought she could get him to put a ring on her finger."

"Andrew was in his midthirties," I pointed out. "Maybe he was ready to be tied down."

"Not with that one."

"Because . . . ?" I prompted.

"She wasn't worthy of him. Anybody meeting her would know that he could do better. She was cheap goods. She worked in the mall, for Pete's sake. Banana Republic. After a customer tried on a bunch of clothes, she emptied out the dressing room. Hanging up pants . . . What kind of career path is that? Oh, wait a minute. Julia didn't need a career. She was going to con Andrew into marrying her and taking care of her for the rest of her life."

"Maybe they were in love," I said.

"They weren't."

"What makes you so sure?"

"For one thing, the harder she tried to nail Andrew down, the more I watched him squirm to get away. That didn't look like love to me. When Julia didn't get the ring she wanted, she pressed too hard about moving into the cottage. That's when Andrew broke up with her. About damn time that he saw her for the gold digger she really was."

"You're very cynical," I told him.

"And you sound like some sort of bleeding heart romantic," March shot back. "Are you married?"

I nodded.

"How long?"

"Nearly three years."

March snorted. "You're practically still on your honeymoon."

"We like to think so," I said.

"Give it another decade. You'll be cynical, too."

I hoped not.

"Back to Andrew and Julia," I said. "So after more than a year together, he broke up with her a couple of weeks ago?"

"That's right. But that girl's still trying to keep her clutches in. You saw her at the memorial service, standing right there like she thought she was family. Now that Andrew isn't here to set the record straight, she's trying to pretend that everything was all hunky-dory between them. That they'd kissed and made up. Nobody's fooled, least of all me."

"Maybe she was trying to cover up how she really felt," I said thoughtfully. "That would be useful."

"How's that?"

I pointed to the second item on March's paper. "We're supposed to be looking for suspects—people besides you who might have had a good reason to be angry with your son. It looks as though Julia Davis just knocked you off the top of the list."

Chapter 12

Well, that made us both feel better.

"See?" March said with satisfaction. "I told you this was going to be easy."

"Don't get too cocky just yet," I told him. "We've barely even gotten started. Not including you, we only have one suspect. Let's talk some more about Andrew's life. Tell me about the people he worked with."

"What do you want to know?"

"For starters, who will succeed Andrew as president of March Homes?"

March picked up his coffee cup and took a sip, then set it aside. The brew had probably gone cold. "If I were only twenty years younger, I'd be at the headquarters right now," he said glumly. "Instead, my doctor has cleared me to drop by twice a week to check on things. That's no way to manage a business."

"So then you must have spent some time thinking about whom you're going to appoint to take over Andrew's position."

"It's impossible not to under the circumstances. You probably saw Walt McEvoy the other night?"

I nodded. "He got up and spoke about Andrew."

"Walt was Andrew's second in command. He started at March Homes as a smart, ambitious kid straight out of business school, and it didn't take him long to find the fast track. For the past few years, he's been CFO."

"So Walt knows where the money is," I said thoughtfully. "And where it goes. How did he feel about your son's plans to expand March Homes?"

March paused for so long that I thought he'd decided not to answer. Finally, he admitted, "Andrew had Walt's backing."

It was obvious but seemed worth stating, anyway. "Meaning that you did not."

"So what are you trying to say? That you think I should turn away an otherwise good man because he made one bad decision?"

"No, not at all. I'm just wondering how the two of you get along."

"We've always had a good relationship. Don't forget, Walt came on board ten years ago, so I'm the one that hired him. I knew at the time he had a ton of potential, and he's proven me right. In siding with Andrew, he thought he was acting for the good of the company. You can't fault a man for that."

"And now he stands to gain a big promotion," I said.

"He deserves it." March's tone was resolute; it allowed no room for argument.

Not that I wanted to argue the decision; I had no reason to doubt that March had chosen the right candidate. But in rushing to the defense of his employee, he had skipped right over the point I'd been trying to make. Walt McEvoy had stood to profit from Andrew's death.

I added another name to our sparse group of suspects.

"Is there anyone else there that you think I should talk to?" I asked. "Maybe someone who had problems working with your son?"

"You're talking about a company I built from scratch," March replied. "March Homes is a family business. Anyone who had problems with the family found another place to work. Period."

It occurred to me—as perhaps it had not

occurred to him—that March's information might be five years out of date. By his own admission, it had been at least that long since he'd been involved in the day-to-day running of the company. At any rate, I intended to ask that question again when I visited the corporate headquarters.

"Just one more thing," I said, standing up. "Do you have a list of the women who received your e-mail?"

"Of course. It's in my computer."

"Do you mind printing a copy for me?"

March swiveled his chair to the side to face a cluttered credenza. He pushed a newspaper and a large rawhide bone aside, and a keyboard and mouse pad emerged from the scattered items. It took him only a minute to find what he needed. Then I heard a printer activate somewhere in the room.

"Behind the couch," March told me.

Why was I not surprised?

A few seconds later, the printer spit out a piece of paper. I picked up the sheet, glanced at it, then quickly looked again.

"Seriously?" I said. "There must be twenty names on here."

So help me, the old goat looked pleased with himself. "There would be more, but I didn't have e-mail addresses for everyone."

I closed my eyes briefly and prayed for patience.

Or maybe March's redemption. I wasn't entirely sure which.

"Let's narrow this list down to the women you heard back from," I said. "The ones who weren't happy to find out about your book."

March frowned slightly. "To be perfectly honest, none of them were exactly pleased."

"And that didn't make you rethink the wisdom of the project?"

"I figured they'd come around in time. After all, what choice did they have? And like I told them, it wasn't as if I was going to paint an unflattering portrait of anyone. That would only make me look bad."

No doubt the women he'd spoken to had been vastly reassured by that fine sentiment.

"Let me see that." March held out his hand.

I passed the list over. He picked up a pen and made check marks next to several names. "I guess if you want to talk to the ones who were really mad, those ladies would make a good start."

I didn't know whether to be irritated by his cavalier attitude or elated to have gathered more names. Bottom line, our pool of suspects was increasing by the minute.

Since I had some extra time, I decided to stop and talk to a few of March's neighbors on my way home. Unfortunately, the basic flaw with that plan quickly became obvious. The other homes along that quiet lane were much like March's own: set well back from the road and surrounded by acres of land. None of their owners would have been able to see what was happening on the road the morning that Andrew was killed unless they chanced to be driving by.

Still, I thought, since I was already there, it wouldn't hurt to spend ten minutes asking around. At least that would entitle me to tick another item off of March's to-do list.

No one was home at the first house I tried. At the second, a maid answered the door and told me that they didn't want whatever I was selling.

"I'm not selling anything," I said quickly.

The door closed in my face, anyway.

On my third try, I had slightly better luck. A well-dressed matron answered the door herself. She didn't look particularly friendly, but she didn't dismiss me immediately, either.

"Yes? What is it?" she inquired briskly.

I introduced myself and asked if she was aware that a man had been killed in a hit-and-run accident on her road the previous week.

The woman nodded shortly. "That had nothing to do with me."

"Even so, I was wondering if you might have noticed anything unusual early that morning. Anything at all."

"Are you from the police?" she asked. "My

husband told me that somebody had already been by."

"No, I'm not—"

"A reporter?"

"No—"

"Is there any reason that I have to talk to you?"

"No, but—"

For the second time that morning, a door started to close in my face.

"You don't have to answer my questions," I said as the gap narrowed. "But it would be the neighborly thing to do."

The door stopped moving. Unexpectedly, the woman began to laugh.

"Neighborly? Where do you think you are? Alabama? Connecticut doesn't do neighborly."

"We do where I live," I said.

"And where is that?"

"North Stamford."

"That's quite a distance. What brings you to Westport?"

"Edward March." I turned and pointed in the direction of his house, in case she truly wasn't acquainted with her neighbors. "It was his son who was killed."

"Yes, I know," she said. "We sent flowers to the memorial. Step inside, would you? I need to shut this door. It's freezing out there."

I was only too happy to oblige. Her front hall

was lovely. And warm. Both were pluses from my point of view.

"I'm afraid I can't help you," the woman told me. "The first I knew of any disturbance was late that morning, when I left to go shopping and saw the police cars parked on the road. I didn't find out what had happened until that evening."

"What was your first thought when you heard?"

"I'm sorry to say that it wasn't very complimentary. I guess that sounds terrible, but Andrew always was a reckless boy. I wondered what kind of trouble he'd gotten himself into now."

"Did the police tell you that he'd been murdered?"

"No, but I read about it in the newspaper. The news sent a chill right down my spine. People live in the suburbs because they want to feel safe. What happened to Andrew was a reminder that the world is changing no matter where you are. Selfishly, I hoped that he'd brought his problems upon himself."

I could understand that. Blaming the victim conferred a sense of immunity. It wasn't fair, but it made bystanders feel better.

"You said that Andrew was reckless. In what way?"

"Oh, you know, the usual teenage pranks. My husband and I have lived here for twenty years. We moved to Westport the year before Isabelle died. She was a lovely woman. And Andrew certainly kept her on her toes."

"What about more recently?"

"I wouldn't really know. The only time we see Andrew now is when he's zipping up and down the lane in that red sports car of his. He's always driving much too fast, and there seems to be a different girl in the passenger seat each time he goes by. But that's no reason to kill someone."

I heartily agreed. I thanked the woman for her time and left.

Friday afternoon after school, Davey had a basketball game. It was the seventh game of the season, and so far his team had won more than they'd lost. When you're in middle school, that's cause for celebration.

As usual, the bleachers in the gymnasium were nearly full. Fairfield County parents aren't rabid about sports, but they do make a point of turning out to show their support. I saw dozens of familiar faces, mostly mothers, but also a few fathers who had made the effort to come and cheer for the home team.

Sam was working, so I had Kevin. I held his hand in mine as we entered the gym. Left to his own devices, the toddler would have run out onto the court to join the players, who were busy warming up and running pregame drills.

I caught Davey's eye briefly, but he was much

too cool to acknowledge his *mom*. Instead, he snagged a high pass out of the air, spun around, and dribbled away down the court.

"Daaaavey!" Kevin shrieked gleefully.

He yanked his small hand away and tried to follow his brother down court. With ease born of practice, I caught him in two steps. I scooped Kevin up and settled him safely on my hip.

"Davey's busy right now. You can play with him after the game."

"Melanie, up here!"

Alice Brickman was standing up in the middle of the bleachers, waving her arms above her head with enough enthusiasm to land an incoming plane. She must have come to the game straight from work, as she was dressed in a trim wool suit and hose. Her strawberry blond curls, gathered into a subdued ponytail at the nape of her neck, began to work their way loose as she bounced.

As always, Alice's smile was wide and infectious. I waved back and headed in her direction.

Alice and I first met in a neighborhood play-group when our sons were less than a year old, and knew immediately that we were kindred spirits. In the ten years that we've been friends, we've supported each other through ear infections, preschool applications, science projects, and the occasional broken bone.

Before Sam and I had married and moved to a

163

bigger house, Alice and I had lived on the same street and had talked daily. But now, with schedules that always seemed to be taking us in different directions, we definitely had some catching up to do.

"I saved you a spot." Alice scooted over and patted the hard metal bench beside her. "Sit down, woman. It's been entirely too long. How's my big boy doing?"

She held her arms open wide, and I passed Kevin over. Alice gave him a loud smacking kiss on each cheek, which made the toddler giggle with delight. He reached up and grabbed at her necklace.

"Shiny," he said happily.

"Watch he doesn't choke you," I mentioned as I shrugged out of my parka, balled it up, and stuffed it under the seat. "The notion of cause and effect doesn't mean much to him when he sees something he wants."

"Oh, please." Alice deftly disentangled the chubby fingers at her throat. Then she reached into her pocket and pulled out a Matchbox car. "I'm an old hand at this."

Instantly diverted, Kevin scrambled down out of her lap. Dropping to his hands and knees, he began to zoom the car along the ribbed lower tier. A more fastidious mother might have picked him back up. Not me. I was just happy he'd found a way to keep himself entertained.

"Where's Carly?" I asked. Joey's younger sister was nine and a budding ballerina.

"One guess."

"Dance class."

Alice nodded. "That child would rather dance than eat. I have to pick her up at Silvermine when the game ends. There's a recital in April, by the way. I have tickets for you and Sam."

"We'll be there," I promised.

Down on the court, a shrill whistle sounded. The game was about to begin. Davey, his maroon and gold uniform hanging loosely on his lanky frame, was running in place near midcourt. When the second-string players had taken the bench, he'd remained. That was new.

"Hey, look," said Alice. "You made the starting lineup."

"Don't read too much into it," I told her. "The flu's been going around. I bet a third of the team is home sick. As soon as everyone's healthy again, he'll be back on the bench with Joey."

The home team scored two baskets in quick succession. The opposing team answered with three of their own. Davey had a rebound and an assist. When a foul was called, followed by a time-out, I turned back to Alice.

"How's work going?"

After nearly a decade as a stay-at-home mom, Alice had dusted off her rusty skills and put her paralegal training back to use two years earlier.

Her husband, Joe, was a partner in a Greenwich law firm, and Alice had taken a job there part-time. Her reentry into the workforce had initially been somewhat rocky, but eventually, things had settled into a satisfying, if hectic, routine.

"Oh, you know."

"Busy?"

Alice rolled her eyes in reply.

"Instead of you always being the one doing the running around, why don't you let Joe pick up Carly a couple days a week?"

"Are you kidding? I can't even get him to pick up the dry cleaning, and he drives right by the store on his way home."

Several other women sitting around us nodded sympathetically. We'd all been there.

The other team's player missed the free throw. Davey's team rebounded and moved the ball down court. Davey scored with an easy layup. I jumped to my feet and cheered loudly. Not to be outdone, Kevin threw in a shriek.

Trotting back into position, my son managed to look both embarrassed and pleased at the same time.

"You look like you've lost some weight," I mentioned as the play resumed.

Alice beamed. "Four pounds since New Year's. It was my resolution. *Again.* But this time I'm actually sticking to it."

"Good for you. New diet?"

"No, the usual. No sugar, no white flour, more vegetables than a rabbit. I'm bored silly, but I can button my jeans, so life is good. What's new with you?"

Between watching the play on the court and keeping an eye on Kevin, it took me a while to get her caught up.

"That's what I like best about you," Alice said at the end.

"What?"

"Your life is better than reality TV."

"Thanks a lot."

"No, seriously. It's been what? Two weeks since we last spoke? Here's my life. Four pounds and a new orthodontist. Your life? Hit-and-run, hoarding, and illicit love affairs. Now, that's exciting."

"Sometimes I could do with a little less excitement," I said. "And just so you know, where Edward March is concerned, we're talking lust, not love."

"Even better." Alice grinned. Then she straightened in her seat and looked at me. "Wait a minute. Edward March, as in March Homes?"

"That's right. He founded the company. Until two weeks ago, his son, Andrew, was running it."

"Oh, boy."

Alice doesn't swear. With two young kids in the house, she's determined to set a good example. So even this mild pronouncement got my attention.

"What?"

She covered her mouth with her hands. "Nothing."

I almost laughed. "You *know* that isn't going to work. What's the problem?"

"Attorney-client privilege."

"You're not an attorney," I pointed out.

"Oh, right." She considered for a minute. "And now that I think about it, they're not our client. The plaintiff was. Anyway, you probably read about most of this stuff in the newspapers."

Now she really had my attention. "What stuff?"

"You know, March Homes, and all the litigation they've been involved in recently."

Chapter 13

"Really?" I said. How very interesting.

A cheer erupted around us when our team scored again. I checked quickly to make sure that Davey hadn't been responsible, and saw that he was busy congratulating another player. Our coach called a time-out. It looked like Joey was going to be sent in.

"What kind of litigation?" I asked.

"Our case was brought by a home buyer," Alice said in a low voice. "The house was new construction. We claimed that promises about quality had been made and not kept, that the builder had cut corners to save money."

With both boys playing, Alice and I kept our eyes on the court. Even Kevin climbed up and stood on the seat beside me to watch. I looped an arm around his waist.

"Did you win?" I asked.

"We settled. I can't tell you the amount. I will say, though, that our client was very pleased by the outcome."

Joey had the ball and was dribbling down the court. Another, much larger player swooped in, elbowed him aside, and stole the ball.

"That's a foul!" Alice cried, jumping to her feet.

The referee agreed. We watched as Joey took his time and lined up his free throw carefully. And then missed the hoop.

"Oh, well." Alice sat back down. "At least he got to try."

"Was there just the one lawsuit?" I asked. "Or more than that?"

"Just one at Plummer, Wilkes. But I know there were others that March Homes had been involved in recently, because I did some of the research for the case. Try Google. I bet you can bring up all sorts of things."

Good idea. I don't know why it hadn't occurred to me sooner. Except that when asked by Detective Wygod, March had assured him that the company hadn't been having any problems. And I'd believed him.

Suddenly, Alice looked worried. "You don't suppose that's related to what happened, do you?"

"I don't know. Maybe."

Davey was now out of the game, sitting on the bench, drinking Gatorade. He'd scored only two points, but I knew he'd be pleased with how he'd played. He turned around, looked up into the stands, and waved at his brother. Kevin's face lit up with a wide grin. He shifted over to stand on my lap and waved back.

"I guess they're far enough apart in age that you don't have to worry about sibling rivalry," Alice said, watching the exchange with a smile.

"There was just a little jealousy at the beginning. It was an adjustment for Davey to come to grips with the idea that he wasn't the center of the universe anymore. But he's always wanted a little brother. And he and Kev are great together. So I know he realizes that he gained a lot more than he gave up."

"I hope you know how lucky you are."

Every day, I thought.

"Kim Kardashian, eat your heart out," I said aloud.

Davey went on to score two more baskets in the second half, and his team ended up winning the game handily. To celebrate, we stopped on the way home and picked up pizza for dinner. Davey spent the rest of the car ride teaching Kevin how to pump his fist in the air.

The two of them went barreling into the house together, Davey still humming with excitement over his team's success. He dropped his backpack and gym bag on the floor and grabbed Kevin's hands. Spinning and whooping, my two children performed an impromptu victory dance in the front hall.

The Poodles, who'd come running to greet us, were happy to join in the celebration. Dogs and children spun together, then landed in a jumbled heap. Judging by the giggles emanating from the pile, no one seemed to have gotten hurt too badly.

"That looks like a win to me," said Sam, strolling into the hall to join us. He leaned down and rescued Kevin as the group began to disentangle itself.

"Thirty to twenty-four!" Davey crowed. "I scored three baskets and had two assists."

Prompted by his brother, Kevin lifted his chubby arms over his head and pumped both fists. A couple of high fives between Sam and Davey followed. The Poodles jumped up and hopped around on their hind legs just to add to the excitement. Any minute now they'd all start to dance again.

Meanwhile, I was still standing there with my arms full of pizza.

"A little help?" I said.

Sam put Kevin down, and the boys ran ahead to the kitchen. Maybe they'd set the table, I thought hopefully. Then I took a step and tripped over Davey's gym bag, still on the floor where he'd dropped it. Yeah, the table thing didn't seem likely.

Sam reached over and took the two wide boxes from me. "There's something I want to run past you," he said.

I pulled off my parka and hung it in the closet. "Shoot."

"Not now. We can talk later, after the kids are asleep."

Preceded by the Poodles, Sam turned and started toward the kitchen. I stood there and stared at his departing back. Seriously? He really meant to leave me hanging like that?

I slammed the closet door shut and scrambled to catch up. "It's nothing bad, I hope."

"Oh, no." He flashed me a quick smile. "Everything's fine."

Well, that told me exactly . . . nada. Geez, a woman would have blurted out the news—whatever it was—as soon as I'd come through the door. But since Sam was still walking away, I guessed I was just going to have to wait.

Davey and Kevin hadn't set the table, but they had managed to take off their jackets and hang them up. And they'd washed their hands. As any mother will tell you, the little victories are important, too.

Over dinner, Davey treated Sam to a blow-by-blow description of the basketball game. Every shot was cheered in hindsight, even those that had missed. Every foul was minutely dissected; even every dribble was accounted for. I helped Kevin with his pizza, ate three big pieces of my own, and wondered what Sam wanted to talk to me about.

It wasn't until much later that evening that I found out. He actually made me wait until the kids were in bed. By then, the suspense was just about killing me.

"What?" I said as soon as we heard Davey's door close upstairs.

Sam walked into the living room and turned on the TV. As I followed along behind, he began looking for the remote. Kevin has a tendency to make off with it when no one's looking. He likes all the shiny buttons.

"Hmmm?" Sam looked up. He was checking under a couch cushion.

"What did you want to talk to me about?"

Down on the floor, head beneath the couch now, Sam said something I couldn't quite catch. It sounded like he mumbled, "Tar."

I glanced around. Eve had remained upstairs with Kevin, but the other four Poodles had come with us into the room. Faith and Casey had hopped up onto the couch. Raven was curled up in a chair. Only Tar was up. He was standing beside the coffee table, convinced that if Sam was on the floor, that must mean it was playtime.

A smarter dog would have taken his cue from the bitches. They'd all watched Sam search for the remote before. Chances were, a couple of them probably even knew where it was. At the very least, they knew that Sam wasn't planning a game that involved them.

The bitches were already snoozing. Not Tar. The big dog was ever hopeful.

I walked over to the sideboard, opened a drawer, and pulled out the spare. "What about Tar?" I asked.

When Sam looked up a second time, I handed it to him.

"Great. Thanks." He took a seat. "Do you remember when we bred Tar to Peter Kirkwood's bitch, Marian, last spring?"

"Sure," I replied. Sam had started offering Tar at stud a couple of years earlier, but he was very picky about the bitches he accepted, so the dog hadn't yet sired many litters. "She was gorgeous."

"Absolutely." Sam nodded. "It was a great mating for both of them. At the time Peter offered me a pick of a puppy in lieu of a stud fee, if I wanted one."

"I didn't know that."

"Yeah, I guess I probably never mentioned it. I was tempted, but things were crazy around here then. Kevin had just turned one, and he wasn't sleeping through the night yet. You were still trying to decide whether or not you wanted to go back to work at Howard Academy. And I seem to recall that you were even trying to make your own baby food."

"Oh, yeah." I grimaced. "That was a short-lived experiment."

Those hectic, sleep-deprived days were just a fuzzy memory now. Thank goodness things had calmed down since then.

"So even though I loved the idea of having a puppy from that breeding," Sam continued, "it just didn't seem like the right time. Marian had the litter last July, and Peter and Sandy kept the best boy."

"I haven't seen Sandy at any shows in a while," I said. "How is she?"

"Not too happy, apparently. That's what I wanted to talk to you about. Peter called me earlier. He and Sandy are getting a divorce."

"That's too bad."

"And they're trying to divide up their dogs."

"That doesn't always go well. I hope for their sakes, and the dogs', that they're keeping things amicable."

"They are. Or at least they're trying to. And apparently, Peter and Sandy both agreed that with things so unsettled between them, neither one had the time or the money to devote to giving a really good puppy the show campaign he deserves."

"Interesting," I said. I was pretty sure I could guess where this was going.

"Augie's six months old now, and they've offered to sell him to me—"

"Augie?" I broke in with a laugh. "As in Augie Doggie?"

"I guess," Sam said. He looked confused.

Maybe he didn't watch cartoons, I thought.

"Anyway, Augie's in hair—at least as much as a six-month-old puppy can be. Peter has him entered in White Plains this weekend to get him out for some experience. I started to decline the offer, but then I stopped and thought about it. Our lives seem much more stable now. And since I retired Tar, I miss having something to show. So I figured I might as well ask. How would you feel about adding another Poodle to the mix?"

"We have plenty of room," I said, considering. "And nothing else in hair. And even though we didn't breed him, being by Tar, he's still a member of the family."

"That's what I thought."

"Have you seen him?"

"Not since he was eight weeks old. He was stunning then."

"Augie Doggie," I said, laughing again. "I hope he's as cute as his name. I think we'd better go to the show and find out."

●　●　●

The Saw Mill Kennel Club Show was a mere half hour away. That was right next door by dog show standards, as exhibitors routinely travel hundreds of miles in search of good judges and comfortable venues. Held at the Westchester County Center, Saw Mill apparently had both, because when we arrived mid-morning Saturday, the building was already packed.

Indoor locations almost always require some forbearance on the part of the exhibitors, especially for those with big dogs. And when set in a metropolitan area, as this show was, just navigating through the crowds of spectators with a carefully coiffed dog can prove a challenge.

Sam parked by the side of the building, and he, Kevin, and I ducked in the exhibitors' entrance. It was just the three of us as Davey was spending the day with Joey Brickman. Both boys had social studies projects due at the end of the month. Joey's was on the Naval Submarine Base in Groton, and Alice had planned an outing to the Submarine Force Museum and a tour of the USS *Nautilus*. Davey had been talking about the trip all week.

Dog shows are old hat where my son's concerned. He's been to so many that the excitement has worn pretty thin. But a submarine tour? *That* was his idea of an adventure.

"Standards aren't on until noon," said Sam, consulting a judging schedule.

Even so, most Poodle exhibitors would have already arrived. We paused at the edge of the grooming area, debating which way to head first. Even there, at the perimeter of the rings, the crowds were so thick that Kevin was pressed close to my leg. I gripped his hand tightly.

"Want up!" he cried.

I could hardly blame him. From where he stood, all he could see was a sea of strangers' legs. Sam reached down and scooped the toddler up, then swung him onto his shoulders. Kevin clung like a monkey and pumped his fist in the air. Now that he'd learned that trick from his brother, it was his new all-purpose gesture.

"Do you want to talk to Peter now, or would you rather see Augie after the judging?" Sam asked.

"After," I said firmly.

That choice was easy. Everyone was more relaxed after they'd already had their turn in the ring. Plus, if we wanted to play with the puppy, we wouldn't have to worry about mussing his hair.

Sam looked off across the room. "In that case, I'm going to go watch Toys. They're about to start, and I see Peg over there by the ring. Coming?"

"No, I think I'll stop by and say hi to Bertie first. And then maybe find a few other people."

"March's list?" asked Sam. He knows me so well.

I nodded. "I'm sure at least a few of the women on it must be here."

"Go to it, then. Just don't forget. Ring eight at noon. Augie will be in the first class."

"I wouldn't miss it."

We parted ways, and it wasn't until half the room was between us that I realized he had the child and I had the diaper bag. Without fail, there's something about being a parent that makes you feel like an idiot at least once a day.

Even in the crowded grooming area, Bertie wasn't hard to locate. She's tall and has flaming red hair and eyes like an eagle. I'd barely begun to navigate my way between the tightly packed tables and the columns of stacked crates before she flagged me down. I changed course and headed in her direction.

Bertie had a Bearded Collie and a Samoyed on side-by-side grooming tables and an arsenal of makeup and applicators laid out on a nearby crate top. As usual, she was moving quickly and efficiently, while at the same time managing to appear neither busy nor stressed.

If I could bottle that skill, I'd be a millionaire. I slipped in between the tables and gave her a quick hug.

"Aren't you missing something?" she asked.

I pulled the cumbersome diaper bag off my shoulder and tossed it into an empty crate. "What?"

"The baby that goes with that bag."

I leaned down and peered into the crate. "There's supposed to be a baby in there?"

She poked me in the ribs with the pointed end of a long-handled makeup brush. I yelped and hopped out of range.

"Kevin is at the Toy ring with Sam and Aunt Peg."

"And you're not," Bertie pointed out.

Unnecessarily, from my point of view.

"So something must be up," she said. "What is it?"

I glanced around. Everyone in the vicinity was busy attending to their own dogs. I lowered my voice, anyway.

"The police think that Edward March murdered his son."

I thought that Bertie might be shocked by the accusation. Or, at the very least, surprised. Instead, she just nodded.

"Did he?" she asked.

"I don't think so." I thought for a moment. "No, strike that. He didn't. He wants me to help him find out who did."

"Well, it's about time."

"Excuse me?"

"And in case nobody else has already said it, welcome back."

"From where?" I asked, utterly baffled.

"Your self-imposed exile. The eighteen-month-long sojourn into mommy-hood, to the exclusion of just about everything else."

"I haven't been that bad."

"You've been worse. Mommy-and-Me Japanese classes? Really? The kid barely even speaks English yet."

I sighed. Another failed experiment.

"The other mothers convinced me that the Pacific Rim was the way of the future."

Bertie wasn't listening. "And that art class?" She shook her head. "Don't even get me started."

"Kevin's very good at finger painting," I mentioned in my own defense.

"What he's good at is splatter. It's the age. At two, they all look like they're going to grow up to be Jackson Pollock."

Good thing she didn't know about the violin lesson, I thought. The one where Kevin decided that the delicate instrument would make a dandy battering ram.

"All I'm saying is, I know you had a rough go of it the summer before last. You never told me the details, but I heard enough to figure out that you needed some time away. But solving mysteries is what you do. It's what you're good at. And it's about time you climbed back on the freakin' horse."

"Melanie's getting a horse?"

Terry was passing by, a Toy Poodle tucked under each arm. As always, he had no compunction about inserting himself into someone else's conversation. Now he stopped and stared.

"Yes, I'm getting a horse," I told him, deadpan. "A black stallion. It's being delivered this week."

"For real?"

"Absolutely. Sam's building me a barn in the backyard. I'm going to ride the horse in the Kentucky Derby."

"Oh." Terry looked disappointed. "Now I know you're pulling my leg. Sam couldn't build a barn if it came with a full set of blueprints and six Amish farmers."

All too true. I love Sam dearly, but handy with a hammer he isn't. But even so, *that* was the part of the story Terry had had a problem with? Amazing.

"That'll teach you to eavesdrop," I said.

"No, it won't." Terry stuck out his tongue and kept moving.

"So here's my question," I said, turning back to Bertie. "I want to talk to some of March's exes. You know, the women he was planning to write about in his book." I pulled out my list and showed it to her. "Have you seen any of these women here today?"

Her gaze skimmed quickly down the paper. "Well, sure," she said with a laugh. "They're dog people, and it's a dog show. Where else would they be?"

Pretty much what I'd figured.

"Maribeth's here. She showed earlier. And India

is judging." Her finger ran down the page. "I saw Patsy Revere, too. In fact . . ." Bertie glanced up. "She's right over there."

Bertie grasped my shoulders and positioned me so that we were facing the same direction. Across the way, I saw an Irish Setter standing on a table, wearing a towel. Another nearby was sitting up on his table and panting. His long pink tongue lolled in and out of his mouth.

"Brunette," Bertie said. "Hair in a bun. Cobalt suit. Bright red nails."

That's how you know you've become a dog person: you automatically notice the canines first. Deliberately, I shifted my gaze from the red setters to their handlers. That done, Patsy was easy to pick out.

"Got it," I said. "Thanks."

It was time to make myself useful.

Chapter 14

Up close, Patsy Revere looked older than she had from a distance. Mid- to late fifties, I guessed, but battling the effects of aging with every weapon at her disposal. Her face was beautifully made up, her brows plucked to a high arch, which lifted her entire expression. Her hairdo was more chignon than bun; the style pulled the skin taut across her cheekbones. A wide belt cinched her jacket tightly around her waist, highlighting an hourglass figure.

Even at the upper end of the range I'd assigned her, Patsy was still at least a decade younger than Edward March. Another reminder that he hadn't always been the crusty curmudgeon I knew now. Indeed, considering his track record with the ladies, at some point March's appeal must have been pretty formidable.

As I approached, Patsy checked her watch, then plucked a tube of lipstick out of her purse. She leaned down to reapply it, using a mirror pasted to the inside of the open lid of her tack box. I waited until she had finished, then stepped up and introduced myself. Patsy rubbed her lips together to blot the deep red stain and stuck out a hand.

"Nice to meet you," she said as we shook. "Are you looking for puppies? I don't have any at the moment, but I can give you my card. I'm expecting a litter in the spring."

As she spoke, my hand lifted automatically toward the Irish Setter sitting on the table beside us. His head was turned in our direction, his large, dark eyes watching us curiously. I had no idea what went into preparing an Irish Setter for the show ring, but experience with Poodles had taught me not to touch anything that looked like it might require grooming. Instead, I simply extended my fingers in greeting. The dog lowered his head and sniffed them delicately.

"Wow," I said. "He's gorgeous."

Patsy smiled. "Thank you. I think so, too. Here's hoping that today's judge agrees."

"Is he a specials dog?"

"Champion Patmore The Patriot," Patsy confirmed. "He's the sire of the litter I have due in April."

"I'm sure your puppies will be wonderful," I said. "But I'm afraid all I'm looking for is information. I was hoping you might have a few minutes to talk. Is this a good time?"

"Good enough, I suppose. We're not due in the ring for twenty minutes or so. What kind of information do you need?"

"It's about Edward March—"

"Oh, Lord." Patsy rolled her eyes. "Not that stupid book of his."

"Well . . . yes," I admitted. "I was wondering how you felt about being included."

"If I thought the project would ever actually come to anything, I'd probably be annoyed. But since that possibility seems remote at best, I'm trying not to waste my time thinking about it."

"Why don't you think it will happen?" I asked curiously.

"Edward writing a book? I can't even begin to imagine it." She stopped and looked at me. "Do you know him?"

I nodded.

"I should have guessed. You're another one, are you? I thought I knew most of the names, but there were a few I didn't recognize. Plus, you look a little young. I never thought of Edward as a cradle robber."

"Oh, no!" I could feel my face growing hot as I hurried to correct her. "I don't know him *that* way. We just met a few weeks ago. My aunt volunteered me to help him write his book."

Patsy snorted under her breath. "Your aunt must not like you very much."

"Sometimes I wonder," I said with a sigh. "But this wasn't really her fault. Neither one of us had any idea what kind of book March intended to write before I met with him. I was expecting it to be about Irish Setters."

"Do you *have* Irish Setters?" Her tone clearly conveyed the fact that if I did, she'd have known about it already.

"No, Standard Poodles."

"Who's your aunt?"

"Margaret Turnbull."

"Well, that explains it."

Any notion I might have had that I was the one leading the conversation was rapidly disappearing. "Explains what?" I asked.

"How you got involved in Edward's business. Peg does love to stir things up."

"Tell me about it," I muttered.

"So . . . ?" Patsy waited expectantly. When I didn't jump in, she frowned as though I'd missed my cue, then continued. "Why are you here? Have you come to hear my side of the story?"

"No, not exactly." I paused. "Unless you want to tell it to me?"

"I can't imagine why I would. Actually, I'd be happier if the whole discussion simply went away."

She gazed at me as though I was missing my cue again. Blandly, I smiled back. I had no intention of going away just yet. Instead, I circled back to something she'd said earlier.

"Why can't you envision Edward March writing a book?" I asked again.

"Because writing is hard work. It requires commitment and perseverance. One look at that long list of Edward's women should be enough to tell anyone that commitment was never his strong suit. He's the kind of man who only wants to be there for the good times. Hit that first little bump in the road and he's out the door and on to the next."

"Is that what happened between the two of you?" I asked. Maybe I did want to hear her story, after all.

Patsy picked up a comb and began to run it idly through the setter's silky ear feathers. I simply stood and waited.

"What happened between us is that Edward

broke up my marriage," she said after a minute. "That's certainly no secret. But it is old news that I'd just as soon not have dredged up again."

She moved on to address the setter's legs. The smooth stroke of the comb through hair was almost hypnotic. As she stepped around behind the dog, Patsy resumed speaking.

"Not that my divorce was entirely Edward's fault. I'm a big girl. I can accept my share of blame. Greg and I were already having problems before Edward appeared on the scene. To tell the truth, I wouldn't be surprised if that's what attracted him to me in the first place."

"That you seemed accessible?"

Patsy lifted her head and looked at me over the setter's back. "No, that I was unhappy. Edward always thought that he was the answer to a woman's prayers. And for a couple of months, I believed him. He had me convinced that he could turn my life around."

"Then what happened?"

"Greg and I separated. It probably would have come to that anyway, but Edward was certainly the catalyst. And then overnight, he was gone. Faced with the fact that I was now free to engage in a nonclandestine relationship with him, Edward couldn't get away fast enough."

"You must have hated him for that," I commented.

Patsy chuckled softly. "I guess I did . . . for

about ten minutes. Then I got real. Me and Edward, long term? That would never have worked. He was just as much of a fling for me as I was for him."

At least that was what she wanted to believe, I thought.

"You must have heard about what happened to his son."

"Yes, I heard." Patsy shook her head. "Those two . . ."

I waited, but she didn't continue. Instead, she slipped the grooming loop off the setter's neck and settled a collar in its place. Then she cupped her arms around the big dog and lifted him down off the table.

All around us, the other Irish Setter exhibitors were preparing to head up to the ring. Patsy's dog danced from foot to foot as he gave his body a big shake. Patsy grabbed a handful of cooked chicken from a Baggie in her tack box and stuffed it in her pocket. In another moment, she'd be gone.

"What about them?" I asked.

She didn't seem to be listening.

"Edward and Andrew," I said, trying again. "What about them?"

Patsy had already skirted around the grooming table, the big Irish Setter following in her wake. I thought I'd lost my chance, but then she paused and glanced back at me.

"Those two were so much alike that they drove each other crazy," she said. "Frankly, I'm almost surprised that something terrible didn't happen between them sooner."

Well, that was a cheery thought with which to start the day. I'd been hoping to find someone with a grudge against Edward March, not someone who would confirm Detective Wygod's theory that March and his son had been their own worst enemies. Maybe I could do better with India Fleming.

The good thing about India was that in the sea of people milling around the large exhibition hall, she was easy to find. The bad thing: she was standing in the middle of a show ring, judging Manchester Terriers. I consulted the schedule posted by the gate and found that she was due for a lunch break in an hour and that her assignment didn't end until three. None of which was helpful at all.

So I went back to my list. The third woman Bertie had seen was Maribeth Chandler. When Terry had pointed her out to me previously, she'd been showing Vizslas. With that in mind, I headed over to the side of the room where most of the sporting breeds were being judged. If Maribeth was like most exhibitors, even though her breed was done, she'd still be hanging out watching her friends and their dogs compete.

I didn't see Maribeth at the Golden ring. Or in the crowd gathered around what appeared to be a large Labrador Retriever specialty. But at the Weimaraner ring, I hit pay dirt. She was standing just outside the gate, conferring with the steward.

Maribeth was tall and slender. With her smooth blond hair and patrician features, she looked every bit as aristocratic as the sleek hunting dogs clustered around her at the gate. I saw her pick up a couple of numbered armbands from the steward. Then she threaded her way back through the crush of exhibitors to deliver them to another woman, who was holding two Weimaraners on slender leashes.

Maribeth ran a couple of rubber bands up the woman's arm, slipped the armbands underneath, and snapped them into place. Then she reached over and took one of the leads. The first class was called, and the congestion began to clear. The other woman headed for the ring with her first entry.

I made my way over to where Maribeth was standing with the second Weimaraner. There were several entries in the Puppy class. Her friend had taken a spot at the end of the line, and it looked as though we had a few minutes before her dog would be judged.

Maribeth glanced my way as I approached, then looked again and smiled in recognition. That was so unexpected, I nearly turned around to see if there was someone else behind me that she was looking at. But then she juggled the looped end of the leash from one hand to the other, shifted the Weim around to her other side, and extended her hand.

"Hi," she said. "I'm Maribeth Chandler. We haven't met, but I know you're Charlotte's friend. She pointed you out the other night."

Charlotte's friend? I had no idea. But if that would give me an entrée, I certainly wasn't above using it.

I grasped her hand, and we shook. The Weimaraner wagged her stubby tail. It looked as though she was pleased to meet me, too.

"Melanie Travis," I said. "You're Charlotte's mother, right? You look just like her."

"Thank you." Maribeth's smile widened. "You've just made me feel ten years younger."

What is it with women and aging? No matter how accomplished she is or how good she looks, every woman I know is insecure about her appearance. Hollywood and the media have a lot to answer for.

"Charlotte is delighted to have someone else to talk to at work now," Maribeth continued. "As I'm sure you've discovered, Edward can be a little . . ."

"Difficult?" I said. "Crotchety? Imperious?"

"All of the above, I gather, depending on his mood. Charlotte does her best to make him happy, but judging by the stories she tells, Edward isn't the easiest boss."

"She told me you were the one who got her the job," I said.

Maribeth nodded. "It seemed like a good idea at the time. Edward was growing frailer. He needed someone to look out for him. And Charlotte has a wonderful liberal arts education that prepared her to do absolutely nothing in the real world. I thought they might suit each other. Of course, I never could have anticipated the recent . . . complications."

That was an interesting euphemism for a sudden, unexplained death.

"Did you know Andrew?" I asked.

"Only in the most superficial way. Edward and I were close a number of years ago. But I imagine you already must know that? Charlotte said Edward hired you to help him with his book."

"That's right."

"Andrew was just a child then. A bright boy, precocious. Always up to some kind of mischief. But under the circumstances, it wasn't as if we would have been spending time together."

If Andrew had truly been a child during their affair, then March's wife, Isabelle, had still been alive. I could certainly understand why March would have made an effort to keep his two lives separate.

In the ring, Maribeth's friend had reached the

head of the line. We both stopped talking while the judge examined, then moved, the exuberant puppy.

"Good boy," Maribeth murmured under her breath as handler and dog gaited in a reasonably straight line, trotting out and back along the mat that bisected the middle of the ring.

"Is he a good one?" I asked. I knew nothing about Weimaraners except that they were beautiful to look at.

"He will be when he grows up. Today he's only here for the experience and to make the major."

Dogs become champions by amassing a total of fifteen points in same-sex competition. A win in the classes—the non-champion portion of the breed judging—can be worth anywhere from one to five points, depending on the number of dogs or bitches beaten on a given day. Included in that total of fifteen points, a dog must also secure at least two majors—awards of three points or more—which ensures those wins have been accomplished against a significant-size entry.

The intent is to guarantee that only quality dogs will achieve their championships. One problem with the system, however, is that in certain parts of the country, and during certain seasons of the year, major entries can be very hard to come by. It's not unusual for dogs that have amassed all their singles to sit out of the show ring and wait, sometimes for months, just for the chance to compete for those elusive big wins. It's also not unheard of for breeders to band together and manufacture majors by filling the classes with inexperienced puppies or dogs that are not quite ready to be competitive.

Maribeth's friend's puppy won the Puppy class. She picked up her blue ribbon from the judge, exited the ring, and waited just outside the gate to return.

"What class is she in?" I nodded toward the Weimaraner bitch. Though she waited patiently at Maribeth's side, her keen eyes were riveted on her owner fifteen feet away.

"Open. She only needs a major to finish. Sue is hoping that today is her day."

The mantra of hopeful dog show exhibitors everywhere.

There were more questions that I wanted to ask, but it was hard not to get caught up in the drama of the judging. The Open class was won by a strong, balanced dog who controlled the show ring effortlessly. It came as no surprise when the judge awarded him the points over Sue's puppy and the winner of the Bred-By Exhibitor class.

Sue quickly exited the ring with the puppy. She reached around and pulled off the top armband to expose the bitch's number underneath, then dropped the first in the trash on her way to where we stood. Maribeth and Sue switched leashes— and dogs with a minimum of fuss. Then Sue was quickly gone again, back to the gate to await her next turn.

As the following class, Puppy Bitches, filed into the ring, I turned back to Maribeth. "We were talking about Edward's book a few minutes ago," I said. "How did you feel about it?"

"Disinterested," she said flatly.

"How come?"

"The life and loves of Edward March? Who'd be crazy enough to publish something like that? Nobody would want to read it. Nobody would care."

She probably had a point.

"Edward is just stroking his own ego. Trust me, he's very good at that. And that e-mail of his was a joke. An honor to be included, my ass. Only a man would come up with a line like that."

Point number two. In case you're keeping score.

"I don't know why he doesn't just make up fake identities for the women. After all, you can be sure that half the stories will be made up. Or at least . . ." Maribeth snorted under her breath. "Significantly enhanced."

We smiled together complicitly.

"I guess I heard wrong, then," I said. "I heard that some of the women on March's e-mail list were upset."

"Maybe some were." Maribeth shrugged, her gaze never leaving the ring. "Not me. I'll be more upset if Sue's bitch doesn't take home this major."

So I stayed and watched until the end of the Weimaraner judging. Sue's bitch won the major handily and then went on to take Best of Opposite Sex. Last I saw, she and Maribeth were hugging each other and jumping up and down in celebration just outside the ring.

It was nice to see somebody go home happy.

Chapter 15

"There you are. *Finally!*" Aunt Peg bellowed. "Where have you been?"

In keeping with accepted protocol, Peg usually whispered her thoughts at ringside. But when she felt the need to take a recalcitrant relative to task, her voice carried. Now it seemed as though half the people in the vicinity of the Poodle ring turned to see what was the matter.

I glanced into the ring just to make sure that I hadn't missed anything crucial. Nope, my watch hadn't stopped. Minis were still being judged.

Sam, bouncing Kevin on his knee, patted an empty chair between him and Peg that he'd saved for me. I slipped into it gratefully.

"I was at the Weimaraner ring," I said.

"Such a lovely breed." Briefly distracted, Aunt Peg brightened. It didn't last. "Not that that's any excuse. You've missed nearly all the Poodles."

"Not the Standards," I told her cheerfully. "Not the ones that matter."

"They *all* matter."

The bellow was back, seemingly louder this time because I was sitting right beside her. Take it from me, it's not easy to be related to a judge.

"You're scaring the dogs," I mentioned.

That got her attention.

Aunt Peg's head immediately swiveled back toward the Poodle ring. The Mini Open Bitch class was lined up on the mat opposite us. Peg looked at each entrant in turn.

"Which one?" she asked.

"The silver." I pointed to the third Mini in line. "She dropped her tail."

"Silvers do that," Aunt Peg muttered.

Did I hear a smidgen of guilt in her lowered tone? I sincerely hoped so.

On my other side, Sam was staring at the ceiling with great fascination. What could I say? It wasn't as if I hadn't warned him before he'd married into the family.

"Here," I said, reaching over to pluck Kevin off his lap. "My turn."

Kevin's face had that pouty look he gets when he's deciding he might be bored. I opened the diaper bag and got out a juice box. That would keep him entertained for at least five minutes. Even more if I didn't open it for him.

"Did you talk to Peter?" I asked Sam. "Have you already seen Augie?"

"No. I decided to follow your lead and wait until after the judging. Everything will be calmer then, and we'll have more time. Plus, I'd hate to meet the puppy and fall in love with his personality and then discover that I don't like what I see in the ring."

Aunt Peg poked me in the shoulder harder than was strictly necessary. She hates to be left out of a conversation, especially one that's taking place right beside her and most likely pertains to dogs.

"What are you two whispering about?" she demanded.

"Poodles," I said innocently. "Isn't that why we're here?"

"Speaking of which," said Sam, "I had an idea."

"I like ideas," said Aunt Peg. "I hope it's a good one. Otherwise, what's the point?"

Seated between them, my head turning back and forth as they spoke, I felt like a spectator at a Ping-Pong tournament. "Would somebody like to change seats with me?" I asked.

"No," Peg and Sam said in unison. They both looked equally perplexed by the question.

I couldn't imagine why. As the monkey in the middle, apparently I was an impediment to their conversation.

Now Aunt Peg leaned forward to speak to Sam, talking over Kevin's head like the two of us were invisible. "Don't worry about Melanie. She'll get herself sorted out. Tell me your idea."

"It's actually more for Melanie," said Sam.

"She appears to be busy with a juice box," Peg noted.

"I'm *right here*," I said. "I can hear everything you're saying."

"Then join in," Aunt Peg said with more than a touch of asperity. "It appears that Sam would like to talk to you."

This, I thought, *must be how the Three Stooges hold a conversation.*

Aunt Peg reached over, grasped Kevin firmly beneath the armpits, and levered him across and onto her ample lap. "Stick with me, young man," she said. "I'll make sure you get something to drink. Unlike some people."

She sounded smug now. Wait until Kevin managed to spill his juice onto her carefully marked catalog. Or started tearing out the pages and throwing them into the ring.

Not my problem, I thought. I angled my body in Sam's direction.

"What have you got?" I asked.

"I've been thinking about Davey," said Sam. "And the fact that even though he lives in a house full of dogs, he's never had one of his own."

It doesn't take much to trigger a mother's guilt. There's always something you feel you could be doing better, especially when there's a newer, younger child in the family taking up so much time. A wave of self-reproach washed over me.

"He had a frog once," I mentioned in my own defense.

"I don't remember that. What happened to it?"

"He took it outside to play and lost it in the grass."

Sam pursed his lips. He might have been trying not to laugh.

"That was a while ago. Davey was much younger then."

"Good to know," said Sam. "I think he's probably old enough now to take responsibility for a pet, don't you?"

I did. And I thought it was a great idea.

"Of course, there's no guarantee that we'll even like Augie," he continued. "Much less that we'll like him enough to want to add him to the family. But if we do . . ."

"Davey would be thrilled," I said. "A dog of his very own? He'd love that. He could feed him and walk him and teach him tricks."

"I know Junior Showmanship wasn't his thing," said Sam. "But I bet he'd enjoy breed competition more. Or maybe even agility. The two of us could work on coat care and then show Augie together."

Sam and Davey already had a terrific bond. But I loved the notion of the two of them having an activity that would bring them even closer.

"The best part," I said, thinking aloud, "is that it

would give Davey something special that was just for him because he's the oldest."

"That sounds brilliant," Aunt Peg said from behind me. Of course, she'd been listening in. "I don't know why you two didn't think of it sooner."

As the Mini judging drew to a close, the Standards began to gather outside the ring. I scanned the group anxiously, looking for Peter and Augie. Earlier, I'd been curious about the puppy, but now it felt as though the stakes had been raised. For Davey's sake, I really hoped that everything would work out.

"There." Sam pointed, and I saw the pair approaching.

Peter Kirkwood was living proof of the axiom that people tend to look like their pets. He had black, curly hair, a long nose, and a ready smile. Now he was looking down, concentrating on the big Poodle puppy bouncing along at his side.

I stood up, hoping for a better view. To my frustration, due to the crowd of people between us, Augie was barely even visible.

In deference to the puppy's inexperience, Peter stopped and waited by the ring's far corner, keeping him well away from the crush of dogs and exhibitors milling near the gate. I caught a quick glimpse as Augie stepped in front of his owner and poked his head over the rail and into the ring.

Then he scooted back, and the two of them melted into the throng.

"Pretty face," I said. It was all I'd had time to see.

As usual, Aunt Peg had done better. "He looks like his sire," she said.

Though Tar was Sam's dog, Aunt Peg was his breeder. And with her decades of experience, she was notoriously demanding when it came to her favorite breed. Coming from her, the comment was high praise.

"I'm still reserving judgment," said Sam. "Let's see what he looks like in the ring."

To our mutual relief, Augie didn't disappoint. Not even close.

There were three puppies in his class, and at just six months of age, he was clearly the youngest. But what he lacked in hair and experience, he more than made up for with correctness and presence. Not to mention his enthusiasm for the new experience.

Augie looked at the crowd of spectators lining the ring and wagged his tail. He tried to lick the judge. He gamboled up and down when he was supposed to be trotting out and back. But when, on the last go-round, he finally settled into stride and showed how he could really move, I heard Aunt Peg sigh.

"That'll do," she said.

Augie placed second in the class, beaten by a

mature white puppy with a profuse coat and a professional handler at the end of his lead. The award was immaterial; we'd already seen what we needed to see. By the time the dog classes ended, Sam and I were standing up.

Aunt Peg and Kevin remained in place to watch the remainder of the Standard Poodle judging, but Sam and I were too impatient for that. We hurried around the ring to follow Peter and Augie back to the setup. We were only a few steps behind when they got there.

Peter hadn't yet had a chance to hop Augie back up onto his grooming table. The puppy stood on the floor beside his crate. With tail up and nose down, he was investigating a tuft of hair that had blown across his path.

While Sam and Peter greeted each other and talked about the class, I hunkered down to the puppy's eye level and waited to see what would happen next. It took Augie only a moment to notice me. One more and he'd tugged Peter closer so that he could bound into my arms and say hello.

The puppy's tail was waving a happy tattoo high in the air. His dark eyes sparkled with mischief. When he hopped up on his hind legs to place his front feet on my shoulders, I unbalanced and tipped over backward. We went down together in a happy heap.

Peter quickly reeled in Augie's leash, gathering

the puppy back to his side. "Sorry about that," he said.

"No." I laughed, getting up and dusting myself off. "That's perfect."

One look at Sam's face and I knew he agreed. We were both in love already. Perfect indeed.

Augie went home with Peter. It would take a few days to work out the details, but as far as Sam and I were concerned, the sale was already a fait accompli. By mutual agreement, we decided not to say anything to Davey until it was time to bring the puppy home.

Usually, I'm great at keeping secrets. This time, I was dying to blurt out the news. So in order to keep myself from spoiling the surprise, I made an effort to stay busy.

The next person I wanted to talk to was Andrew's recently dumped ex-girlfriend, Julia Davis. Although I'd seen her at the memorial service, I had no idea how to get in touch with her. So the next morning I called March's house. Charlotte picked up, and I explained what I needed.

"No problem," she said. "I have her number right here. Julia moved recently. She's living in Norwalk now."

"You seem to know a lot about her," I said. "You two must be friends."

"Julia used to come to the house sometimes

with Andrew. Then, while they were here, Andrew and Mr. March would lock themselves away to talk business. So Julia and I would hang out. That's when we got to know one another."

"What was your impression of her relationship with Andrew?"

"What do you mean?" Charlotte sounded suddenly wary.

"March makes no secret of the fact that he didn't like her. He told me that Julia was trying to trap Andrew into marrying her, that she was only after him for his money."

"That's not fair," Charlotte said heatedly. "Julia was in love with Andrew. She wanted them to have a future together."

"And what did Andrew want?"

"I don't know," Charlotte replied. "You would have had to ask him. But you need to understand something. Mr. March has a way of setting impossibly high standards for everyone around him. He thought that Julia wasn't good enough for Andrew, but that wasn't Julia's fault. I'm not sure Mr. March would have thought that anyone was good enough for his only son."

Charlotte read off the address and phone number, and I jotted them down. Norwalk and Westport were neighboring coastal Connecticut towns, but they were worlds apart in terms of ambience and prestige. I pulled out a map and found that Julia's apartment was located on the edge of an industrial zone near the turnpike.

A quick call confirmed that she'd see me. I imagine it helped that I dropped March's name into the conversation and implied that I was calling on his behalf. We made an appointment for later that morning.

Sam agreed to take charge of the kids and the Poodles. When I left, they were all out in the backyard, building a snow fort. It was one of those sparkling clear winter days where the bright combination of sun and snow smoothed away the world's rough edges and left it looking like a wonderland. I needed sunglasses just to manage the glare.

Julia's apartment complex consisted of two squat, three-story stucco buildings. The landscaping was minimal, and the dual units were framed by a mostly empty parking lot. Improbably, the builder had chosen to name the complex Sound View. Only if you stood on the roof with a telescope, I thought as I locked my car behind me.

In theory I needed to be buzzed into the building, but someone had used a cinder block to prop open the glass door that led to the lobby. Julia's apartment was on the second floor. There was an elevator, but it didn't respond when I pushed the button, so I took the stairs.

Julia was more prompt. She answered my first knock. I heard her release first a chain and then a dead bolt. Then the door drew open wide.

"You must be Melanie," she said with a tentative smile. "Please come in. I hope you can excuse the mess. I'm still unpacking."

I entered the apartment via a narrow hallway that led to a combination living room and dining room. The furniture was sparse, just a couch and a small round table with three straight-backed chairs. Several large cartons, one of which appeared to be acting as a wardrobe, had been pushed up against the wall. A curtainless window looked out over the parking lot.

At the memorial service, Julia had looked sleek and pulled together. Now, with her long dark hair pulled back in a messy ponytail, wearing ripped jeans and a bulky pullover sweater, she was hardly recognizable as the same woman. Her face was pale and gaunt, and there were dark circles beneath her eyes. Her nails were bitten painfully short.

"I'm sorry this place looks so awful," she said, waving me to a seat at the table. "I don't usually live like this. It's just that my life's in a bit of turmoil at the moment. . . ."

I pulled off my jacket and slung it over the back of my chair. "Don't worry about it. It's my fault for coming on such short notice."

Julia smiled at my attempt to assuage her discomfort, and I saw a brief vestige of the lovely woman I remembered. It was difficult for me to envision this fragile-looking girl as the conniving gold digger March had painted her to be.

"Can I offer you something to drink? Water? Juice?" Julia spread her hands helplessly. "I apologize for the meager choices. I'm trying to cut back on caffeine."

"Some juice would be great," I said.

A small kitchenette was separated from the main room by a waist-high partition. Julia scooted around it and opened the refrigerator. "Apple okay?"

"Perfect."

"You said Edward sent you?" Julia said as she opened a cabinet and got out a couple of glasses. "Has he changed his mind?"

"Excuse me?"

"Has he changed his mind? You know, about the baby?"

Holy crap on a cracker.

Julia came out from behind the counter, holding the two glasses of juice. She set one down in front of me, then slid into a seat opposite.

"The baby?" I repeated.

"Yes." Julia's hand slipped down to her stomach in a protective motion. "Andrew's baby. Isn't that why you're here?"

"You're pregnant," I said stupidly.

Julia nodded. "Ten weeks, give or take."

"And Edward March knows that?"

"Of course he knows. I told him myself almost two weeks ago."

That would have been right after Andrew died,

I realized. Interesting that March had seen fit to withhold that important fact. He'd certainly been more than forthcoming about other issues regarding his son's ex-girlfriend.

"That was why you wanted to get married," I said.

"Of course. But it wasn't the only reason. Andrew and I were ready. We'd been together for more than a year."

"His father told me that the two of you had broken up."

Julia's dark eyes flashed with irritation. "He would say that."

"Is it true?"

"Technically . . . yes. But it didn't mean anything. Andrew and I were both passionate people who liked to get our own way. Sometimes we fought like banshees, but we still loved each other. We'd always gotten back together before, and we would have this time, too."

It sounded as though March and Julia each had a different version of the same events to promote. And it was beginning to look like they both had a significant stake in the outcome. I wondered which of the two was more likely to be lying to me.

"What did you and Andrew fight about the last time?" I asked.

Julia took a sip of juice and leaned back in her chair. She took her time about answering. "It was the baby," she said finally.

"Getting pregnant wasn't a mutual decision?"

"It was an accident," Julia admitted. "But once it happened, anyone could see that it was fate pushing us in the right direction."

"Is that how Andrew felt about it?"

"He wanted me to get an abortion." She tossed her head angrily. "That was *never* going to happen."

"So you argued about it. And then broke up."

"Only temporarily."

Hard to tell that by looking at her living situation.

"Why is all your stuff in boxes?" I asked.

"Sometimes Andrew could be a real jerk, that's why. When I told him about the baby and he realized that I had every intention of having it, he told me to get out."

"So you'd been living together then."

Julia nodded. "Since last fall."

Another point March seemed to have shaded to fit his own version of the facts.

"Your boyfriend got you pregnant, then threw you out of his house. That's pretty cold."

Woman to woman, we shared a look.

"You must have been very angry," I said.

"*Angry* doesn't begin to cover it," Julia replied. "I was furious. I was having Andrew's baby, and he didn't even care. I could have killed him for that."

Chapter 16

"Someone did," I pointed out. "Was it you?"

"Me?" Julia's head snapped up. "You must be joking."

"You just said that you were furious at Andrew."

"I was. And he deserved it. But that doesn't mean . . ." Abruptly her eyes narrowed. "Is that why you came here today? Did Edward send you because he's looking for someone to blame?"

"He's looking for the truth. He wants to find out what happened."

"No, he doesn't," Julia said angrily. "What Edward wants is a palatable version of events that makes him feel better about all the ways he was never there for his own son—not when Andrew was growing up and not now. The two of them can't stand each other. Did he tell you *that*?"

"Not exactly. He did say that they didn't always get along."

"They didn't *ever* get along." Julia shoved back her chair and stood. She walked over to the window and stared out through the grimy glass. "Edward was always trying to tell Andrew what he could and couldn't do. He treated him like he was still a child."

"March didn't approve of your relationship with Andrew," I said.

"No." Julia's voice quieted. "He didn't think I was good enough. And yet . . ."

I waited for her to finish her thought. Instead, Julia lifted a hand and traced a word on the cold glass with her finger. *No,* she wrote.

"And yet, what?" I asked.

She turned to face me. "Edward put the moves on me himself. I'll bet he never told you that."

He most certainly had not.

"I wasn't suitable for Andrew, but he thought he'd have a try himself. I shut him down so fast, it made his head spin."

"Did you tell Andrew about that?"

"Of course not. Why would I? Those two already had enough to fight about. I had no desire to make things worse than they already were."

"March thinks you were only interested in Andrew because of his money," I said.

Julia gave an unhappy laugh. "He would."

"Were you?"

"I can't tell you that it wasn't part of the attraction. But not in the way you're thinking. Who Andrew was, the upbringing he'd had, the things he had experienced and had access to, that was all part of what made him the man I fell in love with."

She looked around the small apartment with a wry smile. "Money helps, you know? Who would want to live like this if they could do better? But his assets weren't everything. Not by a long shot. Andrew and I had a real bond. We *got* each other. Do you know what I mean?"

I did. I felt the same way about Sam.

"Where were you on the morning that Andrew was killed?" I asked.

"You mean, do I have an alibi?"

"I wasn't going to be so blunt, but yes."

Julia left the window and sat back down. She picked up her glass and sipped her juice. "The police asked me the same thing, you know."

"I imagine they would have."

She looked at me curiously. "So how does that work, then? Don't they report back to Edward and tell him what they've found out?"

"Not nearly often enough, from what I hear."

"That must really frost his balls."

"I believe it does."

We both smiled at that.

"I was there that morning . . . when it happened," Julia said after a minute. "I was at Andrew's cottage."

My smile melted away. I hadn't expected that.

"What were you doing there?"

"Packing. Getting my things together. I had a lot of stuff to get organized and moved." She gestured toward the unpacked cartons.

"I thought you'd already moved out by then."

"I had, two weeks earlier. When Andrew told

me to go, I packed a bag and went. But that departure was kind of sudden. A lot of my things got left behind."

"So you decided to go back and pick them up at seven o'clock in the morning?" I asked skeptically.

"Nooo." Julia's tone was meaningful. "I went back to get them the evening before."

Oh.

"You spent the night," I said.

"It happens." She shrugged. "Andrew and I might have been pissed at one another, but the sex was still smokin' hot."

Definitely more than I needed to know.

"When you went to Andrew's house that night, were you hoping to make up with him?" I asked.

"No," Julia said firmly. "I went to get my stuff."

"So the sex was just a perk."

"Who are you?" She peered at me across the table. "My mother?"

"Sorry." I waved a hand. "My bad. Then what happened?"

"We had another fight."

"About what?"

"Apparently, Andrew still thought that he could convince me to get an abortion. 'Wipe the slate clean,' he said. 'We'll start over.' When I told him that wasn't going to happen, he got mad. He tossed on his jogging stuff and left."

"He just walked out on you?"

"Pretty much." Julia frowned. "I guess I might

have been yelling at the time. My hormones are all screwed up. And Andrew just didn't want to hear it. He pulled out his phone and dialed Sherm. That was his way of shutting me out, of letting me know that he wasn't listening to me. Then he walked out the door, and I never saw him again."

She sighed softly. "It isn't fair. I never got a chance to make things right between us. And now Andrew will never have a chance to get to know his son."

I agreed with her. *Unfair* didn't begin to cover what had happened.

"The cell phone," I said. "You're sure Andrew had it with him when he left the house?"

"I just said that, didn't I? He was talking to Sherm. They used to touch base in the mornings, before Andrew went into work."

"The police didn't find his cell phone at the scene."

"I know. They made a big deal about that. The detective asked me three times if I was certain about what I saw. Of course I was. Because if Andrew hadn't been on that damn phone, maybe I could have stopped him from leaving. And maybe everything would be different now."

A tear slipped down Julia's cheek. She reached up angrily and brushed it away. I gave her a minute to gather herself. I used the time to take my empty juice glass over to the sink and rinse it out.

"Can you think of anyone who might have wanted to harm Andrew?" I asked on my return.

"I don't know. And I probably shouldn't guess. . . ."

"But if you did?" I picked up my scarf and wound it around my neck.

"Things had been pretty rocky for Andrew at work lately."

"Because he was fighting with his father?"

"No, besides that. That was nothing new. But it seemed like there was something else going on at the office that was bugging him. Maybe a couple of jobs that didn't go right, or somebody reneging on a deal . . ."

Julia lifted my parka off the back of the chair and handed it to me. "To tell you the truth, I didn't pay that much attention. I mean, that's life. It's always something, you know?"

I did.

Together, we walked to the door. "When I first got here," I said, "you asked me if March had changed his mind."

Julia nodded.

"Changed his mind about what?"

"After Andrew died, I told March I was pregnant. I figured he should know. The baby will be his only grandchild. I thought he might want to . . . be involved."

"You mean financially?"

"No," Julia said quickly. "I didn't want Edward's money. I didn't want anything from him. But I've got to be realistic, too."

We both gazed around at the small, dingy apartment. I had to admit, things looked pretty bleak.

"I asked if I could continue living in Andrew's cottage, that's all. You know, until after the baby's born. I didn't see the harm. It's not like Edward is going to be using it for anything."

"I take it he said no."

"He barely even took the time to listen to what I had to say before tossing me out."

Like father, like son, I thought.

I reached out and laid a hand on her arm. "Are you okay here?"

"I will be," Julia said. "I've got my job. I've got insurance. I've met a couple of the neighbors. They seem nice enough."

She gave a halfhearted smile as she opened the door for me. "I guess I just need to get some more unpacking done. Everything will look better then."

"Good luck," I told her.

I meant that sincerely. I'd been a single mother for most of Davey's early life. I knew she had a tough road ahead of her.

"If you get a chance," said Julia, "put in a good word for me with Edward."

"I'll do that."

I bypassed the elevator and took the stairs back down to the ground floor. The entrance was still propped open, and the temperature in the lobby now matched the one outside. Both were barely above freezing. Somewhere, a heating bill was skyrocketing for nothing. I'm a mother. I think of things like that.

As I crossed the lobby, I saw a heavyset man approaching the building. He looked vaguely familiar, but I couldn't immediately place him. Broad shoulders, prematurely receding hairline, wire-rimmed glasses. Where had I seen him before?

He entered through the open doorway and walked past me toward the stairs. Moving with long, deliberate strides, he didn't even glance in my direction. Nor did he try the elevator. He knew it wouldn't come; he must have been here before.

As the man took the steps two at a time, then turned the corner and disappeared, I stared after him thoughtfully. Finally, the brain cells kicked in. Sherm Yablonsky. He'd been at the memorial service. He was Andrew's best friend. One of the people who had eulogized Andrew but had not acknowledged his ex-girlfriend.

So what was he doing here? I whipped around and sped back up the steps, reaching the second-floor landing just in time to see Sherm disappear into Julia's apartment. That was interesting.

• • •

From Norwalk, it was only a short trip to Westport. Considering the price of gas, I figured I might as well kill two birds with one stone. Charlotte had told me that March rarely left home, and he and I had some things we needed to talk about. Hopefully, he wouldn't mind if I dropped by uninvited.

Charlotte answered the door and stared at me, looking perplexed. "Were we expecting you?" she asked.

I walked past her into the house and took off my jacket. "Not unless you're psychic," I said. "Don't you ever have a day off?"

"Yes, of course I do. It varies. And someone has to make sure that Mr. March is eating. . . . Wait a minute, *psychic?*"

"That was a joke." I tossed my parka onto the coatrack.

"Oh." She didn't look reassured.

"I was in the neighborhood. I thought I'd stop by."

Charlotte's expression cleared. "You went to see Julia."

"Yes, I did. I'm glad you're her friend. I think she needs friends."

"Julia's been . . ." Her voice dropped. She glanced toward the closed library door. "It's been hard for her. She's been made to feel like the things that went wrong were her fault, when they weren't. Andrew should have taken better care of her. He should have stood up for her more."

"With his father, you mean?"

"Yes—"

We both heard the click as the library door opened. March appeared in the doorway. Robin was at his side. The setter looked at me and wagged her long plumed tail in greeting.

"Can't a man get any peace around here on a Sunday morning?" March demanded.

"I thought you might like to hear about what I've been up to," I said. "But we can do it another time."

"Don't mind him," Charlotte told me. "He's doing the *New York Times* crossword. He hates to have his puzzle interrupted."

"How long does it take you to finish?" I asked curiously.

"Who says I do?" March glared in my direction. "Oh, for Pete's sake, I've lost my train of thought now. You might as well come in."

"What a pleasant invitation," I said, following him into the library.

He was muttering under his breath. I chose not to listen.

The drapes, I noted happily, were still tied back. The room wasn't exactly bright, but I could easily see where I was going. Also someone, probably Charlotte, had done some more tidying. The ambience was definitely improving.

"Close the door," said March. He headed for his desk.

"I like it open. It's nice to get some fresh air in here."

He stopped and turned. "Why do you argue so much?"

"Seriously?" I said. "Like you should talk."

"Margaret was wrong about you," he grumbled.

"In what way?"

"She said you liked to make yourself useful."

I smiled in spite of myself. Useful people were Aunt Peg's favorite kind.

"She really said that about me?"

"Don't look so pleased with yourself." March settled down into his big leather chair. "I haven't seen any evidence of it yet."

"I'm working on it," I told him. "But first I've had to clear up a few other things. It turns out that you haven't been entirely honest with me."

"In what way?"

"I understand you've been having problems at your company."

"Who told you that?"

"That isn't important," I said. "What is important is that you didn't tell me the truth. I know that one lawsuit was settled recently, and that there have been others, as well."

Alice had recommended that I Google for more details. That was a great idea, except that I'd been too busy since to have a chance. Now I decided to wing it and see where the conversation took me.

"That seems like a lot of litigation for a small company," I said.

"First off," March replied, "March Homes isn't a small company. And secondly, it's the construction business."

"Meaning?"

"That's the way things are done. Everybody sues everybody else."

I had no idea if that was true or not. If so, it seemed like an odd way to do business.

"But you lost," I pointed out.

"No, we settled the claim. Big difference."

"So you knew you were in the wrong."

"We weren't wrong," March's voice rose. "But nobody wants to get involved in long, drawn-out litigation. Corporations settle lawsuits to make problems go away. People who bring nuisance suits are depending on it. That's how business is done."

"So then everything is hunky-dory?"

"Don't put words in my mouth. Like I said a minute ago, it's the construction business. There are always issues that need working out. Have you taken a look at the economy lately?"

I assumed that was a rhetorical question. I tried another tack.

"After Andrew took charge of March Homes, did he keep you informed about everything that was going on?"

"Not every little detail," March admitted. "More like the big picture."

"Julia Davis says that he was worried about things at the office."

"I should hope he was worried," March snapped. "It's a hard job, running a company like that. I ought to know."

"I'm just wondering if Andrew was having problems he didn't tell you about."

"And I'm wondering why you're willing to take the word of an inconsequential ex-girlfriend about anything."

"Julia is pregnant," I said quietly.

"I know that."

"You might have mentioned it before."

"Why? It doesn't mean anything."

I stared at him, dumbfounded. "How can you say such a thing?"

March sighed loudly. "*Now* what's the matter?"

"That baby is your grandchild."

March pushed back his chair. Its movement nudged Robin to her feet. She circled around and laid her head across March's knees. Automatically, his hand lifted to rest on the back of her neck. His thumb began to rub along her long, lean skull.

I envied his position. There's nothing more comforting than having a dog in your lap.

"Maybe it's my grandchild," March said. "There's no proof."

"She and Andrew had been living together since last fall."

"That doesn't prove a damn thing. Women will try to pin something on you whether it's true or not. Once Julia got pregnant, she probably figured she could trap my son into marrying her. That's the oldest trick in the book."

"If you really believe that, I feel sorry for you," I said. "That baby is your flesh and blood. You can do a DNA test if you have to have proof. But in the meantime, I can't believe you want to turn your back on the two of them."

"And I can't believe you think this is any of your business," March retorted.

"You asked me to help find out who murdered your son. That's what I'm doing."

"Is it? Because so far, I'm not seeing any useful results."

"I could let the police arrest you," I said. "That's beginning to sound like a useful result to me."

"Don't think they're not trying. While you've been off wasting valuable time, they've been circling around me like a pack of buzzards who think I'm the only decent meal in sight."

"I warned you that might happen."

"You did," March agreed. "Maybe Margaret wasn't entirely wrong about you."

"Now what?" I asked, exasperated.

"She said you were a sharp cookie. So now you've got me wondering, too. Maybe there were things going on at the company that I didn't know about. That Andrew didn't want me to know about."

"You're back in charge of things again," I told him. "Surely, you can find that out."

"Nominally I'm in charge," March said irritably. "But everybody knows that I don't have the strength or the stamina to do the job. They handle me with kid gloves. Two days a week is barely enough time to work on a smooth transition of power. We don't get down and dirty with the details."

March lifted Robin's head and pushed the setter aside. He stood up and pointed his finger at me. "That's where you come in. Get yourself over to March Homes. Talk to the people that I don't get to hear from. Find out what they have to say."

"I can do that," I said.

Charlotte seemed to have disappeared, so I saw myself out.

Chapter 17

I had to get on the parkway to go home, and once there I found myself driving past the Stamford exits and continuing on to the next town, Greenwich. You know, where Aunt Peg lives. The person who'd gotten me involved in this adventure in the first place.

Talking to Aunt Peg always clarifies my thoughts. Her no-nonsense approach strips away inconsequential details and goes straight to the heart of a problem. Either that or the sugar rush I usually have when we're together makes my brain operate at warp speed. Whatever the reason, it seems to work.

As always, her Standard Poodles announced my arrival before I'd even managed to get out of the car. Aunt Peg opened her front door, and the herd came flooding the steps. All six big black dogs eddied around my legs, jostling each other for position. I extended both hands and ruffled as many ears and topknots as I could reach.

"Just you?" said Aunt Peg.

She stood at the edge of her porch and peered at the Volvo. Apparently, she was hoping that query might conjure up a child or two. Or possibly even my husband. It was easy to see where I fell in the order of importance.

"I'm afraid so," I told her. "Sam has the kids. I've been out running errands."

"On a Sunday morning?"

I ignored her outraged tone. Aunt Peg's approach to the religion we grew up with is every bit as lapsed as mine. "It happens."

With a quick flick of her wrist, she motioned the

Poodles back inside the house. I followed along just as dutifully.

"Is there a reason for this unexpected visit?" she asked.

"I need cake."

Sweets are Aunt Peg's solution to the ills of the world. She pondered the significance of my request briefly, then said, "I can do that."

I'd never doubted her for a minute.

Apparently, in deference to the day of the week, we had coffee cake. It was swirled with cinnamon and had icing on top. The combination was sweet enough to make my teeth ache. Aunt Peg had her ever-present cup of Earl Grey. She plunked a jar of instant coffee on the counter and left me to deal. No surprises there.

"So," she said. "Tell me what's been going on. Start with Augie."

Of course, she would want to hear about the puppy first. But since less than twenty-four hours had passed since her previous update on the Poodle's status, there wasn't much to tell.

"He's wonderful. He's adorable. Davey's going to love him."

"Have you told him yet?"

"No. And don't you dare." I did my best to sound menacing. It was probably a bit of a stretch. "Augie is going to be a surprise."

"When?"

"We're picking him up in a couple of days."

228

"A child's first puppy is a momentous occasion."

My aunt's life revolves around her involvement with dogs—and she wouldn't have it any other way. So the subtext of her statement was clear: *Don't blow it.*

"You know," she said thoughtfully, "once Davey has his own dog, I might even be able to get him back into Junior Showmanship."

It had been Aunt Peg's fondest wish to cheer her nephew on to the junior handling title at Westminster. Unfortunately, as we'd discovered the year before, Davey hadn't shared the same aspirations.

"Don't even go there," I told her. "It's not happening. Sam and Davey are going to finish Augie in the breed ring, then look for something fun. Maybe agility."

"That would work."

I knew she'd agree. When she had time in her schedule, Aunt Peg was an agility maven herself. I used my fork to section off a large bite of coffee cake and pop it in my mouth, then moved on to the topic I'd come to discuss.

"Your friend Edward March," I said.

"What now?" asked Peg.

"For starters, he's a bit of a liar."

"Don't be naive, Melanie. Everyone shades the truth now and then."

"He seems to shade it more than most. Or maybe

he's simply incapable of seeing any viewpoint other than his own."

Aunt Peg sliced off two new pieces of cake and put one on each of our plates. "Are we talking about that regrettable e-mail again?"

"Oh, please," I said. "That's old news. But just for the record, I have yet to meet a woman who would be honored to appear in March's book."

"I'm not surprised," said Aunt Peg. "There's a basic truism I've learned over the years."

"What's that?"

"The male ego is a powerful source of self-delusion."

That made me laugh. "How do they do it?" I asked.

"I don't know, but every single one of them looks in the mirror every morning and sees an Adonis staring back at him. And somehow that carries over into the rest of their lives."

Women should be so lucky, I thought.

"March's business has been having problems," I told her.

Aunt Peg got up, walked over to the refrigerator, and got out the butter dish. In case the coffee cake wasn't fattening enough on its own, I supposed.

"In this economy, I should think that they would," she said as she sat back down. "Even in Fairfield County, new construction is down. And the rest of the state is even worse. Builders have been hit hard, especially ones like March Homes."

"Why them in particular?"

"Most of the houses they build are lower-end construction," said Peg. "March Homes specializes in putting together developments, inexpensive housing meant to give young couples a chance to buy their first homes. But now all those young people can't get mortgages. So everybody's stuck."

"That's not their only problem," I said. "March Homes has also been fending off lawsuits from disgruntled clients."

"That must hurt."

"I would think so. And here's something else. Andrew had a longtime girlfriend named Julia Davis. The two of them had been living together since last fall. Then she got pregnant, and he dumped her—two weeks before he died."

"Oh, dear," said Aunt Peg. "That's a rather revolting development. Have you met her? Does she seem like the murderous sort?"

"I'd say that she's more unhappy than vindictive. She also appears to be struggling financially. And despite the fact that she's carrying his only grandchild, March doesn't want anything to do with her. He says she's nothing more than a gold digger who was trying to trap his son into marriage. How cold is that?"

"Yes, well . . ."

Aunt Peg put down her fork and stared at some distant point. Her fingers began to drum idly on the tabletop. The Poodles, lying around us on the floor, raised their heads to see what was going on. If I were a dog, I'd have pricked my ears, too. I wondered what she was thinking.

"About that," she said after a minute. "It could be that baby isn't Edward's only offspring."

"What do you mean?"

"You know how people gossip at dog shows?"

Of course I did. Sometimes that was half the fun of being there. On losing days, when the judge hated your dog, it might be all the enjoyment you had.

"Let's just say that at one time there were rumors floating around. It seems there was a possibility that one of the women Edward was involved with had gotten pregnant."

"Who?" I asked quickly.

"I don't have any idea. That's the whole point of a rumor, isn't it? Maybe what you hear is true and maybe it isn't—and there's always some vital piece of corroborating information that seems to be missing."

"When was this?"

"A good long time ago. It would have been years, maybe even decades. It was just a wisp of titillating information that floated around the handlers' tent for a while and gave us all something to talk about while we were busy brushing."

"But March never acknowledged a child?"

"Not that I know of. And as I said, it could be that there never was one. Maybe the story was started by a disgruntled competitor who wanted to make Edward look bad."

"That's rotten," I said.

Aunt Peg shrugged. "That's life. People do all sorts of nasty things when there's winning and losing on the line, and they've managed to get their egos involved in the outcome. Really, Melanie, considering some of the situations you've seen, you, of all people, should have learned that by now."

As usual, she was right.

"So what happens next?" asked Aunt Peg. "While you've been busy nosing around in Edward's private affairs, what have the police been doing to make themselves useful?"

"Good question. March is keeping tabs on the investigation, so I've purposely been staying away. Unfortunately, it sounds as though rather than looking for other suspects, the police are trying to build a case against him."

She nodded. "It wouldn't be the first time something like that happened. Edward is, after all, Andrew's closest relation. Under the circumstances, I can see why you might want to lie low until you have some sort of fantastic revelation to spring on them."

My aunt was ever the optimist. And she usually had higher expectations for me than I had for myself. Her point about lying low was well taken, however.

My past dealings with various police forces have consistently proven less than gratifying. One thing the authorities all seemed to agree upon was that sleuthing was a job best left to the professionals. Even when—or perhaps especially when—I'd managed to beat them to the punch.

Either way, I had learned not to expect a warm welcome when I took myself down to the local police station and attempted to share the nuggets of information I'd uncovered. And now, with Edward March determined to run interference with the authorities on his own behalf, my self-serving plan was to draw as little official attention to myself as possible.

"You're assuming that I ever have such a revelation," I said.

"For Edward's sake, let's hope so."

I devoted the next twenty-four hours to doing the Mommy thing.

That meant tobogganing on the big hill at the Greenwich Country Club on Sunday afternoon, cooking a delicious and nutritious dinner that evening, then helping Davey with his rather tedious homework on the Normans and the Saxons. Monday morning, Kevin and I went to Gymboree, then stopped at the supermarket, the post office, and the dry cleaner on the way home. Along the way I also found time to clip three Poodles' faces and twelve feet, then run the pooper-scooper around the backyard.

It was no wonder the police thought they ought to be the ones investigating crime. Looking at my schedule, I had to agree.

Monday afternoon I got back on the road. This time I was on my way to Route 7, a congested highway that passes through industrialized areas of Norwalk and Wilton on its way north to Danbury. It was also the location for the corporate headquarters of March Homes.

I hadn't called ahead to make an appointment. Nobody at March Homes was expecting me. In my experience, giving people advance notice only offers them the opportunity to think about what they should or shouldn't say. Or, worse yet, to refuse to see me all together.

My plan—such as it was—was to ask to see Walt McEvoy. Especially now with the company's management hierarchy in a state of flux, I couldn't imagine that he'd be available. That was fine with me. What interested me was who I'd be delegated to instead, and what that person might have to say.

Considering that March Homes was in the business of custom construction, their corporate headquarters was surprisingly plain. It was just a square, two-story building, situated beside the highway and surrounded by an unadorned parking lot. If it hadn't been for the sign by the road, I would have missed it entirely.

The building was painted industrial gray, and its windows needed cleaning. At least the lot was freshly plowed. It was also mostly empty. I wondered what, if anything, that signified as I parked and went inside.

Considering the building's ordinary exterior, I wasn't expecting much. Which is why the lobby I entered came as a revelation. Spacious and well lit, it seemed to be as much a showroom as a reception area.

Floor-to-ceiling images of March-built homes and developments covered the walls. A model of a subdivision in Danbury—construction currently in progress, according to the sign affixed to the front—was spread out over a large platform to the right of the entryway. A reception desk was on the left.

A slender, earnest-looking young man was speaking on the phone when I entered. A nameplate on the desk identified him as David Hunt. Seeing me, he immediately hung up and stood. "May I help you?"

"Yes. My name is Melanie Travis. I'd like to speak with Walt McEvoy please."

"Do you have an appointment?"

Such an efficient-looking receptionist must surely have known the answer to that question, but I humored him, anyway. "No, I don't. Is he available?"

"I'll check for you." David picked up the phone again. "May I ask what this is in reference to?"

"No."

I smiled to soften the blunt denial. It didn't help. David still looked affronted. Nevertheless, he pushed a few buttons and spoke to someone in a low tone, angling his body slightly away, as if he didn't want me to overhear what was being said.

The call seemed to go on for quite a bit longer than I would have thought necessary. At the end, David hung up and gestured toward a suite of chairs grouped around a low table. "If you wouldn't mind having a seat, someone will be with you shortly."

Only a minute or two passed before the elevator situated in the back wall of the lobby opened and an attractive woman came striding out. She had short blond hair and pretty features, which were all but hidden by a pair of large, dark-framed eyeglasses. She wore chunky gold jewelry at her ears and throat, and her rounded figure was accentuated by a snug floral wraparound dress. Navy blue heels, high enough that I would have been tottering on them, tapped a tattoo on the floor as she approached.

"I'm Rose Mooney, Mr. McEvoy's assistant," she said. "I'm afraid he's busy right now. But if you'd like to come to my office, maybe I can help you."

I introduced myself; then Rose and I took the elevator to the upper floor in silence. Once there we walked past a glass-walled conference room and several other offices, whose doors were all closed, before reaching Rose's work space at the end of the hall.

Her desktop was immaculate; her shelves were organized by function. The only decoration on the walls was a single March Homes poster headlined with the slogan BUY WITH CONFIDENCE! and displaying a picture of a presumably happy family underneath. Blinds over a small double window had been angled to cut the glare from the early afternoon sun. There was a low couch along one side wall of the room, and Rose steered me that way.

"Let's sit down," she said. "I'm sorry Mr. McEvoy isn't able to see you, but hopefully, I can answer any questions you might have. As you probably know, March Homes is the most highly respected builder of custom residences in Connecticut."

"So I've heard," I told her.

"Excellent." Rose cupped her hands around her hips, then slid them downward as she sat, smoothing her skirt into position. She crossed her legs demurely at the ankle. "Maybe you have a friend who's used our services?"

"I'm afraid not. And I'm not looking to do so, either."

"Oh." Rose managed to imbue the single word with a wealth of disappointment. "Then how may I help you?"

"I'd like to learn more about your company," I said. "Your COO died recently under suspicious circumstances—"

"You're a reporter," Rose said flatly. "You should have started with that information. David would have stopped you at the door, and I wouldn't have wasted my time."

"I'm not a reporter," I said. "And I can promise you that nothing you tell me will be made public."

Rose tipped her head to one side, studying me intently through her thick lenses. "Who sent you here?"

"Edward March. He's asked me to gather some information for him."

"Don't be ridiculous. I know Mr. March. If he needed information, he'd have gone to Mr. McEvoy directly."

"Not if he's under the impression that McEvoy is telling him only what he thinks he wants to hear. And that perhaps Andrew had been doing the same thing for some time. Mr. March has every intention of finding out what was going on here prior to his son's death. I'm hoping you can help me with that."

"You think I'm going to report on my boss behind his back?"

"You're the one who volunteered to answer all my questions."

"Not questions like these. I thought you'd want to know about construction costs or scheduling or choosing tile for the bathroom."

Rose stood up, walked over to her desk, and sat down behind it. Even an amateur psychologist could read that body language. She was placing a big solid barrier between us.

"Lawsuits," I said.

This time I'd done my homework. Three had been settled by March Homes over the past two years, including the case Alice's firm had been involved in. Another had recently been initiated.

"What about them?"

"It looks like there's been an increase in the amount of litigation the company has been dealing with."

Rose's answer mirrored the one March had given me the day before. "That's just the cost of being in the construction business. When people design a home, they make choices based on blueprints and pictures. And then inevitably, in the middle of the process, when things begin to take shape, they change their minds. They thought two bathrooms were going to be enough, but now they want two and a half. The cheaper flooring was going to be fine in the kitchen, but now they want to upgrade.

"And somehow customers never seem to understand that when they ask for more expensive materials, the price is going to go up. Or that when they change a floor plan mid-construction, that costs us time and money. And unfortunately, there's an unemployed lawyer on every street corner who's willing to tell them that the extra charges aren't their fault and that they shouldn't have to pay."

"One of the lawsuits alleged that the quality of the workmanship done by March Homes was subpar," I said. "That Andrew had made promises about quality that weren't kept."

"People can allege anything they want," Rose pointed out.

"Yes, but when a company repeatedly settles claims, it makes it look as though the allegations most likely had merit. I know the economy has taken a toll on the construction business. Was Andrew cutting corners to cut costs? Was he making poor decisions that impacted the company's bottom line?"

"I wouldn't know anything about that," Rose said sharply.

She hadn't been happy to answer my questions in the first place. Now her patience was wearing thin, and I was clearly running out of time.

I stood up. "You know that Andrew's death wasn't an accident," I said.

Rose's head dipped in a brief nod.

"He must have made someone very angry. Maybe an unhappy client who didn't want to resolve things in court? Or a disgruntled employee? As Mr. McEvoy's assistant, you must have seen things and heard things. . . ."

I let the thought dangle, but Rose didn't take the bait.

"If you're looking for someone willing to tell tales, you've got the wrong person," she said firmly.

"Your boss is lucky to have such a loyal assistant."

"Mr. McEvoy is a good man and an excellent executive. And Edward March is the one who's lucky to have someone of Walt's caliber in place and ready to take over management of the company. After five years of baby-sitting Andrew, he certainly deserves the top spot."

Baby-sitting? I blinked in surprise, wondering if I'd heard right.

And in that moment of hesitation, I lost my chance to find out.

Rose quickly stood up and stepped out from behind her desk. Her lips were pursed shut; her arms crossed over her chest. She had the look of a woman who thought she'd said too much already.

"That's all the time I can possibly spare," she said. "Let me show you out."

Chapter 18

It wasn't as if I was being given a choice. Rose waited until I'd preceded her through the doorway. Then she closed the office door behind us and escorted me down the hallway.

"I can find my own way," I said.

"No problem. I'll walk you to the elevator."

No problem indeed. I felt like a prisoner being conducted out of a cell block. This level of surveillance within the company headquarters was curious, especially since Rose knew that March himself had sent me there. What was she afraid I might see?

With that in mind, I used the stroll down the corridor to have a good look around. The conference room was still empty. But the door to one of the offices we'd passed earlier was now ajar, revealing a big, beautifully appointed room complete with an oriental rug and a polished cherrywood desk.

As we walked past the open doorway, I caught a brief glimpse of someone inside. A woman was standing with her back to the door, pulling books off a high shelf and loading them into a cardboard box. Immersed in her task, she didn't look around as we went by.

"Whose office is that?" I asked.

"It was Andrew March's."

Rose's clipped tone was clearly meant to discourage further discussion. Which did nothing to stop me from speculating on my own. Rose reached out and pushed the elevator button. The doors slid open.

"Thank you for your time," I said pertly as I walked inside. "You've been very helpful."

I sincerely hoped *that* gave her second thoughts.

Quietly, the doors slipped shut between us. The elevator ride was brief. Just long enough for me to make a plan.

When the doors opened on the floor below, I remained inside and hugged the corner near the button panel. From David's vantage point, the elevator would appear empty. After a brief pause, the doors closed again. I pressed the button to go back up.

Returned to the second floor, I saw that luck was with me. Rose had disappeared. Hopefully, she'd gone back to her office. The corridor in front of me was now empty.

I scampered out of the elevator and made my way quickly down the hall. Silently, I slipped into Andrew's office and closed the door behind me. The woman inside glanced up at the sound of the small click. She was older than I'd thought at first, probably approaching retirement age. With her plump cheeks and kindly eyes, she looked like someone's favorite granny.

She wedged the books she was holding into an empty space at the top of the box and said, "Can I help you?"

"I hope so," I replied. "My name is Melanie Travis. I'm a friend of Edward March's. He sent me here to ask some questions."

"What about?"

"He wants to get reacquainted with his company."

"As well he should, under the circumstances." The woman leveled me a look. "I thought Walt McEvoy was in charge of that."

"Mr. March is open to hearing other opinions, as well."

"I can get Rose for you. She's Walt's assistant."

"I've already spoken with Rose."

The woman's gaze turned speculative. "You didn't get the answers you wanted?"

"No. Mostly, I just got the party line."

"I can't say I'm surprised by that. I'm Bonnie Raye. Maybe I can help you. What kind of information are you looking for?"

I liked Bonnie. She looked like the kind of woman who would appreciate an honest approach.

"To put it bluntly," I said, "I want the dirt."

She nodded, waiting for me to continue.

"What's your position here?" I asked.

"Until very recently, I was Andrew March's

assistant. He was the COO," she added helpfully, in case I didn't know.

"And now?"

"Now it looks as though I've been made redundant. Demoted back downstairs to the bull pen, where I started twenty years ago, answering phones and taking orders. Apparently, the company's moving in a younger direction."

"I'm very sorry," I said.

"Thank you." Bonnie studied me for a minute. "Maybe you could buy me a cup of coffee."

"Sure. I'd be happy to."

"Not here. There's a Starbucks just up the road. I could meet you there in, say, twenty minutes?"

"That sounds great. Are you sure you can get away?"

Bonnie chuckled as she slapped the carton shut and unspooled a roll of tape across the top. "I can get away, all right. What are they going to do if they don't like it? Fire me?"

Half an hour later, Bonnie and I were settled at a corner table. Mid-afternoon the Starbucks was mostly empty. Aside from the two of us, the only other occupants were a teenager, who was thoroughly engrossed in his laptop, and a ladies' tennis group from the nearby indoor facility.

Bonnie chose a caramel macchiato, and I had a mocha latte. Between the two beverages, we were probably about to consume an entire day's worth of calories. I took a sip, licked the foam off my upper lip, and decided it was worth it.

"First off," said Bonnie, "how is Mr. March doing?"

"His health isn't great," I told her. "I assume you know that."

She nodded.

"And, of course, he's very upset about what happened to his son. He told me he's been going in to work a couple of times a week. You haven't seen him?"

"Seen him, sure." Bonnie used her spoon to scoop up a drizzle of caramel. "Talked to him, no. His time is monopolized by the powers-that-be from the moment he gets out of his car."

"But you were Andrew's assistant," I said, puzzled by that revelation. "You must have been on top of everything that was happening prior to his death. March didn't want to meet with you?"

"As far as I can tell, no one's taken the time to stop and ask Mr. March what *he* wants. They've just channeled him in the direction they needed him to go."

"What do you mean?"

"As I'm sure you can imagine, there's been a lot of upheaval at the headquarters recently. Maybe even what you might call a seismic shift. With Andrew out of the picture, that left a big hole at the top. Most of us, well . . . I guess we sat around and waited to see what would happen next."

Bonnie stopped for a sip of coffee, and her gaze slid toward a tray of hazelnut tarts behind the glass-fronted counter. *I'm not above using bribery to achieve my aims;* I filed that thought away for future use.

"And the others?" I asked.

"The others were mainly Walt and Rose. The two of them saw an opening appear and *bam!* They were right on top of it. Not that Walt didn't deserve the promotion. He did—and I'm sure he'd have gotten it, anyway. But instead of waiting to find out what Mr. March's plans were, he just moved in and assumed control."

"Maybe he thought someone had to," I said.

"Or maybe he figured that the best way to rise to the top was to cut everybody else off at the knees. So no, I haven't spoken with Mr. March. Why else do you think I'm here?"

"Maybe because you like the hazelnut tarts?"

Bonnie chuckled and started to stand up. I pushed back my chair and beat her to it.

"It's on me. I'll be right back."

"Better make it two," said Bonnie. "They're not very big."

I made it three, two for her and one for me, and tossed all thoughts of a nutritious diet out the window for the day. When both of us were chewing blissfully, I reopened the conversation.

"Rose seemed pretty dismissive of Andrew," I said. "She referred to Walt as his baby-sitter."

"That sounds like something she would say."

"Is it the truth?"

"Not even close. Don't get me wrong. Andrew was no saint. He certainly had his faults. But when it came to March Homes, he'd worked his way up from the bottom, and he knew what he was doing. Not to say that all his decisions were the right ones. Andrew could be a little impetuous and maybe hotheaded at times. But he understood the business, inside and out."

"Those impetuous decisions he made," I said. "Could any of them have resulted in someone being angry enough to want to harm him?"

Bonnie finished the rest of her first tart before speaking again. Daintily, she licked the last of the sugar off her fingertips. Then she looked at me thoughtfully. "Are we off the record here, or what?"

"I'll do my best to keep anything you tell me confidential," I told her. "And if that's not possible, you have my promise that I won't reveal where the information came from."

"Fair enough," said Bonnie. "How well do you know Edward March?"

"Pretty well, I guess."

"Then you know he has a way with women."

I laughed at that. "So I've heard. In fact, he's writing a book about it."

Bonnie's eyes grew wide. "No!"

"I'm not kidding. Although he's put his literary

ambitions on hold for the time being, until he gets the company sorted out."

"I should hope so." Bonnie snorted. "Writing a book, indeed. What is that old fool thinking?"

There was no way to answer that. I didn't even try.

"Back to Andrew," said Bonnie. "The first thing you need to know is that the apple didn't fall far from the tree. He had quite an eye for the ladies himself. And not a lot of willpower. That could be a dangerous combination, if you know what I mean."

"He got involved with someone at March Homes," I guessed.

"More than once," Bonnie confirmed. "It seemed like he thought of the bull pen as his own personal happy hunting ground. Usually, he didn't get in too much trouble. That boy had charm to spare when he needed it. But once or twice that kind of risky business came back and bit him in the butt."

"How?" I asked. "Who are we talking about?"

Bonnie lowered her voice, even though there was no one within earshot. I leaned in closer across the small table to hear.

"Melissa McEvoy, for one."

"As in *Walt McEvoy?*"

Bonnie nodded. "She's his wife. Now, let me be clear. This is past history I'm talking about. Three or four years, at least. That boy, I don't know what he was thinking. It's one thing to dip your pen in the company inkwell, but to go after another senior officer's wife? That's just way out of bounds."

"Then what happened?"

"Somehow Walt found out. I don't even know how it all blew up, but when it did, it got ugly fast. Next thing, Andrew and Walt were threatening to come to blows in the conference room. A couple of the other guys had to pull them apart. And suddenly something that should have been a private matter had everybody in the whole building talking about it."

"But they continued to work together?" I asked incredulously.

"Not easily. And not happily, either. Mr. March had to get himself back in the office and smooth things over personally. He told Walt he'd be foolish to throw away a career opportunity like the one he had here over something as meaningless as an affair."

"That must have gone over well," I said drily.

"Probably not, but it didn't matter. One way or another, Mr. March got the job done. Eventually, Andrew and Walt shook hands and made up. At least publicly, anyway."

"And in private?"

"If I had to guess, I'd say that there are still some bitter feelings there and they've been festering for a long time."

Amazing, I thought, that March hadn't deemed this fracas important enough to mention when he'd spoken so fondly of his son's handpicked successor.

"You said there'd been a couple of times. . . . What else?"

"George," said Bonnie. "Has anyone told you about him?"

"No. Who is he?"

"George Weiner. He worked for March Homes for five years. Then he was passed over for a promotion, which he thought he should have gotten. He quit his job and sued."

"For what?"

"Sexual discrimination."

"Did he have a valid complaint?"

"George thought so."

"Did anybody else?"

Bonnie smiled. "You mean, besides his lawyer?"

"It sounds like you weren't entirely convinced."

"You got it."

She picked up her second tart and bit into the flaky crust. It looked so good that I considered going back for seconds myself. Then I thought about the size of my pants versus that of my hips and asked another question instead.

"When did this take place?"

"George quit the company last fall. We got notice of the lawsuit right before Christmas.

As far as I know, the legal department's still deciding which way to go with it. But Andrew was adamant. He wasn't going to settle under any circumstances. He wanted to take the case to court."

That seemed like an unexpected position for him to take. Based on what I'd learned so far, Andrew's decision would have been directly opposed to company policy.

"Do you know why he felt that way?" I asked.

"He said the suit had no merit, and he was sure that a judge would agree."

"What do you think?"

Bonnie's shoulders lifted in a small shrug. "To tell you the truth, I'm not sure. George's claim is that Andrew favored women when it came time to make promotions—and that he especially favored women who were willing to trade sexual favors for advancement. George contended that, as a man and through no fault of his own, he had no possibility of fair treatment at March Homes."

"Was he right?"

"Hard to tell, really. Maxine—she's the woman who got the promotion George didn't—she's a real hard worker. But George had been with the company longer. I guess he figured he had seniority."

I sipped my latte and thought about what she'd said.

"The fact that George had been at March Homes

for a while means he probably knew about the company's propensity to settle lawsuits rather than defend them," I said after a minute. "It could be that he initiated his case under the assumption that it would never go to court—especially since what he was alleging could be seen as potentially embarrassing to the company."

"That makes sense," said Bonnie. "Do you think it matters?"

"It might, if the only thing standing between George and an easy settlement was Andrew's determination to fight him to the bitter end."

Bonnie smiled admiringly. "You have a devious mind. I like that in a woman."

"It's one of my better qualities," I told her. "Thank God I have a couple."

She saw me eyeing the last piece of hazelnut tart. Bonnie pushed the plate across the table. "Go ahead and finish it. I've had plenty."

I was happy to comply. I washed it down with the last of my latte. I guessed we were about done.

"You've been pumping me for information," said Bonnie. "Now it's my turn."

Or maybe not. I stared at her with interest.

"Andrew's girlfriend, Julia? She used to come into the office sometimes. Now that he's gone, what's going to happen to her?"

That was a question I hadn't expected. "You do know that she and Andrew had broken up, right?"

"Pffft!" Bonnie brushed a hand through the air. "Those two were always breaking up. And then they'd turn around two weeks later and get right back together again. It was just their way of doing things."

"You and Julia must have been friends," I said.

First Charlotte, then Sherm, and now Bonnie. It looked as though Andrew's ex had supporters in all sorts of interesting places.

"That girl makes friends easily. We'd talk sometimes when she came to meet Andrew. Most people coming to see the boss, they didn't even notice me. But Julia did. She cares about people." Bonnie shook her head. "Probably more than anybody ever bothered to care about her."

"Julia has moved into an apartment in Norwalk," I said. "I got the impression things are a little difficult for her right now."

"Because of the baby?"

"You know about that?"

Bonnie laughed. "I had three of my own. I think I probably knew before she did." Then her smile faded. "Julia's not as strong as she wants people to think. She needs someone to take care of her."

"Unfortunately, that person won't be Edward March," I told her.

"Kind of a shame the way things turned out," said Bonnie. "Somebody up and killed the son. They should have gone after the father."

Chapter 19

I'd just turned out of the Starbucks parking lot when my cell phone rang. A glance at the screen revealed a number but no ID. I pulled off my glove, transferred the steering wheel to my other hand, and fitted the phone to my ear.

"Melanie?" said a breathless voice. "It's Charlotte. Can you come right away?"

"I'm in Wilton," I told her. Spurred by the urgency in Charlotte's tone, I put on my turn signal and pulled into the fast lane. "Not too far north of the parkway. I can probably be there in fifteen minutes—"

"Please hurry. I didn't know who else to call."

"I'm on my way. What's going on? What's the matter?"

"Detective Wygod just called. Do you remember him?"

"Sure."

"He's coming here," said Charlotte. "I think he's going to arrest Mr. March."

Well, damn.

"March needs to call his lawyer," I said quickly. "Legal representation will be a lot more useful to him than I will."

"I told him that," Charlotte wailed. "But he won't do it. Mr. March thinks that having a lawyer here will make him look guilty. He said the detective just wants to talk to him, to go over some of his statements again."

"Okay calm down for a minute," I said. My foot eased up off the gas pedal. "That doesn't sound so bad. Talking is a long way from making an arrest."

"Maybe." Charlotte didn't sound convinced. "But Mr. March calls the police station constantly, looking for news. He's always complaining that he can barely even get the detective on the phone. So why would Wygod suddenly decide to come here?"

"Maybe he's coming to tell March to stop bugging him and let him do his job," I said. I was only half kidding.

"Just come," Charlotte said softly. "So he won't have to meet with the detective alone. Please?"

"Now I'm ten minutes away," I told her. "Don't worry. I'll see you soon."

A plain, unmarked sedan was already parked in the driveway when I arrived. Charlotte had the front door open before I'd even parked my car. The moment I entered the house, she grabbed my coat and purse and pushed me down the hall.

"They're in the library," she said.

Of course. Where else would they be?

Not unexpectedly, the door was closed. "Do they know I'm coming?" I asked, pausing in front of it.

Charlotte hesitated, then shook her head. "I didn't have a chance to tell Mr. March I'd called you."

I didn't believe that for a minute. So now, on top of being unsure why I'd been summoned with such urgency, it appeared that my presence might not even be welcome.

"I can't just go barging in there," I said.

"But somebody has to stand up for Mr. March!"

"From what I've seen, he does an excellent job of standing up for himself," I muttered.

Charlotte didn't reply. Her eyes were large and imploring.

I looked at her and sighed. Then I raised my hand and knocked.

"What?" March yelled from within, polite as ever. "We're busy in here!"

I opened the door but didn't enter the room. March was seated behind his desk. Wygod had taken my usual chair across from him. Both men turned to look in my direction.

"Is everything all right?" I asked.

"Of course," said March, his voice full and firm. The image of strength he was trying to project seemed at odds with the frailness of his body. "Why wouldn't it be? The detective is just catching me up on a few details of the investigation."

"I'm glad to hear that." I moved forward into the room. "Have there been any new developments?"

Wygod stood as I approached.

"You remember my friend Melanie Travis, right?" said March.

"We met the last time you were here," I told him. "In the kitchen."

The detective nodded. "You were the one who asked all the questions."

Really? That wasn't how *I* remembered my participation in the conversation. A little warning bell went off in my brain. Unfortunately, it was too late for me to retreat now.

"Melanie's good at asking questions," March was saying. "In fact, I sent her around to talk to some people for me. You know, in case maybe you didn't have time to get to everyone."

"Is that so?" This time the hostility in Wygod's tone was hard to miss. "So you've been doing a little detecting on your own?"

"I was simply gathering some information for Mr. March," I said. I found myself adopting the demeanor I'd have used with an aggressive dog. I moderated my voice to a soothing level and didn't make direct eye contact.

"I hope that's all it was. Because I would hate to think that you might be impeding an official police investigation."

That brought my head up. I stared at Wygod.

"It's been two weeks since Andrew died," I pointed out. "How is the *official investigation* coming along?"

The detective lifted his shoulders in a small shrug. "Like I was telling Mr. March, we've been very busy. There are a lot of different avenues we need to explore before we begin to zero in on specifics. I think he agreed with me that it's always better to have a job done well than done fast."

March was nodding as Wygod spoke. I was not. All I heard was a string of cover-your-butt platitudes. In other words, it sounded as though the police had diddly.

If that was the case, Charlotte had been right to worry about the reason for Wygod's visit. The longer the authorities went without settling on a primary suspect, the more appealing Edward March—with his motive and his proximity to the crime—was going to appear to them.

"I guess that means you must have a lot of potential suspects to sort through," I said.

Detective Wygod wasn't in a mood to share. His answering grunt was neither confirmation nor denial.

Briefly, I considered mentioning the things that I'd uncovered: Julia's resentment at the way she'd been treated, Walt McEvoy's lingering bitterness and dogged quest for promotion, George Weiner's anger with the company and subsequent lawsuit. Then, just as quickly, I decided against it.

For one thing, I wasn't sure March wanted me airing his company's dirty laundry. For another, judging by the detective's attitude, he wasn't likely to take anything I said seriously. And since the police would probably have already discovered much of the same information, there was simply no point in my irritating the detective further.

"We'll keep in touch," Wygod was saying to March. "Please be assured that we're doing everything we can to bring your son's killer to justice."

He spun on his heel and headed for the door. As the detective passed me, he nodded curtly. "Ms. Travis. Stay out of trouble."

"I'll certainly try," I replied.

Charlotte appeared in the doorway to escort Detective Wygod out. March and I both watched him leave.

When we heard the outer door close, March waved me to a seat and said, "So I hear Rose is still guarding access to Walt McEvoy like she thinks he's the Holy Grail and she's the last line of defense."

"That was fast," I replied. "I was there only a couple of hours ago."

March grinned, happy to have caught me out. "What? You think I don't have my sources?"

"Did your sources also tell you that after twenty years on the job, Bonnie Raye has been demoted back down to the bull pen? Or that the entire office knows about your son's affair with Walt McEvoy's wife? Or that George Weiner's lawsuit against March Homes alleges that Andrew had a history of promoting women who were willing to trade sexual favors for advancement?"

March's smile faded. For several moments I had the satisfaction of seeing my information render him speechless.

"Where'd you get all that from?" he asked finally.

"What? You think you're the only one with sources?"

I was only teasing, but March's expression didn't lighten. He sat back in his chair and blew out a windy breath.

"Melissa McEvoy," he said. "That was a mess."

"I'm sure it was. Why didn't you tell me about it before?"

"Why would I? It's over and done with. Everybody put it behind them."

Or so he wanted to believe.

"Don't waste your time worrying about George," March said. He was already moving on. "George is small time. Weiner the Whiner, that's what Andrew used to call him."

"If anything, that makes me worry about him more. Aside from not promoting him and blocking the settlement of his lawsuit, your son apparently also exposed the guy to public ridicule."

March gave a distracted nod. He didn't appear to be listening to what I was saying.

"Are you sure Bonnie's been sent back downstairs?" he asked.

"That's what she told me. Now that Andrew's gone, her job has been made redundant."

"That's not fair."

"I agree. Maybe you can do something about it."

"I damn well can," March snarled. "I may be old, but March Homes is still *my* company. Nobody's going to tell me how to run things."

He sat for a moment, staring off into space. "Jeez, Bonnie Raye. I haven't seen her in a couple of years. How is the old girl, anyway?"

"Doing well, I believe. She asked after you." I figured there was no point in mentioning how she felt about March's treatment of Julia.

"She would. Bonnie was like a den mother. She wanted to take care of everybody. That was why I made her Andrew's assistant when he moved up to a job at headquarters. I figured she'd be able to keep him from getting into too much trouble."

"I'm sure she did her best." I stood up to leave.

"You never did tell me," said March. "Why are you here today?"

"Charlotte called me. She was worried about you. She thought you might like some support when you talked to Detective Wygod."

"That one." March shook his head. "She's another mother hen."

"She cares about you," I said. "God knows why."

He cackled at that. "Can't be my looks anymore. Must be my sterling personality."

"Must be," I agreed, heading for the door.

Charlotte met me in the hallway as I was pulling on my coat. "Is everything all right?"

"As far as I know." I dropped my voice. "Charlotte, what's really going on?"

"What do you mean?"

"Why did you call and tell me I had to come?"

"I was afraid. . . ." She glanced toward the open library door, and her voice trailed away.

"Of what?" I pressed.

"Let's go outside," said Charlotte. "We can go grab Robin and take her for a walk. Do you have boots with you?"

I laughed at that. It was January in Connecticut. I was already wearing them. I had gloves tucked into my pocket, too.

The Irish Setter was in the kitchen, snoozing in a cedar-filled dog bed situated in a patch of sun. As soon as Charlotte called her name, she leapt to her feet, happy to join in the adventure. I opened the back door, and a burst of cold air came rushing in. As I paused to zip my parka and pull on my gloves, Robin squeezed past me and flew down the steps. Before Charlotte and I were even outside, the setter was already halfway across the yard.

"Robin loves this." Charlotte pulled a knitted cap low over her ears. "I try to get her out for a really long walk at least once a day. Mr. March used to make sure that she got plenty of exercise, but now it's my job."

Robin zipped on ahead of us through the snow. She danced; she bounced; she gamboled happily. Then she caught a scent and lowered her nose into the white powder, leaving a shallow tunnel in her wake as she raced away.

I started to run after her, but Charlotte called me back.

"Don't worry," she said. "We don't have to keep up. Robin will circle back around and wait for us if she gets too far ahead. All this land out here belongs to Mr. March. It's not like she can get into any trouble."

We tramped through the snow in silence for several minutes. Now that we'd achieved a measure of privacy, I expected Charlotte to tell me what she hadn't wanted to say inside. Instead, she seemed to have relaxed, content to simply enjoy a stroll through the open fields behind the house.

"So," I said finally. "What really happened earlier?"

Charlotte shrugged uncomfortably. "I don't know. I'm sorry I made you come all the way out here for nothing. I just had this awful vision of the police showing up and dragging Mr. March away in handcuffs. And I didn't know what I was supposed to do about that."

All at once she looked both very young and very vulnerable. The ten-year gap between our ages seemed like an eternity.

"It looked to me like Detective Wygod only wanted to talk," I said.

"I know that now. I guess maybe I overreacted a little."

I thought of my headlong, high-adrenaline drive from Wilton to Westport. Charlotte had over-reacted a *lot*. Not only that, but I got the impression there was something she wasn't telling me.

"You seem like a pretty levelheaded person," I said.

Charlotte's chin lifted. "I am."

"So what made you think that Detective Wygod was going to arrest Mr. March?"

Her eyes tracked the red setter, now racing toward a belt of trees. Robin hit a snowdrift running flat out, and a shower of powder sprayed in all directions. It didn't even slow her down. Charlotte watched for another few seconds, then turned back to me.

"Because that's what my mother said is going to happen. She told me that Mr. March seems like a nice man on the surface, but underneath he's a black-hearted scoundrel."

I was pretty sure that anyone who thought

March seemed like a nice man had probably never spent much time in his company. The scoundrel part sounded about right, though.

"Does your mother think March had something to do with his son's death?" I asked curiously.

"I don't know. Maybe."

That was interesting.

"What do you think?" I asked.

"I think that it doesn't pay to disagree with my mother," Charlotte said firmly. "No matter what she says."

As we approached the trees, Robin came flying back out into the open. Small hard balls of ice swung from the feathers on her tail and legs. Charlotte called the setter over and checked the pads of her feet. She dug out several chunks of snow from between the setter's toes.

"Your mother's the one who got you the job working for March," I said as I watched her work.

Charlotte released the dog and dusted the snow off her hands. "That's right."

"Why would she do that if she thought so poorly of him?"

"I don't know. She's her own woman. She does what she wants. I gave up trying to understand my mother a long time ago."

It was a shame that so many mother-daughter relationships were so difficult, I thought. I'd lost my own mother unexpectedly when I was just about Charlotte's age. There were so many things

I would have done differently had I known how limited our time together was going to be.

"Maybe your mother used to have a higher opinion of him," I said, thinking out loud. "And then she changed her mind. Has anything happened between them recently?"

"Not that I know of. They don't really keep in touch." Charlotte paused, then added, "I guess she heard about that stupid book. But my mother didn't seem to care about that."

"She told me the same thing."

Charlotte glanced my way. "You talked to her?"

"At a dog show over the weekend. She said she didn't think the book would ever really happen."

"Well, as usual, my mother was right. Because now it looks like it won't."

We reached the crest of a small hill and stopped to admire the view. A snow-covered meadow spread out before us, pristine and unspoiled. Open land was a luxury in Fairfield County. A property this size was testament to March's financial success.

"Look down there," said Charlotte.

After a last headlong dash down the hill, Robin had finally succeeded in wearing herself out. I'd been watching as she came trotting back to us, but now I turned the other way and saw what looked like a hunting lodge nestled in a shaded hollow.

"That was Andrew's cottage," Charlotte told me.

"Have you been inside?"

"Just one time. I took the police there on the day he died so that they could have a look around."

"And?" I asked curiously.

"There wasn't much to see. The place was a bit of a mess. I guess Julia had been there earlier that morning, packing things up."

"You knew she was here?"

"Of course I knew. Julia had just gotten her apartment, but before that she'd been staying with me."

I looked at her, surprised. "How did that come about?"

"When Andrew tossed her out, she didn't have anywhere else to go. I told her she could come to my place for a couple of days. At that point, neither one of us figured that they'd be apart any longer than that."

Charlotte and Julia had to be closer to each other than I had realized. "Did you know she was pregnant?" I asked.

"Not before she showed up that night. That's when I found out. You know how it is when you have a fight with your boyfriend. You want to talk to someone about it. You want to dissect every detail and figure out what went wrong. . . ."

"You want a friend who will tell you that he's being an ass."

"That too. Of course, once she told me what

269

their argument had been about, it wasn't hard to come to that conclusion. My father left my mother before I was born. I never even got to meet him. So it was easy for me to take her side."

"I'm sorry," I said.

"Don't be." Charlotte turned around and started back the way we'd come. I could see the main house off in the distance through the trees. "I never knew any different, so it seemed normal to me. And my mother made sure that I had more parenting than any one child could ever possibly need."

"I'm sure she meant well," I said with a laugh.

"She would agree with you," Charlotte replied cheerfully. "Me, not so much."

As we walked back, I pondered Julia's situation. At least it looked like she was surrounded by plenty of friends. That would definitely help. Then that thought led to another, and I remembered something I'd meant to look into.

"What do you know about Sherm Yablonsky?" I asked as we climbed over the low stone wall that marked the edge of the yard.

Robin was once again running on ahead. The setter bounded across the last expanse and hopped up the steps that led to the back door.

"Just that he and Andrew were old friends," Charlotte replied. "Andrew really made an effort to keep his personal life separate from what went on up here."

I could readily understand why. I certainly wouldn't want to live my life with Edward March looking over my shoulder.

"Why do you ask?"

"No reason," I said lightly.

At least none that I wanted to divulge just yet. But I couldn't help but wonder why Andrew's old friend had looked so comfortable visiting his buddy's ex-girlfriend's apartment.

Chapter 20

I crammed that all into one afternoon and still managed to beat Davey's bus home. Once there, I relieved Sam of Kevin duty and got the two boys settled on the living-room floor with a castle blueprint and a full box of Legos. That freed up fifteen minutes, which I used to run the Poodles around the backyard a couple of times. An hour later, I had a pot of spaghetti sauce bubbling on the stove and a loaf of garlic bread in the oven. A generous glass of red wine completed the agenda. That's what I call multi-tasking.

After dinner, when Kevin was in bed and Davey was working on his homework, Sam asked how things were going. By mutual agreement, we never talk about what I'm working on in front of the kids. The Poodles, however, gather around us and listen to every word.

I'm sure Faith would have valuable insights to add if only she were able to communicate them. Since we haven't figured out a way around that barrier, I have to settle for Sam.

He and I were sitting side by side on the couch, and I snuggled into the crook of his arm. "This whole group of people I'm dealing with makes me feel very old-fashioned," I said.

"You?" Sam laughed. "Ms. Low Tech? How is that possible?"

I reached around and swatted him. "That's not the problem. *That,* I could understand."

"What is the problem, then?"

"Edward March has a string of ex-girlfriends a mile long. And now it looks as though his son continued the tradition. Apparently, Andrew considered his company's pool of female employees to be fair game."

"That could lead to lawsuits," Sam pointed out.

"It already has. At least one that I know of."

"It sounds to me like Andrew's the one who was out of touch with current standards."

Eve hopped up onto the couch. I pulled her into my lap, and she lay down, spreading her body across my legs.

"Even worse than that," I said, "Andrew dumped his girlfriend when he found out that she was pregnant. They'd been living together in his house, and he kicked her out, with no place to go."

"I hope she's the one who hit him with the car."

"I don't. She seems like a nice woman."

"Then I hope you find someone else to blame it on."

I sat up and looked at him. Sam was smiling.

"You're not taking me seriously."

"On the contrary, I take you very seriously. It's the loony people you seem to get involved with that I refuse to give credence to."

Sam's arm was wrapped around my shoulder. His fingers played idly through the strands of my hair. When his hand slid up and his palm cupped the side of my jaw, I leaned into the caress and sighed.

"Kevin's asleep," Sam mentioned.

"In an hour Davey will be in bed, too," I replied.

It was all we needed to say. That's the great thing about being married. We both understood the shorthand.

Charlotte had given me Sherm Yablonsky's contact info and had told me that he was a lawyer in downtown Stamford. That sounded easy enough.

When I looked him up online, I found that the legal offices of Grady & Yablonsky were located on a side street just off of West Broad. According to their website, they specialized in cases involving personal injury, wrongful death, auto accidents, and disability. Walk-ins were welcome.

So Tuesday morning I went to Stamford and paid Sherm a visit. Considering the kind of law his firm practiced, I probably shouldn't have been surprised to discover that the picture painted by the website was far grander than the reality. At first I didn't even recognize the small clapboard building, now sadly in need of a paint job, as the same tidy office I'd seen online.

There was plenty of parking on the street out front. I crossed the cracked sidewalk, hopped up two steps, and opened the door. A bell chimed to announce my arrival as I entered a small stark room that looked as though it had been furnished at Big Lots.

The desk and two chairs were generic; the carpeting was industrial grade. A collection of legal tomes was scattered across a low bookshelf. The ficus tree by the window appeared to be badly in need of water. The most interesting thing in the room was a large banner on the back wall, proudly emblazoned with the firm's slogan, WE WILL FIGHT FOR THE VICTIM! Aside from me, the plant, and the banner, however, the room was empty.

"Hello?" I called out.

A voice answered from behind a door in the back wall. "Have a seat. I'll be right out."

I looked around at the available choices and opted to remain standing. Sherm exited the bathroom a minute later, still drying his hands.

Though he'd been wearing a suit and tie on the website, today he was dressed down in khaki pants, a V-neck sweater, and a button-down shirt that was open at the throat. Maybe the casual look was meant to put potential clients at ease.

Sherm paused a moment to form an impression of me. Then he balled up the paper towel in his hands and tossed it in the trash. He took two steps, and I took two steps, and we met in the middle of the room.

"Sherman Yablonsky, Attorney at Law," he said pompously.

He extended a still damp hand, and I shook it briefly as I introduced myself. Sherm took my coat and offered me a cup of coffee, which I declined. We sat down opposite each other in the two modular chairs.

"How can I help you?" he asked.

"I'm here to talk about Andrew March."

Sherm's surprise was evident. With his job, I'd have expected him to have more of a poker face. I wondered if that was a problem when he argued cases in front of a jury.

As I watched, he rearranged his features into a more suitable expression. "It was a terrible shame," he said, shaking his head. "To lose a good guy like that so young. What a tragedy."

"I heard your eulogy at the memorial service," I said. "You and Andrew must have been close friends."

"He was my best friend. We met in college, so I knew him more than half my life. That leaves a huge hole, now that he's gone. I guess you probably know about that. You were a friend, too?"

Sherm reached over and placed his hand on top of mine. The gesture was probably supposed to be comforting. I found it kind of creepy.

"Not exactly." I slid my hand away. "We'd only just met."

"Ahh."

There seemed to be a wealth of meaning contained within that single syllable. Abruptly, I got the impression that Sherm was formulating all the wrong assumptions about my relationship with Andrew.

"Actually," I said crisply, "I'm a friend of Andrew's father."

"Oh."

Again with the single word. I was beginning to think that law school had been wasted on this guy.

"Obviously, the police are looking into what happened," I said. "But Mr. March asked me to make some inquiries, too."

"With regard to what exactly?"

"He wants to know what happened to his son."

"You mean, who's responsible?"

"Yes."

"I'm afraid I can't help you with that," Sherm said firmly. "Any problems Andrew might have had, they had nothing to do with me."

What an interesting response.

"What kind of problems are we talking about?" I asked.

"You know. The usual."

"Perhaps you could elaborate for me."

"Like any guy might have. Work, women." Sherm winked at me complicitly. "Those are the typical complaints, aren't they?"

"If you say so. Are we talking about any work or woman problems in particular?"

"You know Andrew," Sherm said.

I took that to be a figure of speech and nodded.

"Even back in our college days, he was always up to his ears in girls, and not much has changed since. Usually, it worked out great for him. But sometimes it backfired, and then he'd have to scramble around to make things right."

"I heard he'd been doing quite a bit of scrambling lately," I said.

Sherm nodded. "You must know Julia, then."

"I do."

"And Miranda too?"

"Excuse me?" I sputtered. "Who?"

"Miranda . . . Andrew's girlfriend."

Good thing I was sitting down.

"I thought Julia was Andrew's girlfriend," I said.

"She was, but . . ." Sherm spread his hands helplessly. "Andrew wasn't a big believer in monogamy. You know what I mean?"

More and more every moment.

"So while he was living with Julia, he was also seeing Miranda on the side?"

"Well, yeah. I guess you didn't know about that?"

"No, I didn't. Did Julia?"

"Not at first. But later on, she found out about it. Miranda made sure of that."

"Miranda sounds like a real sweetheart," I said.

"She can be," Sherm replied.

Clearly, my sarcasm had gone right over his head. Then he saw the expression on my face and began to backpedal.

"Well, obviously, Julia didn't think so."

"Obviously not," I agreed.

Sherm babbled on, still trying to cover his gaffe. "Anyway, she pretty much ignored what was going on with Miranda. I guess Julia figured that eventually Andrew would come back to her, like he always had before. Especially since she had an ace of her own to play."

"The baby," I said. "Andrew's child."

"Precisely. Julia was convinced she was going to get a marriage proposal."

Sherm paused expectantly, like he thought he'd come up with something I didn't know and maybe I'd want to applaud. Instead, I simply sat and waited him out.

"Well, that didn't happen," he continued finally. "Not even close. Instead, Andrew was pissed. He wasn't the kind of guy who was going to let some girl manipulate him into doing something he didn't want to do."

"Not even one he was supposed to be in love with?"

"Love?" Sherm laughed. "Where did you get that idea?"

"They were living together, weren't they? That sounds like a serious relationship to me."

"On Julia's part, sure. As for Andrew, I don't think he even knew what a serious relationship was."

"She must have been very angry about the way Andrew treated her," I said.

"Hell, yeah," Sherm agreed.

"Angry enough to want to hurt Andrew?"

That brought him up short. "I don't think I like what you're asking."

"Why not? Obviously, somebody was furious with Andrew. From everything you've just told me, it sounds like that person could have been Julia."

"No way!"

Sherm jumped to his feet. He stalked across the small room and glared at me from the other side. Clearly, I'd hit a nerve.

"Again," I said calmly, "why not?"

"Because Julia's not that kind of person, okay? She could never do something like that. And besides, like you said earlier, she was in love with

Andrew. All she ever really wanted was for him to love her back."

As he stood there and pleaded Julia's case, a piece of the puzzle suddenly fell into place. All at once I understood the subtext I'd been missing. Andrew might not have been in love with his girlfriend, but his best friend was.

"I saw you," I told him. "On Sunday, at Julia's apartment. You went to visit her, didn't you?"

"So what if I did?"

"No problem. I'm just wondering why."

"I wanted to make sure she was all right, that's all. Julia's got a lot on her plate right now, between the move and the baby and what happened to Andrew . . . . What kind of a friend would I be if I didn't check up on her?"

"You sound like you're a very good friend," I said.

"I try." Sherm lifted a hand and raked it back through his hair, a nervous gesture that must have worked better before his hairline began to recede.

"So you've been helping her out."

"Someone has to. It's not like Edward March is going to step in and do what's right."

"Julia told me that she wanted to move back into Andrew's cottage until after the baby was born," I mentioned.

"It wasn't much to ask, but he turned her down cold. That was a mistake. Julia only wants what's coming to her."

"As the mother of March's grandchild, you mean?"

Sherm nodded. "Her child will be Edward March's only remaining family, and Julia wants her baby to be recognized as such. She wants him to inherit the legacy he's entitled to. That's what we're fighting for."

I swiveled all the way around in my seat and stared at him. *Fighting for?*

"What do you mean?" I asked.

"It was my idea." Sherm was clearly proud of himself. "Andrew died intestate. No surprise there. He wasn't big on planning ahead. So his assets revert back to his closest living relative, his father. But I'm going to file a claim in probate court on behalf of Julia's unborn child. He or she should be named as the beneficiary of Andrew's estate."

Well, that was a new wrinkle.

"Does Edward March know about that?"

"Not yet. But he will just as soon as I get all the paperwork in order. And since Andrew never had a chance to properly acknowledge the child, we're also going to file a civil suit. One way or another, March is going to pay. That old bastard is going to be sorry that he ever even thought of leaving Julia standing out in the cold with no place to go."

Either that, I thought, or March's experienced legal team would squash Sherm Yablonsky like an annoying bug.

I rose to my feet. "I'm happy to know that Julia has found herself such an ardent supporter."

"I'm only trying to do what's fair." His tone was filled with a smug sense of righteousness.

Lucky for Sherm, what he thought was fair would also succeed in lining his own pockets. Not to mention make him look like a hero in front of the damsel in distress. At least he appeared to take his firm's motto seriously.

As I slipped on my coat, Sherm strode to the door and opened it for me.

"I hope I succeeded in answering all your questions," he said. It sounded like the kind of stock phrase that was issued to all departing clients.

"Sure," I told him. "You were great."

Sherm beamed at the praise. Talk about easy.

I glanced at the name stenciled on the window, GRADY & YABLONSKY, ATTORNEYS-AT-LAW, and then back at the single desk in the small room. "Where's Grady?"

"He has Tuesdays off."

"So how does that work? On the other days of the week, do you guys share a desk?"

"Not exactly. He's like a roving lawyer."

"I've never heard of that."

Sherm was growing pink around the ears. "Yeah, well . . ."

"You made him up, didn't you?"

"Okay, look," he said. "There is no Grady. But

two names on the masthead makes it sound like the firm is a more important place. The clients think they're getting twice the representation."

"Good to know," I said.

As I walked back to my car, I pondered that. I thought about a guy who was in love with his best friend's girlfriend, and wondered what other kinds of things Sherm might bc willing to lie about.

Chapter 21

After meeting with Sherm, I returned home, and Sam, Kevin, and I had lunch together. The Poodles eddied around our chairs as we ate, like sharks trolling for chum. With an almost two-year-old at the table, they knew that their chances of getting lucky were pretty good. Someday our younger son will have table manners, but it doesn't seem likely to happen anytime soon.

Kevin ate half of his small turkey sandwich, then blithely tossed the other half on the floor, where Raven quickly scooped it up. Sam and I both ignored the transgression. I handed out peanut butter biscuits to the other dogs to even things up, then sliced up an apple for Kevin. He adores fruit, which was probably the only thing that kept the Poodles from getting lucky twice in one meal.

After lunch, Sam disappeared into his office to do some work, and I called Bonnie to get George Weiner's phone number.

"What are you going to do with it?" she asked before giving it to me.

"Call and see if he'd be willing to meet with me."

"He will be," she said with certainty.

"How do you know?"

"George likes to hear himself talk. Once he finds out you're willing to listen to him grumble about the company, you'll be lucky if you can shut him up."

It turned out that Bonnie was right. As soon as I explained why I was calling, George agreed to see me. The fact that I implied I was an adult graduate student writing a thesis on sexual harassment in the workplace probably helped things along.

George lived in Norwalk, so we settled on a meeting place halfway between us: a café on Forest Street in downtown New Canaan. I bundled Kevin up, grabbed the diaper bag, and headed out.

Parking was tight on the small side street. And since Kevin tends to get distracted easily, walking in a straight line isn't his strong suit. By the time he and I reached the café, George was already there. The only man sitting by himself, he wasn't hard to pick out.

George was a middle-aged man with a sizable paunch and a disgruntled expression that was framed by a pair of out-of-control eyebrows. He was slouched in his seat, plump fingers playing with a dirty napkin. Even though I was no more than a minute late, it looked as though he had already finished his first cup of coffee.

Or maybe his second. Judging by his speedy response to my call, George seemed to have time on his hands.

Weiner the Whiner, March had called him. And the first words out of George's mouth did nothing to dispel that image.

"Hey," he said, sounding reproachful as Kevin and I made our way to his table. "You brought your kid."

"His name is Kevin, and he's pretty easygoing," I told him. "Just let me get an oatmeal cookie to keep him busy, and then you and I can talk."

His movements slow and cumbersome, George picked up his things and moved them to a larger table. In the time it took him to get resettled, I had whipped Kevin out of his snowsuit, found a child seat and dragged it over, and purchased a cookie that was half the size of a hubcap.

I strapped Kevin into the seat, then broke off a piece of cookie and handed it to him. For insurance, I pulled out a couple of Matchbox cars and placed them on the table in front of his seat. George watched this flurry of activity with his head cocked to one side.

"What?" I asked as I finally sat down, too.

"Wouldn't it have been easier to leave him at home?"

"Sure," I said with a laugh. "That would have been easier. I'm guessing you don't have kids."

"Nope. Married, divorced, no kids."

"Sometimes they're inconvenient," I told him.

"So I see." He squinted in Kevin's direction. "He looks like you."

"You think so?" That made me happy. I thought Kevin took after his father, but maybe since I often saw them together, it was easier for me to discern Sam's features in our son than my own. "Thank you."

"So you want to talk about the work environment at March Homes."

"Right."

"And my lawsuit."

"That too. Maybe you could start by giving me a little bit of background."

It was like turning on a faucet. Words flowed out of George in a steady stream of recrimination. He'd worked for March Homes for five years, and in all that time, he'd felt underappreciated, mishandled, and misunderstood. He had worked incredibly hard and had watched while other employees advanced and his own career remained stagnant.

"So initially, you were hired by Andrew March to fill the position of sales associate," I said when George finally paused after talking for three solid minutes. "When you left the company last fall, what was your job at that point?"

"Same thing, sales associate. There were half a dozen of us at that level, and I worked as hard as anybody. I was always bringing in new business."

I slipped Kevin another chunk of cookie. "Which is why you thought you'd earned the promotion."

"Right. When the job of sales manager opened up, it should have been mine. And it would have been except that Andrew March was too busy playing games to reward real talent."

"What kinds of games are we talking about?"

George glanced at Kevin, like he thought maybe I should cover my son's ears. Kevin had a piece of cookie in one hand and a toy car in the other; he was happily oblivious to our conversation. I could have promised that child a pony, and he wouldn't even have noticed.

"You know," George said. "With the women in the company. Andrew had all the breaks. He was a single, good-looking guy, and on top of that, he was the boss. When it came to the female employees, he got around pretty good."

There was naked envy in George's tone when he

spoke about Andrew. If he ever had to give a deposition for his lawsuit, he was going to need to work on that. Or if the police got around to questioning him about his former boss's murder.

"I take it you didn't like Andrew March much," I said.

"It was nothing personal. What I didn't like about Andrew was that he didn't play fair. I worked my ass off for that company. I deserved that promotion. The only thing holding me back was that I was the wrong gender to play footsie with the boss."

"So a woman sales associate got promoted over you?"

George nodded glumly. "Maxine Wood."

"Was she good at her job, too?"

"Yeah, I guess."

"Maybe she got promoted on merit," I mentioned.

George's bushy brows lowered over suddenly narrowed eyes. He glared at me like I was a cute, fluffy puppy who'd unexpectedly bitten his finger.

"She got the promotion because she slept with the boss," he said.

"That must have made you pretty angry."

"It did. Anyone would have been angry in my place." George was determined to make me see things his way. "What Andrew did wasn't right."

"I guess you must think he deserved what happened to him."

"Let's just say I didn't shed any tears when I found out."

"How did you find out?" I asked curiously.

"I heard about it on the news. 'A murder in Westport' . . . That was the big headline, so I stopped to listen. It's not like that happens every day."

"Were you shocked when you found out who it was?"

"Nah." George leaned in close, like we were pals sharing a secret. "Tell you the truth, first thing I did was laugh."

"Because Andrew's death cleared the way for your lawsuit to be settled?"

"Hell, no. I'll ride that thing all the way to trial if I have to. I got a lawyer working on contingency, so it makes no difference to me. The reason I laughed is because Andrew March was one of those guys who led a charmed life. He thought he could do whatever he wanted and nothing bad would ever happen to him. And then it did."

George smiled then. For the first time since we'd sat down, he looked happy. "I'll tell you what. Andrew got what he had coming to him, and I'm glad he did."

When Kevin and I got home that afternoon, Sam had good news.

As I undressed Kevin and listened to what Sam had to say, the Poodles leapt and pirouetted around us in a frenzy of excitement, as if they knew we were talking about them. Since they've been eavesdropping on our conversations for years, maybe they did.

"I just got off the phone with Peter," he said. "We can pick up Augie this afternoon if we want to."

"What do you mean, *if?*" I asked with a laugh. "I can't wait. We'll go as soon as Davey gets home from school."

I pulled Kevin's shoes off and stepped him out of his snowsuit. The moment he was free, he pushed my hands away and trotted purposefully down the hallway toward the kitchen. I had no idea what he was after. Neither did the Poodles, but they followed along anyway.

All except Faith. She remained behind, her body pressed close to my legs, her expressive face tipped upward in my direction. The other Poodles might not have understood, but she had. I could read the question in her dark eyes.

Faith had been my first dog ever. She'd also been an only dog for several years. Like an only child, she'd been accustomed to receiving all the attention and to ordering her world as she saw fit.

First to redefine the easy balance of that relationship had been Faith's daughter, Eve. And although the younger Poodle had slipped seamlessly into the family, I knew that Faith had had to make some adjustments. Davey and I were no longer just *her* people.

Then Sam had moved in. With him came three more Poodles, and still more adjustments needed to be made. Time and space were ceded to the newcomers, and Faith's and my relationship had had to adapt again. Gracious as ever, Faith had made accommodations, and the two canine families had merged smoothly.

Now here we were once more, asking her to accept another new puppy into the fold. Faith was six years old now. For a Standard Poodle, that was well into middle age. There was no gray around her muzzle yet, no loss of spring in her step. But even so, at her age Faith could be forgiven for thinking that she'd already done her duty when it came to welcoming rambunctious newcomers into her home.

So when the other four Poodles ran on ahead and she remained behind, wrapping her body around my legs, I knew that the gesture was a mute plea for reassurance that nothing would change too much. I squatted down so that we were face-to-face, and cupped her long muzzle between my palms. For a minute, we simply breathed in and out together.

"You're the best dog in the world," I told her.

Faith's tail wagged slowly back and forth

in acknowledgment. She already *knew* that.

"You'll always be my favorite." I paused, then added fervently, "Always. No matter what." Just to make sure that she understood.

Faith did. Her long pink tongue came out and licked the bottom of my chin.

"I know," I said. "I love you, too."

We left it at that and went to join the others.

Luckily, Davey didn't have basketball practice that afternoon. His bus dropped him off at the end of the driveway just before four o'clock. Sam and I were waiting impatiently.

We watched through a front window as he quickly left the plowed driveway, hopped over a small drift, and skipped toward the house across the snow-covered lawn. Only an eleven-year-old boy would not only choose the path of most resistance, but also look positively cheerful about it. When he stopped to scoop up a handful of snow and form it into a snowball, I strode to the front hall and yanked the front door open to hurry him along.

My timing was impeccable. In the few seconds it took me to reach the door, Davey had cocked back his arm and let fly. A snowball the size of a small grapefruit went hurtling past my ear and smacked into the wall behind me.

I know I jumped to one side. I might have let out a small shriek. The way my life works, you'd think I might have lost my capacity to be startled by now, but apparently not.

All five Poodles came scrambling into the hall to find out what had happened. Tar won the race. He leapt up and snagged the icy missile before it even hit the floor.

"Uh-oh," said Davey. He hopped up the front steps. "What'd you do that for?"

"I might ask you the same thing," I said.

"Because the door was *closed*," my son replied with perfect preteen logic.

Then he saw Sam and Kevin waiting behind me and hesitated. His whole family doesn't usually turn out to welcome him home from school. At his age, we trust him to find his own way up the driveway and into the house. Sometimes he even grabs a snack before bothering to hunt us down and say hello.

Slowly, Davey slid his backpack off his shoulders and let it fall to the floor. "Am I in trouble?" he asked.

My son has a very expressive face. I watched his brow pucker and realized that he was thinking through a list of recent infractions, checking for the likely crime. The mother in me found it interesting that doing so should take more than a second or two.

"Not at all." Sam's answer was quick. "In fact, just the opposite."

"That's . . . good," Davey said carefully. He

still looked confused. "What *is* the opposite?"

"Your mother and I have a surprise for you."

"Awesome." Davey's trepidation vanished; his face split in a grin. "What is it?"

Sam glanced my way. "Maybe your mother wants to tell you."

"No," I replied. "It was your idea. You go ahead."

Sam and I had already discussed how we were going to play this. We'd decided that Davey and Augie should meet first. Then once we saw how they got along, we'd ask Davey if he wanted to have the puppy for his own.

"You know I've been missing having a dog to show," said Sam.

Davey nodded.

"Your mom and I thought that since things are finally beginning to calm down around here, it might be a good time to add a new puppy to the family. How would you feel about that?"

"Great!" Davey agreed happily.

If there was a boy anywhere that would turn down a puppy, he certainly didn't live in my family.

"A friend of mine has a puppy available," Sam told him. "And guess who his sire is?"

He didn't have to think long. There was only one male Poodle in the house. "Tar!"

"You got it."

"Awesome!" Davey cried. It seemed to be the word of the day.

"We can go pick him up this afternoon," I said.

Davey's eyes widened. "Like *today?*"

"Right now, if you want."

"Cool," said Davey. "Let's go!"

The drive to Ridgefield took half an hour. Being midwinter, it was dark by the time we arrived. Davey chattered with great animation for the duration of the trip. When he hopped out of the car at the Kirkwoods' house, he'd already compiled more information about Augie from Sam than I had.

He skipped ahead to the house and rang the doorbell while I was still unfastening Kevin's car seat. "I guess we don't have to wonder how Davey feels about this plan," Sam said with a laugh. He took Kevin out of my arms and gave me a little push. "Go on. Go catch up."

Sandy Kirkwood answered the door. She was a slender woman about my age with pale blue eyes, translucent skin, and worry lines bracketing the sides of her mouth. She smiled happily at the sight of us, however, and we were quickly ushered into her home.

"Our kennel is in the basement," Sandy said, leading us to the living room. "Peter just ran down to get Augie. They'll be back up in a minute."

We heard the muffled sound of pounding feet, and then a door slammed in another part of the house. Sandy called the puppy's name and a low, throaty woof replied. Then Peter and Augie rounded a corner and came through the doorway together.

The big black puppy had just enough hair to require a single rubber band in his topknot and one on each of his ears. His face, his feet, and the base of his tail were clipped close. The rest of his body was covered with a plush coat of dense inky hair. His tail, topped by a round black pompon, was wagging enthusiastically.

Augie started to race toward Sandy, then abruptly slid to a stop at the sight of all the extra people in the room. I crouched down and held out a hand. Davey did the same. Sam, still holding Kevin, hung back.

It took the puppy only a few seconds to recover. His tail snapped back up. He bounded forward once more. Augie reached me first, but when Davey said his name, he quickly changed direction. Davey held out his arms, and the Poodle puppy romped straight into the embrace as if they were already the best of friends.

Davey opened his mouth to say something, but when Augie's tongue snaked out and tickled his ear, he sputtered a laugh instead. His fingers were already stroking the thick hair over the puppy's shoulders. Between the two of them, it was a toss-up as to which one looked happier.

"That looks like a match to me," said Peter.

Sam caught my eye, and I nodded.

"Me too," he agreed. "Let's sit down and finalize the paperwork."

The two men went off to another room. Davey remained on the floor with Augie. Sandy and I took a seat on the couch. She told me what kind of food Augie was currently eating and where he was on his vaccination schedule.

"Peter has this all written down," she said. "He'll give the information to Sam with the papers. But I figured I'd run through a few things in case you had any questions."

I was already well acquainted with the breeding program that had produced Augie. Sam had received verification of Maid Marian's genetic testing before allowing her to be bred. And since Tar was the puppy's sire, roughly half of his ancestors were living in Aunt Peg's house. So aside from the day-to-day details, there wasn't anything else I needed to know.

"I was sorry to hear about you and Peter," I said instead.

Sandy gave a small shrug. "It happens. We'll get through it. At least we're both managing to act like adults. And not having children makes things easier. I'm really happy that Augie's going to a good place. That's a huge relief."

"He's a beautiful puppy, and we're thrilled to have him." I gestured toward the pair on the floor. "As you can see."

"Kids and dogs," Sandy said with a sigh. "There's nothing better."

"Who gets custody of Maid Marian?" I asked.

"She'll go with me. Marian's the only one I'm taking. Peter will keep the rest of the bitches and the Kirkwood kennel name. Just getting that all separated out has been a huge undertaking. I think the Louisiana Purchase took less negotiation than we've been through."

"I can imagine."

"While we have a minute to talk," said Sandy, "I heard about what you're working on. You know, with Edward March."

I looked at her in surprise. "How do you know about that?"

"Are you kidding? The dog show grapevine has been buzzing about his book for weeks."

Oh, right, the book.

"Do you know India Fleming?" Sandy asked.

"Not personally. I know who she is. I've shown under her."

"Close enough."

In dog show circles, it was.

"If you haven't already done so, you might want to talk to her. India's pissed as hell about Edward's plans, and she has plenty to say on the subject."

"Thanks," I said. "I'll do that."

"Just don't tell her I sent you."

"Why not?"

"India has a temper. She also has power and

the cojones to use it. Maybe it's cowardly of me, but I'd rather not get on her bad side."

"Like Edward March is?"

Sandy nodded. "The funny thing is, the two of them have a lot in common. India is also very aware of her stature in the dog show world and of the legacy that she's creating. Because of that, she has no intention of letting some dumb book tarnish her reputation."

"I'll definitely talk to her," I said.

I'd overlooked India before. It was beginning to look as though that might have been a mistake.

Chapter 22

We waited until we got home to tell Davey about the rest of his surprise.

He was every bit as talkative on the car ride back from Ridgefield as he had been on the way there. On this trip, however, Davey pulled the big puppy into his lap, and his steady stream of chatter was directed at Augie rather than the car's human occupants. I listened with a smile as Davey pointed out local landmarks, extolled the virtues of our large fenced backyard, and acquainted the puppy with the names and personalities of the other Poodles he was about to meet.

As we pulled into the garage, Davey wrapped up his monologue. "The best thing is that at our house you won't have to live in the basement."

"I'm sure the Kirkwoods' basement is very nice," Sam said as he turned off the car and hit the button to close the garage door. Apparently, he'd been listening in, as well.

"Maybe, but sleeping on someone's bed is better." Davey let that thought dangle for a moment, then added, "Until Augie gets used to being in a new house, maybe he could sleep in my room. What do you guys think?"

I turned around in my seat. Kevin's head was tipped sideways to rest on his shoulder. Lulled by the long ride, he was fast asleep. At the other end of the seat, Augie was still lying across Davey's lap. Davey's arms were clasped around the puppy's neck, holding him close. Both boy and puppy gazed up at me hopefully.

"Up until now, Augie's been a kennel dog," I reminded him. "So he's going to have to sleep in a crate until he's housebroken. But I don't see any reason why his crate can't be in your room. Besides . . ."

I glanced over at Sam and gave him a nudge. In the car's half-light, with the seat between us, Davey shouldn't have been able to see the small gesture. Even so, he seemed to sense that something was up.

"Besides, what?" he asked.

"We think it ought to be your decision where Augie sleeps," Sam told him. "Considering that he's going to be your dog."

For several seconds there was only silence. I watched Davey's eyes grow wide. Then he tilted his head and gazed down at Augie as if he was seeing the puppy in a whole new light. Augie's tail thumped up and down obligingly on the seat.

"Really?" Davey managed to say finally. *"My dog?"*

"If you want him to be."

"Well . . . yeah!"

"Great," said Sam. "Then it's settled."

"So what does that mean?" Davey asked eagerly. "Can I do anything I want with him?"

"Within reason," I said with a laugh. There isn't a mother in the world who would give an eleven-year-old boy total carte blanche.

"I promised the Kirkwoods that we would finish his championship," Sam told him. "I thought you and I could work on that together. But afterward, if you want to try something different with Augie, like agility or disc dogs, or if you'd rather do nothing at all, it's totally up to you."

"Wow." Davey exhaled slowly. "Awesome."

"I'm glad you think so." I reached around and ruffled my son's hair, then slid my hand down and did the same to Augie's abbreviated topknot.

"Hey, be careful with my dog's hair!" Davey said with a grin. He'd been the recipient of many similar warnings over the years. "If we want Augie to finish, we need to start protecting his coat."

"You're a child after Aunt Peg's heart," I said.

Not everyone would take that as a compliment, but it only made Davey's smile widen. Sam's, too, for that matter.

Beaming like a kid who thought he'd won the lottery, Davey started to get out of the car. Then he looked back at his little brother, still asleep in the car seat, and stopped.

"What if Kevin gets upset that I have my own puppy and he doesn't?" he asked hesitantly. "I don't want him to feel left out. I guess maybe I could share if you guys want me to."

I could see how much it cost Davey to make the offer. And if I hadn't known that he'd object to a display of maternal affection, I'd have run around the SUV and scooped him up in a hug. Instead, I settled for shaking my head.

"No way," I said. "Augie is all yours."

"Are you sure?" he asked hopefully.

"Having a dog is a big responsibility," said Sam. "You're going to have to exercise Augie and feed him and help with his housebreaking. Kevin's much too young for stuff like that. Maybe when he's older, he'll get his own puppy, too. But only if he earns the privilege by being a really good kid, just like you did."

Sam slipped Davey a wink. Immediately, my son's expression cleared. Eased of guilt, he hopped Augie out of the car, and the two of them skipped across the garage toward the door that led to the house.

"You'd better go, too," I said to Sam as I stayed back to get Kevin. "Davey may need help with the introductions."

"Right." Sam had had the same thought. He was already on his way.

"Thank you," I called after him.

"For what?" He paused.

"You're great with Davey. I don't know how you do it, but you always manage to say just the right thing."

"Are you kidding?" Sam asked. "Who do you think I learned it from? I've been watching you all these years."

Then, like Davey and Augie, he disappeared into the house. Good thing, otherwise he might have heard me start to sniffle.

Aunt Peg showed up early the next morning.

Like that was a surprise. I'd half expected to find her waiting for us in the dark when we arrived home the night before. Now I'd barely managed to get Davey away from Augie and onto the school bus before the front door opened and Peg let herself in.

As always, the Poodles went racing to welcome her. Only Augie—the newest and the youngest member of the pack and not yet certain of his place—hung back with me. And of course, he was the one that Aunt Peg most wanted to see.

She greeted the adult Poodles first, calling each one by name, scratching their ears, and chucking them under the chin. When that group felt properly acknowledged, Aunt Peg then stooped down, lowering herself to Augie's level. She beckoned to the puppy with her fingers.

"What a gooood boy you are," she trilled. All six Poodles looked around. They pricked their ears and cocked their heads. "Come over here, young man, so I can get a good look at you."

Resistance was futile. Any one of us standing there could have told Augie that.

Not that it mattered. When it came to dogs, Aunt Peg was an irresistible force. And Augie, just like the other Poodles, was highly susceptible to her charms. He left my side without a backward glance and trotted straight into her open arms.

"What an excellent puppy you are," Aunt Peg praised. She's a big believer in positive reinforcement.

Her hands skimmed over Augie's body with quick professional strokes. She checked his bite, his shoulder angle, and the depth of his chest—all the conformational details that she hadn't been able to examine from ringside when she'd seen him at the show.

"Still happy with your choice?" Sam asked, coming to join us in the hall.

"Very much so." Aunt Peg rocked back on her heels. Then she realized what he'd said, and arched a brow upward. "*My* choice?"

"You know we'd never make a decision like that without your approval."

Peg fixed him with a beady eye. "As if I'd believe that. Not that the flattery isn't welcome, mind you."

"Anytime." Sam grinned.

He held out a hand and pulled Aunt Peg to her feet. She dusted off her palms and had a look around. "Where is my nephew?"

"One just left for school," I said. "The other is sitting at the kitchen table with a box of Cheerios. If you're nice to me, I might not tell him that the new puppy got a very thorough greeting before you asked about him."

The implied insult didn't even slow her down. "Harrumph," Peg said under her breath as she headed for the back of the house. "If he's going to be a member of this family, he had better get used to that."

Indeed.

I made Aunt Peg a cup of Earl Grey. Sam brewed another pot of coffee for the two of us. Kevin scrambled down off his chair and wandered into the pantry, where the cereal box he'd taken with him became the foundation for his next building project.

Several of the Poodles opted to follow Kevin,

hoping for either a handout or an accidental spill. Tar went and stood by the back door; Augie followed him there. No doubt about it, housebreaking is easier when you have older dogs willing to show a younger one the ropes. I opened the door and let the two Poodles outside.

"How old is that puppy again?" asked Aunt Peg.

"Six months. Barely."

"Two males in a house with several bitches," she mentioned. "You'll need to keep an eye on that as he matures."

"We will." Sam nodded.

"You're going to want to stop any problems before they have a chance to start."

"We'll worry about that when the time comes," I said cheerfully. Through the window on the upper half of the door, I watched Tar and Augie as they ran around the yard together, bounding and leaping in unison through the deep powder. "But not today."

"Right." Aunt Peg's tone was mild. "Today we're going to talk about how it's been more than two weeks since Andrew March died and you still don't seem to know who was responsible."

Way to kill a good mood.

I grabbed the cup of coffee Sam had left for me on the counter. It was my third of the day, but when my aunt's in the vicinity, I tend to need fortification. I added a dollop of milk and joined her at the table.

"I heard from Edward earlier this morning," said Aunt Peg. "Like me, he's wondering how much longer it's going to take you to figure things out."

"He called you?"

"Why is that surprising? Don't forget, I'm the one who offered him your services. So he holds me responsible for what you accomplish." She stared at me over the rim of her mug. "Or don't."

"You offered him my services as an organizer and a coauthor," I pointed out. "Not a sleuth."

"Fair enough," Peg shot back. "How much writing have you gotten done?"

A quickly muffled chuckle came from Sam's direction. So much for support from that quarter.

"The book is on hold for now," I told her. "And as for the murder, I'm working on it."

"I should hope so!"

"There are a lot of people I need to see. It turns out that the March men—father and son both—have more than their share of detractors."

"I could have told you *that,*" Aunt Peg sniffed. "And it wouldn't have taken me two weeks to figure it out."

"Maybe you should do this for me," I said.

The offer wasn't a serious one, but Aunt Peg stopped to consider. While she thought about things, I got up and walked over to the window to make sure that Augie and Tar were still getting along. The puppy was wearing a new coating of snow on his neck and back, but other than that, things seemed to be going well.

"I'm free this morning," Aunt Peg replied after a minute. "Let's do it."

It wasn't as if I didn't deserve that. But if Aunt Peg said that she intended to solve Andrew March's murder in the next several hours, I was not going to be amused.

"Do what, exactly?" I asked.

"How should I know? That's for you to tell me. Surely, you must have a list of things to do or people to see. Who's the next person on your agenda?"

I didn't even have to think about that.

"India Fleming," I said.

"India?" Aunt Peg blinked. "Really?"

"Really." A chat with India was long overdue.

"If you say so."

Peg reached inside her commodious purse, fished around, and pulled out a cell phone. Sam and I shared a meaningful glance. We couldn't help but notice that she had India's number on speed dial.

I've been known to invent all sorts of reasons to get people to talk to me. Not Aunt Peg. She just pulled strings.

Her conversation with India didn't last long. Aunt Peg snapped the phone shut and tucked it away. "I told her it was important. India will see us in thirty minutes. She lives in North Salem. We'd better get going."

Sometimes I can only shake my head in wonder. In Aunt Peg's world, it's just that easy.

Chapter 23

Bucolic is a word I don't get to use often, but in North Salem's case, it applies. Unfortunately, I wasn't able to enjoy the scenery, however, because Aunt Peg was driving. As we zipped north along a succession of back roads that took us into Westchester County, I spent the majority of the trip with my eyes half closed and my hands clenched in silent prayer.

Peg thinks that speed limits are for sissies. Not only that, but she seems to have a sixth sense concerning the location of speed traps and patrol cars. It's a dangerous combination on a dry summer day. Midwinter, the end result can be positively hair-raising.

We did, however, reach India's home in record time. The judge lived in a trim town house in a wooded setting. No fenced yard, I noted automatically. In fact, not much yard at all.

"Good thing it's midweek," Aunt Peg mentioned as she parked in the driveway. "Otherwise, India would be on the road."

The life of a successful dog show judge is a peripatetic one. The AKC mileage rule prohibits judges from accepting assignments within a two-hundred-mile radius more than once every thirty days. As a result, in-demand judges spend a good deal more time doing their jobs in distant locales than they do near home.

Over a weekend, a top-tier judge like India might be anywhere from Florida to California. Which probably explained why her yard wasn't fenced. Ironically, given the nomadic demands of their busy careers, many judges aren't able to keep dogs themselves.

India must have been waiting for us, because she answered our knock almost immediately. She was a petite woman in her late fifties, with sharp features and discerning gray eyes. In the show ring, she was known for her sense of fair play and her no-nonsense demeanor. She commanded respect from experienced exhibitors and neophytes alike, and heaven help the handler who had the temerity to question her authority.

India invited us in, and she and Aunt Peg shared a quick hug. Then Peg stepped back and introduced me.

Like all good judges, India had an eye for detail. "I've seen you in my ring," she said as she took our coats and hung them up.

"Yes, you have," I agreed with a smile. "Several times."

"With a Standard Poodle, I assume?"

"Of course."

India led the way to the living room. "If it was one of Peg's, you probably won under me."

"I did. Thank you."

"I like what I like." India bobbed her head in a sharp nod. "Consistency is a virtue in a judge. I wish more would cultivate it."

She waved us toward a deep red couch with a high curved back and plump cushions, then sat down in a wing chair opposite. Scattered across the coffee table between us were the latest issues of the *Canine Chronicle*, *Dog News*, and *ShowSight Magazine*. Framed win pictures on the walls of the room showed a several-decades-younger India handling a variety of dogs to Best in Show wins at top events like Westchester, Ox Ridge, and Montgomery County. Above the mantelpiece was an oil painting of a Smooth Fox Terrier who, even to my amateur eye, looked vaguely familiar.

"Champion Tumblebrea The Terrorist," India said, following the direction of my gaze. "He was the best dog I ever bred. But believe me, he well deserved that name."

"When Terror was on, he was unbeatable," said Aunt Peg.

"And when he wasn't . . ." India rolled her eyes. "Oh my, that dog had a mind of his own. There were days when I just wanted to slink out of the ring and hide."

The mental picture made me smile. It also produced an unexpected feeling of kinship. I'd suffered through similar experiences myself, without ever suspecting that someone of India's stature might have done the same.

"I hope you don't mind if we get to the point," she said. "My schedule's rather full, but Peg said it was important you see me. Something about Edward March . . . ?"

"I wanted to talk to you about his book," I said.

"*Proposed* book," India corrected me.

"Right. I heard you weren't very happy about the fact that he intended to include you."

"Not happy is an understatement. I'm mad as hell about the whole mess. What does that have to do with you?"

"In theory, I'm Edward March's coauthor."

India's eyes narrowed. "What do you mean, *in theory?*"

"I took the job before I knew what the book was going to be about. Once I found out, I was going to quit. But then March's son was killed—"

"Andrew," India said with a sigh. "What a terrible accident. Furious as I am at Edward—and believe me, I may never forgive him—he didn't deserve that."

"It wasn't an accident," I told her. "Andrew was murdered."

India looked surprised by the news. She glanced quickly at Peg, who nodded, then turned her gaze back to me. "By whom?" she demanded.

"Presumably, someone with a score to settle against one of the March men."

She thought that through. It didn't take her long.

"Someone like me, you mean?"

"Yes."

"Now, India," said Aunt Peg.

I glared in her direction, willing her to butt out. That's never worked in the past. Nor did it this time.

"No one's accusing you of murder," Peg continued.

"It seems to me that's exactly what your niece is doing," India retorted. "Although I can't imagine why. Edward isn't an easy man. No doubt he's made more than his share of enemies. Surely, I wasn't the only person who was furious enough to want to kill the old coot."

"Perhaps you'd like to rephrase that statement," Aunt Peg said mildly.

"No, I would not." India's tone was firm. "When I first heard what Edward intended to do, I could scarcely believe it. The extent of his hubris was unbelievable. The confidences he meant to expose, the secrets he planned to reveal . . . What gave him the right to make those decisions for everyone else? My God, if I could have gotten my hands around Edward's scrawny neck, I'd have finished him off myself."

India took a deep breath and composed herself. "But then time passes. And tempers cool."

"It doesn't sound as though yours has," I said.

"My fight is with the father, not the son. I didn't even know Andrew. If I had wanted to strike out at Edward, I'd have attacked him directly. I wouldn't have gone through someone else."

"Even though Andrew's death is the reason the book has been put on hold?"

"A fortuitous circumstance," India pointed out. "But not necessarily one that I would have foreseen."

So she said.

"Frankly, I'm surprised at you." India shifted her gaze in Peg's direction. "I'd have expected you to be every bit as angry as I am about this maelstrom Edward intends to create."

Aunt Peg lifted her chin. "Maybe I don't take myself as seriously as you do, India."

"Maybe you should," her friend retorted. "A reputation is a fragile thing. Once tarnished, it can never be entirely regained. Edward's book will turn us all into laughingstocks. You must know that."

"Oh, pish," said Peg. "That book, if indeed it ever gets written, will be nothing more than a trifle. People will read it and titter, and then everyone will move on."

"Perhaps you're willing to take that chance, but I most certainly am not."

Peg and I shared a look.

"India," she said carefully, "what did you do?"

"I've taken certain precautions, that's all. Since Edward is the one who chose to open up this Pandora's box, it seems only fair that he should share in the fallout with the rest of us."

India leaned back in her chair and chuckled softly, as if amused by her own private joke. "He never even saw it coming. And why would he? Edward has never appreciated women for who we truly are. To him, we're just a means to an end. It probably never even crossed his mind that a woman's accomplishments and good name could be every bit as important as his own."

"Even so—" I said.

India held up a hand, the gesture a peremptory request for silence. "Humor me for a moment. Let me backtrack and put things in context for you. In my generation, women had to fight to be taken seriously. Rights and privileges that you take for granted weren't even available to us."

Beside me, Aunt Peg nodded.

"You probably don't even remember when women's rights—women's lib, as it was belittlingly called—was a hot-button issue. You've grown up with the opportunities that women like Peg and I fought for. We marched on Washington. We burned our bras. . . ."

I tipped my head in Aunt Peg's direction, gazing at her with fresh appreciation. This was a side of

315

my aunt I'd never heard about. "You burned your bra?"

"I most certainly did," she said crisply. "We had a point to make, and no one was listening."

"And the smell of burning underwear got their attention?"

India snorted. "The act was symbolic. It let men know that we weren't going to be subservient anymore."

"I am woman, hear me roar," I said.

"Just so."

India smiled with satisfaction. Whether it was because she'd enjoyed her own history lesson or because she'd succeeded so deftly in changing the subject, I wasn't entirely sure. While I tried to figure out how to get her back on track, Aunt Peg stepped in and did it for me.

"We've been friends a long time, India," she said. "You know I'm on your side."

"Of course, Peg. And I like to think that I have your back, too."

"You need to tell us what you did to protect yourself from Edward March."

"Oh, that."

Yes, that, I thought. The reason why we'd come.

"It was simple, really. I decided that Edward should also know what it felt like to have something to lose. So I threatened him."

Looking at the tiny woman sitting before me, I

assumed she didn't mean physically. "With what?"

"Exposure. I told him that if he went ahead and violated my privacy, I would feel no compunction about doing the same to him."

Aunt Peg leaned forward. "Which secret were you going to tell?"

A sly smile played around India's lips. "Is there more than one?"

"I don't know *any* secrets," I said impatiently. "Maybe someone would like to clue me in?"

"In a moment," said India. "First, I need your assurance that we're speaking in confidence. After all, I can hardly use this information as a bargaining chip if it's going to become common knowledge."

Aunt Peg and I both nodded. I don't know about her, but I had my fingers crossed in my lap. If India had information that might point the way toward Andrew's killer, there was no way I was going to keep it to myself.

"Maribeth Chandler has a daughter," said India.

"Charlotte," I agreed quickly, eager for her to move things along. "She works as Edward's assistant."

"Maribeth got her that job. It's always interested me that no one else ever stopped to wonder why."

"According to Charlotte, it was because she was at loose ends and needed something to do."

"Charlotte doesn't know the whole story," said

India. "Maribeth never told her. That's part of the reason that I've kept Maribeth's confidence all these years."

"Oh," I said.

Just like that, another missing piece fell into place. It had been right in front of me all the time; I probably should have realized sooner. Now it was like slipping a new lens onto a microscope: suddenly everything became clearer. Edward March was Charlotte's father. And that single fact realigned almost everything I thought I had known about the two of them.

"Oh, indeed," said Aunt Peg. "I guess the rumors were true."

"They were," India confirmed. "I didn't know Maribeth back then, but some years later she and I ended up socializing at a judges' symposium. We were sitting in the bar late at night. We were miles from home. . . . You know how that is."

We all did.

"She mentioned that she missed her daughter, whom she'd left at home in her mother's care. I asked about her husband, and one thing led to another. Over a pitcher of margaritas the whole story came pouring out."

"I've spoken to Maribeth," I said. "She's quite open about the fact that she had an affair with Edward. So why is Charlotte's paternity such a secret?"

"Maribeth had no choice about that. Don't

318

forget, twenty-five years ago, when she got pregnant, Edward's wife, Isabelle, was still very much alive. Andrew was a young child, and Edward was a married man. When Maribeth told Edward she was pregnant, he gave her money and told her to get rid of it."

Like father, like son, I thought again. It was not a complimentary refrain.

"Obviously, she refused," said Aunt Peg.

India nodded. "Maribeth wanted a child. She was in her thirties, unmarried, and was having an affair with a man who was unavailable. She thought that pregnancy might be her only chance. She said she never even considered terminating it."

"Then what happened?" I asked.

"When Edward found out she hadn't done what he wanted, he went ballistic. He told Maribeth that he would never acknowledge the child and that if she tried to contact Isabelle or tell her about the baby, he would make her very, very sorry."

"What a jerk."

"My sentiments, as well," Aunt Peg agreed. "How is it that none of us knew about this before?"

"Maribeth was very careful to adhere to Edward's dictates. You and I might have made different choices, but she was a single mother who was struggling to make ends meet. After Charlotte

319

was born, she and Edward reached an agreement. He would contribute to the baby's upbringing in return for Maribeth's silence. He kept his word, and she kept hers."

"How much of that does Charlotte know?" I asked.

"Almost none," India replied. "Maribeth concocted some story about a sailor or a traveling salesman. She said things were simpler that way."

I shook my head. "Simpler for Maribeth maybe, but not necessarily for Charlotte. I can't believe she's been working for her father for two years and doesn't even know it."

"That was why Maribeth convinced Charlotte to take the job. She wanted father and daughter to get to know one another. I think she harbored a secret hope that once Edward realized how wonderful Charlotte was, he would finally acknowledge her as his own."

"I'm afraid I don't see that happening," said Aunt Peg. "Edward doesn't have that kind of sentiment in him."

"But now Charlotte is March's only remaining child," I pointed out. "That has to make a difference."

"It would to me," India agreed. "But with a man like Edward, who knows?"

"Charlotte had a half brother," I realized suddenly. "And she never even knew it. What a shame."

"That whole story is shameful," Aunt Peg said sharply. "Edward's behavior was reprehensible. I'm beginning to regret ever recommending you to him in the first place."

India sputtered a laugh. "That was *your* doing, Peg? You encouraged your niece to get tangled up with Edward March? That's like sending a lamb into the lion's den."

"I didn't know that at the time. Now it's beginning to look as though I may have made a small error in judgment."

It was as close to an apology as Aunt Peg had ever come. I reached over and squeezed her hand.

"You meant well," I told her.

"I always do," she replied.

Chapter 24

"Now where are we going?" asked Aunt Peg. We were back in her minivan, careening southward toward Connecticut.

"Now you take me home and drop me off."

"That doesn't sound very exciting."

"I should hope not," I said. "After two trips in your passenger seat, I'm not sure how much more excitement I can stand."

"Don't be ridiculous. Speed limits are just guidelines, not hard and fast rules. Nobody obeys them but you."

A deer grazing by the side of the road lifted its head and gazed thoughtfully in our direction. Aunt Peg never even lifted her foot off the gas pedal. Instead, she leaned on the horn and went hurtling past.

I waited until my heart had dropped down out of my throat, then said, "There are so many things wrong with that statement, I don't even know where to begin. You drive like a maniac. What if that doe had decided to leap into the road in front of us?"

"Then I should think she would have been very sorry."

"She's not the only one," I muttered.

Aunt Peg's eyes left the road as she turned to look at me. "Were you talking to me?"

It was no use. Attempting to modify Aunt Peg's behavior was like trying to reason with an Afghan Hound. Nothing changed, and everyone just ended up frustrated.

"Let's talk about something else," I said. I definitely needed a distraction.

"Edward March," Aunt Peg said immediately. I got the impression that she'd only been waiting for me to give her an opening. "The more I find out about that man, the less I like him. Maybe the two of us should go pay him a visit."

"You make it sound so civilized." I leveled her a look. "I know you better than that. What you really want to do is read him the riot act."

"What's wrong with that? It certainly sounds as though somebody ought to."

Leave it to Aunt Peg to volunteer.

"Somebody," I agreed. "But not you. Don't forget, you just told India that you would keep her confidence. So you can hardly go running to Edward and yell at him about a story that you're not supposed to know."

"If we hadn't consented, India wouldn't have told us. So there you are. I'm quite certain that oaths given under duress don't count."

"Kind of like speed limits?"

"When you get a notion, you are as tenacious as a dog with a marrowbone." Aunt Peg frowned in annoyance. I was glad to see, however, that her foot had eased up slightly on the gas pedal.

Half an hour later, we both arrived home in one piece. Aunt Peg and Sam decided to sit down over lunch and plot Augie's future show career. I reminded them that they needed to consider Davey's input. Both of them agreed with me, but that didn't slow them down for a minute.

Two devoted breeders dazzled by the potential of a pretty new puppy? Augie was simply too much temptation to ignore. He was like a shiny new toy they couldn't resist taking out of the box and playing with, even though it didn't belong to them. I grumbled under my breath and left them to it.

While they sat down and went to work, I gave Julia Davis a call. She'd been in my thoughts since we'd met, and I hoped she was doing well. But beyond that, I also wanted to hear what she had to say about the things that Sherm and I had discussed. I wondered whether filing a claim against Andrew's estate had been her idea or that of her crusading lawyer, and whether or not she'd thought through the ramifications of taking such an action.

As I'd hoped, Julia was home and agreed to see me.

I stuck my head in the kitchen and waved good-bye. Sam and Peg were hunched together over a dog show calendar, penciling in notations under various dates. Kevin was munching happily on a carrot. At some point it would probably occur to the three of them that they were hungry, and Sam would fix a proper meal. Or not.

He looked up when I said good-bye. "Where are you going?"

"Norwalk. I won't be gone long."

It did not escape my notice—or Sam's—that Aunt Peg used that moment of inattention to stealthily erase a note he had just made.

"Sounds good." He got up, walked over to the desk, and replaced his pencil with an indelible pen.

"You've got Kevin," I pointed out.

"I know." Still distracted, Sam looked around, saw his son pushing a Matchbox car across the floor, and pointed. "Right there. We're good."

I could only hope. Since the adults in the room outnumbered the child two to one—make that seven to two if you counted on the Poodles' help—presumably the level of supervision would prove adequate.

In the week since I'd last seen Julia's apartment, not much had changed. With its unpacked boxes, bare walls, and meager assortment of mismatched furniture, the living situation still had the look of a temporary arrangement. The only new addition was a spindle-back rocking chair painted a deep shade of blue. It sat in a shaft of sunlight beside the small living-room window.

Julia had been slender before; now she looked positively skinny. Her pale skin was drawn tight across her features, and there were new hollows beneath her cheeks. Her wrists, extending out from the sleeves of her chunky sweater, appeared frail and bony.

"Are you all right?" I asked. I took off my coat and tossed it on top of a box.

"Well enough, I guess. Pregnancy is kicking my butt. I thought I was supposed to be glowing. When does that part start?"

"Don't ask me," I said. "I never got there. I

feel like I ought to make you a sandwich or something."

"Not much point. I wouldn't be able to keep it down."

"Crackers?"

"Had those for breakfast."

Been there, I thought.

I crossed the room and had a look at the rocker. "This is nice."

"Thank you. It was a gift from a friend."

"Sherm Yablonsky?"

"Yes." Julia sounded surprised. "How did you know that?"

"I saw him arriving when I was on my way out last time I was here. And then a couple of days ago I went to talk to him about Andrew, and he mentioned that the two of you had been in touch."

Julia took a seat on the couch. I walked over and joined her.

"Sherm's a great guy," she said. "He's been a big help to me."

"I'm glad you have someone on your side," I told her honestly.

She studied my expression. "That sentence sounds like it should end with the word *but.*"

"I just think that you ought to make your own decisions about what you want to do next. I hope you won't let yourself be talked into anything that doesn't seem right to you."

"Sherm told you about the lawsuit," Julia said flatly.

"And the claim against Andrew's estate. He seemed very pleased with himself. He said it was all his idea."

"What's wrong with that?"

"Nothing, except that Sherm is a lawyer. And from the looks of his office, he's one who's in need of business. It's probably debatable whether or not he has your best interests at heart."

Julia laughed softly. "My business isn't the kind that Sherm needs. I'm not even paying him."

"Not yet," I allowed. "But if you win, I'm sure he'll be entitled to a portion of the proceeds."

"Well . . . yes. That's the way it will work."

"Edward March will be a formidable legal adversary. Sherm may well find that he's in over his head, and by the time that happens, you'll have lost your chance to settle things amicably. Why make an enemy of March if you don't have to? Once your baby is born, maybe this can all be resolved in a less confrontational way."

I'd learned only that morning that March had contributed to the care and upbringing of Maribeth's child. Even though there'd been extenuating circumstances in that case, it still gave me hope that he could be convinced to do the same for Julia's baby.

"Edward and I are already on opposing sides," Julia said, her expression hardening. "And none of that was my doing. Don't make me out to be the bad guy here, because I'm not."

"I know that," I said. "I just thought maybe if you tried talking to Edward one more time, before Sherm has a chance to build a wall between the two of you—"

"He won't see me."

"Excuse me?"

"I did try. I called. I even asked Charlotte to put in a good word for me. None of it helped. Edward said that Andrew had made his feelings clear when he broke up with me, and that he intended to respect his son's wishes."

So much for wanting to play the mediator. Now I was angry on Julia's behalf, too. "That's bullshit!"

"Of course it is. But there's the truth, and then there's Edward's truth. The only thing that matters to Edward is what he wants to believe."

Julia picked at a loose thread in the hem of her sweater. Her nails were unpolished and bitten short; her cuticles were ragged. "I was talking to an old friend of his a couple weeks ago, and she said the same thing. Edward doesn't even care whether or not he's right. He just wants to get his own way."

Unfortunately, that sounded about right.

"Who told you that?" I asked.

"Charlotte's mother. Do you know her?"

I nodded.

"I stayed with Charlotte for a few days before I got this place. One night her mom dropped by."

"Did you tell her you were pregnant?"

"Not on purpose." Julia grimaced at the memory. "I was in the bathroom, puking my guts out, when Maribeth arrived. Right away she went all maternal on me. She wanted to know if I was sick and what my symptoms were. Believe me, it was easier just to confess the real reason."

Looking for a sympathetic reception, Julia had certainly landed in the right place, I mused. Her next words confirmed that thought.

"Maribeth was wonderful to me," she said. "Especially when Charlotte told her why I was there. She was furious on my behalf. I appreciated the support, even though I didn't think I needed it. At the time I just figured that everything would be back to normal in a day or two, and Andrew and I would be back together."

Worried by her fingers, the thread abruptly pulled loose. Julia continued to tug, and several stitches unraveled. A small hole appeared, and Julia stared at it intently. She looked uncertain what to do next.

"You were that sure that you'd be going back to Andrew," I said, "even though you knew by then that your relationship wasn't as solid as you had previously thought?"

"What are you talking about?" Julia's gaze lifted.

"Sherm mentioned a woman named Miranda."

"Miranda was nobody."

"That's not what he thought."

"Sherm's always been a sucker for a pretty face." Julia's tone was dismissive. "It's not surprising that he was impressed."

"And yet he wasn't the one involved with her. Andrew was."

"*Involved?* No way. Maybe he was briefly infatuated, but that's all it was. The only commitment Andrew made was to me."

"So Miranda was just a fling. Even so, you must have been pretty upset. Especially since you were pregnant with Andrew's child."

"Sure I was upset," Julia said. "But I understood, too."

I stared incredulously. "That's big of you. In your shoes I don't think I'd have been nearly as complacent."

"You didn't know Andrew, did you?"

"We met briefly," I said. "But no, I didn't really know him."

"He was just like his father in a lot of ways. Andrew always had to be the one in charge. He had to make the decisions. I like a forceful guy, but marriage is a partnership, you know?"

I nodded.

"Andrew was taking his time getting used to that idea. I think he was afraid that when we got married, he'd be giving up some of his control.

And that made him uncomfortable. So maybe he needed to rebel a little just to prove to himself that he was still his own man."

Or maybe having girlfriends on the side and tossing Julia out of his house was Andrew's way of telling her that he was planning to rebel *a lot,* I thought. Julia saw herself as tolerant and understanding. To me, it was beginning to look more like she'd been missing the Big Picture.

"From the way you describe him, Andrew doesn't sound like someone who could be coerced into doing something he didn't want to do," I said.

Julia's hand went to her stomach. "You don't get it. I wasn't trying to coerce Andrew. Having a child together was something we'd both dreamed of. Maybe the timing was a little unexpected, but Andrew would have come around. I'm sure of it."

"According to Sherm, Andrew wasn't ready to settle down. Even though he was living with you, he was still seeing other women."

"Sherm doesn't know what he's talking about."

"He was Andrew's best friend."

"So he says." Julia's tone was sharp. "The only thing still holding those two together was nostalgia for their shared past. He and Andrew had almost nothing in common anymore. Sherm knew that, and he resented everything about Andrew. He envied Andrew his successful career, his position in his father's company, even his cars."

"What Sherm resented was the fact that Andrew had you," I said quietly.

"That's not true." The denial was swift. Julia didn't even stop to think before blurting it out.

"You know it is."

"No, I don't."

"Sherm is in love with you."

Julia closed her eyes and shook her head, as if she wanted to block me out completely.

"That's why Sherm's been so helpful since Andrew died, checking up on you and bringing you gifts," I said. "Sherm is happy that Andrew's gone. Now he can have you all to himself."

"You're wrong," Julia replied. "It's not what you think."

"Then tell me what it is."

"Sherm . . ." She stopped and blew out a breath. "Okay, maybe he has a little crush on me. But that's not my fault. I've never encouraged him, not even once. Sherm was just always around. It seemed like we could never get rid of him. Sometimes he used to tell me things. That's how I found out about Miranda. Sherm told me."

"It sounds to me like he was trying to drive a wedge between the two of you."

"I don't know. Maybe he was. I never thought about it before. I guess I always hoped that Andrew would be a little jealous when Sherm paid attention to me, but he never was. He just thought it was funny."

Julia stopped and frowned. "That night when Andrew and I argued and he told me to get out? I said, 'It's cold and dark out there. Where do you expect me to go?' But Andrew just laughed. He said, 'Why don't you go to Sherm? You know he'll take you in.' "

"But you didn't."

"No, of course not. I would never have done that. I called Charlotte. She let me sleep on her couch."

"The morning that Andrew was killed, do you know where Sherm was?"

Julia chewed on her lip, considering her reply. "Right before he left the cottage, Andrew took out his phone and called Sherm. That was his way of ending the argument, of telling me that he didn't want to talk to me anymore. All I know is that Sherm was on the other end of the line. He could have been anywhere."

"He could have been at the end of the driveway," I said.

Julia didn't disagree with me. Instead, she crossed her arms over her chest, clasped her shoulders in her hands, and shivered.

Chapter 25

I was back in my car once again when my phone rang. It was Charlotte.

I couldn't hear what she was saying. For some reason, she was whispering.

"You have to speak up," I said. "I'm driving, and I can't hear you."

"You have to come," she said. "It's important."

Oh Lord, I thought. We'd been here before.

"Where are you?" I asked.

"Westport."

Only one town over. That was good. I was beginning to feel like I lived in my car.

"You're with Edward?"

"Not exactly."

I sighed and pulled over onto the shoulder. "Charlotte, tell me what's going on."

"I have something to show you. Something you really need to see."

"What is it?"

"Please," she implored. "I can't do this over the phone. You have to come here."

I hadn't planned on making another stop, but considering that I was already in Norwalk, this wouldn't be too far out of my way. Besides, even though only two days had passed since I'd last talked to March, a lot had happened in the meantime. It seemed to me that it was time for him to call Detective Wygod and arrange another meeting. After I saw Charlotte, I'd sit down with March and bring him up to speed.

Plan made, I pulled back out onto the road.

"Tell me where you are," I said to Charlotte.

"I'm at Andrew's cottage. You know where it is, right? We saw it the other day, when we were out walking."

"Got it," I said. "Sit tight. I'll be there in fifteen minutes."

The agitation I'd heard in Charlotte's voice made me nervous, and I made the trip in ten. I'd never used Andrew's driveway before, but I'd seen it on earlier visits. Like the main entrance to the property, it was at least a quarter mile long and lined with mature trees whose naked branches snaked upward like gnarled fingers reaching toward the gray sky.

Charlotte had told me that Andrew liked his privacy, and he certainly would have had it here, I thought when the cottage finally came into view. The small home was tucked into a remote corner of the expansive property. Whoever had built it— possibly Andrew himself—must have wanted to put as much distance between it and the main house as possible.

The driveway came to an abrupt end just outside

the front door. A dark blue SUV was parked to one side, and I pulled the Volvo up next to it.

The cottage was made of stone, with beveled-glass windows framed by thick wooden shutters. The red oak door looked equally solid. When I lifted my hand and knocked, I couldn't hear a sound from within.

Nor did Charlotte answer. I knocked a second time and waited another minute. Even sheltered in the hollow, I still felt the bitter cold. A north wind, blowing down off the hill, rattled the branches high above me. I had left my gloves and hat in the car and thought briefly about going back for them.

Instead, I reached out and tried the doorknob. To my surprise, it turned easily. I pushed the door open and let myself inside.

The room I entered was lit only by the weak sunlight filtering in through the windows, but I could see that it was comfortably furnished. Two plump love seats faced each other in front of a stone fireplace, and a rough-hewn coffee table sat between them. There was a dining area on one side of the room. An arched doorway beyond that appeared to lead to the kitchen. One wall was lined with bookshelves; another held an enormous flat-screen TV.

A fine layer of dust covered every visible surface, and there was a faintly musty smell in the air. The temperature inside the cottage wasn't much warmer than that outside. I knew that the police had been there and had performed a search; it looked as though the place had simply been closed up and left alone ever since.

"Charlotte?" I called out. "It's Melanie. Are you here?"

"Coming! I'll be right down."

A narrow stairway led to an upper floor. Even as Charlotte replied, she was already running down the steps. I stared at her as she approached; I couldn't seem to help it. Even knowing her bond with Edward March, I still couldn't see any trace of him within her.

"That was quick." Charlotte's cheeks were flushed, and her gaze quickly shifted away. "You made good time."

"You said it was important. What were you doing upstairs?"

"Just looking around."

The cottage had belonged to Charlotte's half brother. Not that she'd ever known that. Under other circumstances—in a more normal family— she might have been a frequent visitor.

"Have you been here before?" I asked.

"Only when I let the police in. I waited outside until they were finished. I'd never been upstairs."

Charlotte's eyes were bright. Like me, she still had her coat on and fastened shut. Her hands were bare; she was twisting and untwisting her fingers together in front of her. I hadn't imagined her agitation on the phone; she still seemed ill at ease.

Something didn't feel quite right. I just couldn't figure out why. I nodded toward the stairway. "What's up there?"

"Andrew's bedroom. And another room, that he turned into a home office. I asked Mr. March last week if he wanted me to start packing things up, but he said to just leave it alone. He didn't even want to think about it."

"So why are we here?" I asked.

"I wanted someplace where we could talk in private. I have something to show you."

Charlotte reached into her pocket and withdrew a cell phone. She held out her hand and offered it to me. I took the phone and pushed a few buttons, trying to turn it on. Nothing happened. The battery was dead.

Charlotte was watching me closely, as if something momentous had happened and I was supposed to form an appropriate response. I had no idea what that might be. Without access to what the device contained, I might as well have been holding a lump of lead.

"Whose phone is this?" I asked.

Charlotte dropped her voice to a whisper, even though we were the only two people there. "It's Andrew's."

It took a moment for the information to register. When it did, I drew a sharp breath.

"This is the *missing* phone?" I said, wanting to be absolutely clear. "The one that was supposed to have been with him when he died?"

Charlotte dipped her head in a nod.

"Are you sure?"

"Yes."

A frisson of shock rippled through me. This changed everything.

"Where did you find it?" I asked. "Was it upstairs? You have to tell the police."

"I can't," said Charlotte.

"Of course you can. This is huge. They need to know right away."

My thoughts pinballed in several directions at once. If the phone was still in the cottage, why hadn't the police found it during their search? And why had Julia told me that Andrew had been talking on the phone when he left to go running?

"That's why I asked you to come," said Charlotte. "I want you to take it to Detective Wygod."

"I'm not the one who found the phone," I told her. "The detective will want to talk to you, not me."

"That's the problem. I have nothing to say."

"Charlotte, think for a minute. One of the reasons the police assumed that Andrew's death wasn't an accident was because his phone—which should have been with him—was missing. But if it was never there to begin with—"

"I can't," she said again. She looked like she might be on the verge of tears.

I slowed down and tried to summon more patience than I felt. "All you have to do is tell Detective Wygod how you came to have Andrew's cell phone in your possession."

She shook her head stubbornly.

What was going on? What was Charlotte so afraid of?

"How about this?" I said. "I'll go with you."

She looked up hopefully. "You'll tell them that you found the phone?"

"No, I can't do that." My tone was absolutely firm. "I'm not going to lie to the police."

"But they know that you've been asking questions. So now you can tell them that you found something."

I blew out a long breath. In the cold, the vapor floated in front of me like a cloud. "Charlotte, what is this all about? Is this really Andrew's phone?"

"Of course it is. Just like I told you."

"Then why won't you take it to the police? This is information they're looking for. Detective Wygod will be happy to hear from you."

"Maybe I can explain things better."

I whipped around at the unexpected sound of another voice, this one coming from behind me. Charlotte's mother, Maribeth, was standing at the top of the stairs.

So much for thinking that we were alone. And for believing that Charlotte had wanted to talk in private.

"I'm the one who found Andrew's phone." Maribeth's hand trailed along the banister as she walked down the steps to join us. "But given my past history with Edward, I have no intention of getting involved. That's why I asked Charlotte to deliver it to you."

I held out my hand, the cell phone nestled in my palm. "Then you're the one who needs to talk to Detective Wygod."

Maribeth glanced down at my outstretched hand. She made no move to take the phone from me.

Charlotte was staring hard at her mother. "What past history?" she asked. "I thought you and Mr. March used to be friends."

"It's nothing you need to worry about, sweetie. Melanie spoke with a friend of mine this morning. I'm afraid she was given information that should have been kept private."

"What information are you talking about?"

"Really, Charlotte, don't be tiresome. It's none of your concern." Maribeth stepped over to her daughter's side, wrapped an arm around her shoulder, and squeezed gently. "It's time for you to go now. I'm sure Edward must be wondering where you are. Melanie and I have a few things to discuss, and then I'll be on my way, too."

Maribeth walked Charlotte past me to the door. She stood in the doorway and watched as her daughter began to walk away, tramping through the snow up the incline, toward the meadow that led to March's house.

So the car belonged to Maribeth, I thought. And she was the one who had had the missing cell phone. Seeing the device in Charlotte's hand, I'd assumed that she had found it in the cottage earlier.

Idly, I flipped the phone end over end in my palm. For a minute it felt as though my thoughts were tumbling and resetting, as well. The picture I thought I'd been looking at disappeared. A new one emerged in its place.

Abruptly, my breath caught in my throat as I realized how wrong that earlier assumption had been. Julia wasn't the one who had lied to me. Andrew *had* taken his phone with him when he left that morning. And the person who had picked it up on the road outside and had taken it away with her was right here with me now in Andrew's cottage.

Maribeth waited until Charlotte had disappeared over the top of the rise. Then she came inside and shut the door.

"It was you," I said.

"Pardon me?" Maribeth inclined her head to one side. Her expression was one of polite bafflement. I wasn't buying it for a minute.

"It was your car that hit Andrew. That was why you had his cell phone. You've had it all along."

I half expected Maribeth to tell me I was wrong, but she didn't. Instead she sighed. "Ah, Melanie, things would have been so much easier if you could have just done what Charlotte asked you to do."

"Take the phone and lie to the police? I don't think so."

"That's your problem. You think too much."

She walked past me toward the fireplace and sat down on one of the love seats. Her hand gestured toward the second sofa opposite. "Have a seat. Let's see what we can do to fix this."

Fix this? I thought incredulously. How was that even remotely possible? Could Maribeth seriously think that murder was an event that could be mended, like a broken bicycle chain or a lost electric bill?

Apparently she did. Maribeth was looking very relaxed, settled in the far corner of the love seat. Her shoulders reclined against the sofa's cushioned back; her hand was draped casually over its high-curved arm.

Judging by her demeanor, she truly seemed to believe that we were going to discuss the problem and come up with a solution. And if Maribeth wanted to talk, I was game. I had questions that needed answers.

She watched with a small smile as I sidled in her direction and took a seat in the near corner of the other love seat. Maribeth might have been relaxed, but I was not. I sat up straight and kept my feet on the floor. I perched on the edge of the cushion and rested my hands in my lap.

There was a coffee table and several feet of distance between us. That seemed like a safe enough margin.

"I know why you were angry at Edward," I said. "But what was your grievance with Andrew? Why would you want to harm him?"

"I didn't," Maribeth replied. "I didn't mean for any of that to happen. All I wanted to do was talk to Andrew."

I lifted a brow skeptically. "Outside, on the road? In the middle of winter?"

"That's where he was when I arrived," Maribeth said with a small shrug. "I can hardly be blamed for that. I was on my way here, to this cottage. I had hoped to catch him before he left for work. And then, suddenly, there he was, running along the road."

I was pretty sure I knew the answer, but I asked, anyway. "What did you want to talk to Andrew about?"

"Julia, of course. Her situation was shameful."

"It was the same situation you'd found yourself in twenty-some years earlier. Was that why you were upset?"

Maribeth's eyes narrowed. "India shouldn't have talked to you behind my back."

"But she told me the truth, didn't she?"

"Yes," she admitted quietly. "Edward is Charlotte's father."

"Why did you never tell her that?"

"How could I?" Maribeth demanded. She paused for a minute, then asked, "Do you have children?"

"Yes, two."

"Then you know that you'd do anything in the world to keep them from being hurt."

I nodded in agreement.

"How could I tell my little girl that her father was alive and well, and living nearby—and that the only reason that we had no contact with him was because he had no interest in her?" Maribeth's expression was pained. "Edward didn't want anything to do with my baby when I was pregnant, and nothing changed after she was born. What purpose would it have served for Charlotte to know that her own father would have been happier if she'd never existed?"

I'm not in the habit of agreeing with murderers. But put that way, I could see her point. "So what did you say to Andrew?"

"Almost nothing," Maribeth replied grimly. "I had a speech all worked out in my mind, but he didn't want to hear any of it. Maybe I was naive. I thought I could make Andrew understand that

345

his decisions impacted others besides himself and Julia—that there was a child's life at stake, as well. When I saw him on the road, I pulled over, rolled down my window, and asked him to get in the car so we could talk."

"I take it he didn't do that?"

"He barely even paused. Even when he spoke to me, he was still jogging up and down in place. Like I wasn't even important enough for him to interrupt his run."

"He had just had another fight with Julia," I told her. "Andrew was already angry before you even got there."

"That's not my fault," Maribeth replied sharply. "He asked what I wanted to talk to him about, and when I started to tell him, he just smirked and ran away. I couldn't believe Andrew would turn his back on me like that. So I drove after him. I never meant to hurt him. I only wanted to get his attention."

"But you hit him with your car," I said.

"That was an accident. I only meant to tap him, just something hard enough to make him turn around. But then the car skidded on the snow, and I lost control."

I didn't know if Maribeth's story was the truth or whether it was a more palatable version of events that she'd concocted after the fact. Or maybe it was simply what she wanted to believe.

In any case, the supposedly innocent tap Maribeth had intended to deliver had resulted in serious injury. And rather than seeking help, she had left Andrew bleeding and unconscious by the side of the road. Maribeth was going to have a difficult time explaining all of that away as an unfortunate accident.

"Then what happened?" I asked.

She shook her head. "I'm not really sure. I must have been in shock. I got out of the car to see if Andrew was all right."

"But he wasn't."

"No. He was unconscious and . . ." She spread her hands helplessly, unable to convey the horror of what she'd seen.

"Why didn't you call for help?"

"I was going to. . . ."

I waited a few seconds for her to continue. When she remained silent, I said, "But you didn't."

"No," Maribeth said softly. "I looked down at Andrew, and my vision blurred for a few seconds. Suddenly, instead of Andrew's face, all I could see was Charlotte. In that moment, the two of them seemed so very much alike. Except that Andrew was the sibling who had been given everything, while my little girl had nothing. Andrew was running his father's company. Charlotte was nothing more than his glorified gofer."

A position that she herself had placed her

daughter in, I thought. It didn't seem like the right time to remind Maribeth of that.

"All at once I realized that if Andrew was gone, Charlotte would be the only child. She would be all that Edward had left. Even *he* couldn't continue to turn his back on her then."

"So you took Andrew's phone and left him lying there."

"The sins of the father . . . ," Maribeth said softly. Her voice trailed away. Then she gave her head a sharp, angry shake and added firmly, "He got what he deserved."

Chapter 26

Was she talking about the father or the son? I wondered. Or maybe it didn't matter which one. Both had suffered from Maribeth's revenge.

I looked at her across the expanse of the table between us. "You must know we can't fix this. You're going to have to tell the police what happened."

"No," she replied calmly. "I'm not."

Later I thought about that: how composed she had sounded, when I might have expected a display of anger or fear. But Maribeth was a better actress than I gave her credit for. Or maybe my instincts were rusty. Because the fact that she remained so unruffled meant that I wasn't nearly as apprehensive about the situation as I should have been.

Since I was sitting across from someone who'd done what she had, my reflexes should have been on high alert. Instead, in the midst of this oddly civilized conversation, they were a beat slow.

"It would be better if you told them," I said. "But if you don't, I will."

We were finished here, I thought. I glanced down to check the position of the coffee table, braced my hands on my knees, and started to rise. Unbalanced for only a few seconds, I saw a flash of movement out of the corner of my eye and felt a whisper's breath of air brush against my cheek.

And suddenly realized the magnitude of my mistake.

Maribeth hadn't relaxed in the far corner of the love seat to be comfortable. She'd done it because that gave the hand she'd hung so casually over the side of the sofa access to the supply of dried wood stacked beside the fireplace.

Now she capitalized on my brief moment of inattention and came up swinging. Maribeth's crimson-tipped fingers looked incongruous wrapped around a thick, bark-covered log. Momentum carried the sturdy piece of wood toward my head with bruising force.

I ducked quickly to one side, tangled a leg in the

table, and stumbled sideways. Reflexively, I threw up an arm. It was too late and not enough. The blow landed just behind my ear. I felt it as both a lacerating source of pain and also a heavy weight that sent me sprawling.

My knees began to crumple, as if my bones had melted away and there was nothing left to support my weight. Spots danced before my eyes. I wanted to brush them away. I wanted the searing pain to stop. I wanted to kick myself for allowing this to happen.

Then none of that mattered. Everything went black.

Cold. So cold.

I think it was the shivering that woke me up. My teeth were chattering so hard that my jaw hurt. My body was shaking in place. The force of that involuntary movement was bouncing my head on the hardwood floor.

If I hadn't felt like I was going to throw up, I might have smiled at the irony. One blow to the head had knocked me out. Another brought me back.

Damn, it was freezing. Gingerly, I rolled onto my side. The small rotation was enough to make bile rise in my throat. Tears leaked from the corners of my eyes as I retched on the floor, then wiped my mouth on the sleeve of my sweater.

Sweater? I thought, my brain processing

information sluggishly as the rough wool scraped at my lips. That wasn't right. Where was my parka?

With effort, I tried to remember. It had been cold in the house when I arrived. Almost as cold inside as out. I knew I hadn't taken my jacket off. I hadn't even unzipped it. Now it was gone.

How long had I been unconscious? I wondered. Slowly, I tipped my head to one side and looked up at a window. It wasn't dark yet. That was good. Dusk arrived early in January, which meant that it must still be afternoon.

I settled back on the floor with an involuntary groan. I had a vague memory of piercing pain. Now my head just throbbed.

Cautiously, I reached a hand upward. My fingertips probed the spot on the side of my head where the blow had landed. My hair was sticky and matted together. My fingers came away stained with blood.

Oddly, that discovery was almost a relief. At least it explained why I was having so much trouble putting two coherent thoughts together.

Where was Maribeth? Gone, I hoped. Gone for good . . .

I closed my eyes just for a minute.

Once again, the cold woke me up. It had seeped into every corner of my body now, its progress as relentless as it was ominous. My fingers had stiffened, even my bones shook from the icy chill.

It wasn't just my head anymore: now my whole body hurt.

I was still lying on the floor.

I had to get up, I realized. I had to move.

If I didn't, I would die right there where Maribeth had left me.

Just as she must have intended, I thought. That was why she'd had Charlotte lure me to this isolated cabin. Here it was possible that my death could be explained away as an accident.

Maribeth didn't have to kill me. The cold would do that. She only had to leave me. Just like she'd done with Andrew.

Idiot, I told myself. *You used to be smarter than this.*

That galvanizing thought helped me push myself up into a sitting position. Back braced against the table, I took several deep breaths, concentrating hard until the nausea passed. Now that I was upright, I hoped I'd be able to think better. Surprisingly, I actually could.

Phone! There was a cell phone in my purse. I just had to find it.

The light around me was growing dimmer. Outside, the winter sun was setting. There wasn't much time before I'd be left in total darkness.

Marshaling every bit of energy I could muster, I leaned heavily against the love seat and used the table to lever myself to my feet. For a minute I simply stood and swayed in place. The room swam wildly around me, colors and objects blurring together as they looped and whirled. I closed my eyes to blot out the sight and tried to find a centered spot.

When I opened them again, I was still dizzy but feeling slightly steadier. Slowly, I turned from side to side and looked around the room. My purse, with cell phone and car keys, was nowhere to be seen. Like my parka, it had disappeared.

Well, damn.

There was a light switch on the wall near the dining area. Bracing my hands on passing furniture to maintain my balance, I shuffled across the room and flipped it up. Nothing happened. As I'd suspected, the utilities that powered the cabin had been turned off.

I peered out a nearby window and saw my car, still parked in the driveway. But without my keys, the Volvo might as well have been missing, too. It was of no more use to me than the powerless light switch.

Think! I told myself. *Think of something. Anything.* There had to be a way out of this predicament. If I could get my brain to work, I could find it.

I had begun to shiver again. The vibrations shuddered through my body in relentless waves. I wondered how much time I had before the bitter cold succeeded in completely draining my ability to respond.

Already I could feel myself starting to grow numb. I knew I needed to fight back, but the loss of sensation offered its own comfort, tempting me to give in. My addled brain felt lethargic, indifferent. It would be just that easy to lie down and go to sleep again.

I gazed out the window once more. In the fading light, the accumulation of snow looked like a calm, unbroken sea. I could chart a course, I thought fancifully. I could leave the cottage and walk to the main house. There would be people there . . . and warmth.

But even as I formulated the plan, I knew I'd never be able to make the trek. The cold, the dark, the distance, and my lack of adequate attire would all work against me. Add to that a bitch of a headache, which would muddle my sense of direction as surely as it was muddling my thoughts. If I left the dubious shelter of the cottage, who knew where I might end up?

I turned away from the window and faced the room again. My eyes went immediately to the fireplace. Where there was one piece of firewood, there ought to be more, right? I knew how to build a fire. I lived in Connecticut. I'd done it all my life.

Equilibrium slowly beginning to stabilize, I staggered back across the cottage. Skirting carefully around the love seats, I saw a small pile of firewood banked beside the hearth. Perfect. Now all I had to do was find a lighter.

Ten frustrating minutes later, I was forced to concede that Maribeth had left nothing to chance. If the small abode had harbored a supply of matches or a fire starter, she must have taken them with her when she left.

The disappointment felt like another blow. It sapped what little drive I had left. My head was still throbbing. My lips felt cracked and swollen. And I was quickly running out of options. Soon it would no longer matter if I came up with a good idea. I would simply be too cold to implement it.

My gaze flickered in the direction of the narrow staircase that led to the second floor. Considering my precarious balance, I wasn't at all sure I could navigate the steep steps without falling. But Andrew's bedroom was up there. Surely, a bed would have a comforter or a blanket. Something I could wrap around me to ward off the biting cold a little longer . . .

I should have been moving toward the stairway. Instead, my legs wobbled under me, then gave out. I sank downward and sat unsteadily on the floor. The hardwood seemed to tilt beneath me, and I closed my eyes. A pervasive feeling of weariness overtook me; I just didn't want to struggle anymore.

And then I heard it.

Somewhere nearby a dog was barking. It was the joyous, deep-throated cry of a big dog on the run. I smiled faintly at the sound, my thoughts drifting contentedly with no particular ambition or purpose. Dogs always make me happy.

Then slowly my eyelids fluttered open. The dog's voice was carried clearly by the crisp, cold air outside. And suddenly I realized that it sounded familiar. It sounded like March's Irish Setter, Robin.

Surely, I had to be imagining things, I thought. Maybe I was dreaming.

The dog barked again. Before the sound had even faded, I was already moving. With effort, I pushed myself up off the floor. Once more, the room spun. I swallowed heavily and kept going. Stumbling on feet I couldn't feel, I crossed the cottage to the front door.

My hand reached out and clasped the icy metal doorknob. My fingers, stiff and aching, wrapped around it. I took a breath, drew the door open, and stepped out onto the stoop.

The frigid cold outside hit me like a shock wave. The biting wind I'd felt earlier was still careening through the trees. It swirled down into the hollow and slammed right into me. I hadn't thought it was possible to be any colder, but I was wrong. The powerful gust knifed through my clothing like it wasn't even there. My skin felt like it was on fire.

I stumbled back in surprise, lost my balance, and ended up crumpled on the front step. Now that I was outside, the dog I'd heard only moments before had quieted. All around me was only silence.

I stared hard into the murky darkness. A pale moon had begun to rise, and the winter night looked oddly peaceful. The only illumination was provided by the soft sheen of moonlight reflecting on the snow.

Then, at the top of the rise, a movement caught my eye. It took me a few seconds to figure out what I was seeing. The shadowy motion resolved itself into a figure—a person approaching the crest of the incline from the opposite side. A moment later, a dog bounded up alongside.

I saw her only in silhouette, but the outline of Robin's elegant frame was unmistakable. The Irish Setter lifted her nose to the wind and gave a small woof.

"Down here!" I yelled. "Help!"

The slender figure turned to look toward the cottage, and I saw that it was Charlotte. She lifted her arm and trained the beam of a powerful flashlight in my direction.

"Oh my God, Melanie!" she cried. "What happened to you?"

Together, she and Robin half ran, half skidded down the icy slope. The setter reached the bottom first. She raced across the driveway and bounded right into me. Another day I'd have had the strength to meet her charge. That night, she simply bowled me over.

The greeting was all I could have asked for. Robin felt warm and vibrant and everything I was not. She felt wonderful. Charlotte came running close behind.

"Robin, get down!" She grabbed the setter's collar and pulled her off. "Melanie, why are you still here? Aren't you cold? What are you doing on the ground?"

The barrage of questions was entirely too much for my muddled brain to process. I tried to speak, but it was difficult to push the words out.

"We have . . . to talk," I managed to say finally. "But first . . . but first . . . I'm freezing. I need . . . to get warm."

"Of course." Charlotte sounded perplexed. "How long have you been out here? Where's your coat? Where are your gloves? Why are you sitting in the snow?"

"A long . . . story," I said. "Help me . . . get up."

Charlotte extended a hand downward. It wasn't nearly enough. I still couldn't find the strength to propel myself to my feet. Beginning to look alarmed, she hunkered down beside me.

"What's the matter? Are you hurt?"

"Yes." My hand rose to touch the spot behind my ear. "Bleeding."

"Stay right there," said Charlotte. As if I had a choice. She whipped out a cell phone and began to dial.

"Call Detective Wygod," I told her.

358

"You need a doctor."

"That too. Wygod first . . . It's important."

Charlotte didn't look convinced, but she dialed the Westport Police Department. As she spoke, Robin returned to my side. The setter pushed her nose into my face and blew out a heated breath.

I tunneled my hands in her coat and pulled her close. Robin climbed into my lap and pressed her body against mine. I had my arms around a big warm dog. Everything was going to be all right now.

Chapter 27

"Detective Wygod will meet us at the house." Charlotte shoved her phone back in her pocket. "Let's get you into your car."

"No keys," I said. "They were . . . in my purse."

"Where's your purse?"

"Gone."

That carned me a hard look. "Your parka?"

"Charlotte . . . we need to talk."

She didn't answer. Instead, she walked around behind me, looped her arms beneath mine, and hoisted me to my feet. Lighting our way with the flashlight, she walked me into the cottage and deposited me on a love seat.

"Be right back."

With an agility I could only envy, Charlotte dashed up the stairs. A minute later she returned holding a large sweatshirt and a polar fleece jacket. A puffy down comforter, thrown over her shoulder, trailed along behind.

She added the layers to my attire one by one, dressing me with brisk efficiency, as if I were a child who'd been left in her care. When she was finished, Robin hopped up onto the love seat and climbed back into my lap. The setter seemed to understand that I needed her there.

Charlotte stepped around behind me. She trained the beam of the flashlight on the side of my head and sucked in a breath.

"You were here with my mother." Her tone was flat, devoid of emotion, as if she had already begun to think things through and knew what I was going to say.

"Yes."

"She did this to you?"

"Charlotte, there are things you don't know—"

"Obviously." It was hard to tell in the unlit room, but it sounded as though her voice caught on a sob. She leaned down and gathered me into an awkward hug. "Melanie, I'm so sorry. I had no idea. . . ."

"I know." If my arms hadn't been bundled up inside the comforter, I'd have hugged her back. "It's not your fault."

"I shouldn't have left you here with her. Maybe on some level I already knew that. But she's my mother. . . ."

"I know," I said again.

"She gave me Andrew's phone and told me to bring you here and give it to you. I thought that was all she wanted. When she left the cottage, she called and told me that you were on your way home, too."

I nodded. Once again, Maribeth had been careful to cover all the bases.

"So what brought you back?" I asked.

"I didn't understand what was going on. I asked her why she had Andrew's phone, and she wouldn't answer me. She was treating me like I was still a child, like she thought I should just take her word for things no matter what she said. But I couldn't do that. Not anymore."

Charlotte lifted a hand and scrubbed it across her face. "I told Mr. March I was going to take Robin for a walk. I needed to be alone. I wanted to think about things and decide what I was going to do next. But as soon as we got outside, Robin took off. She came running down here to the cottage. All I did was follow her."

"I'm glad you did."

"Me too," Charlotte said softly.

After that, things seemed to move quickly. Although I probably wasn't in the best position to judge. Considering the severity of the concussion I'd sustained, my perception of time was unreliable at best.

Charlotte left Robin with me in the cottage while she ran back to the main house to intercept Detective Wygod. It must have taken longer, but it seemed like only minutes had passed before the two of them returned. By then I was considerably warmer and a good deal more lucid.

Nevertheless, the detective took one look at me, bundled me into the back of his car, and headed for the hospital. We spoke along the way.

I told him about Maribeth's past connection with Edward March and the truth about Charlotte's paternity. Then I skipped ahead to Julia's pregnancy and the reason that Andrew's callous behavior had so enraged Maribeth. I ended with the argument that had left Andrew lying in the snow by the side of the road.

Some things about that conversation remain fuzzy in my mind. I'm pretty sure that somewhere along the way I informed Detective Wygod that my son had a new puppy named Augie. I might have also mentioned that my aunt believed in free love in the sixties.

Despite the extraneous details, the detective seemed to take everything in stride. He had nearly all the same pieces that I did; he'd just been looking at them in a different order. But once everything was properly aligned, he immediately knew what I was talking about.

By the time Detective Wygod delivered me to the emergency room, Charlotte was already giving a statement to another officer. An arrest warrant was issued for Maribeth, who hired a lawyer and turned herself in later that night. She claimed that Andrew's death had been a tragic accident and that she had no knowledge whatsoever of what had happened to me.

Perhaps having learned her lesson when she kept Andrew's cell phone, Maribeth had left my parka and my purse, with phone and car keys, locked inside my car in the driveway. She insisted that I'd been fine when she left the cottage. It wasn't her fault, she maintained, if I'd been stupid enough to stumble around in the dark and injure myself.

I learned most of this from Sam the next morning. He had arrived at the emergency room as a doctor with very gentle hands was finishing putting four stitches in the side of my head. Luckily, I didn't have a skull fracture. I was only slightly dehydrated, and my body had returned to the normal temperature without incident.

Sam and the doctor shared a joke about my hard head, which I pretended not to hear. All of us were grateful that my injuries weren't worse. Sam took me home, tucked me into bed, and watched me like a hawk for several days.

By the time I surfaced again, Maribeth's lawyer had gotten her released on bail, and she was proclaiming her innocence to anyone who cared to listen. In the spirit of confession, Maribeth had told Charlotte the truth about her father the night I went to the hospital. That revelation, coming on top of everything else, was too much for Charlotte to process and she quit her job as March's assistant.

Three days later she came to see me. Though I'd told Sam repeatedly that he didn't need to treat me like an invalid, I found his desire to pamper me hard to resist. I was reading a book in the living room, Faith and Eve curled up contentedly on either side of me, when Charlotte arrived. Sam showed her in, then left the two of us alone.

"I'm glad you came," I said. "I wanted to say thank you in person."

Charlotte smiled wanly. "And I wanted to apologize."

"There's no need."

"I appreciate your saying that." Charlotte perched on the other end of the couch. Her hand reached out to stroke Eve's back. The Poodle's tail wagged gently in acknowledgment. "My mother . . . she's always had issues. But even so, I can't quite seem to wrap my head around everything that happened. She says Andrew's death was an accident."

I nodded. Maribeth was the only family

Charlotte had ever known. I wasn't about to tell her what to believe or not believe.

"So what now?" I asked.

Charlotte shrugged. "I guess I'll have to see. You heard I quit my job?"

"I did."

"Under the circumstances, I figured Mr. March was going to fire me, anyway. But . . ."

I pulled Faith over into my lap and waited.

"He says he doesn't blame me for what happened."

"Of course not," I told her. "Nobody does."

Charlotte shook her head. She didn't look entirely convinced.

"Mr. March wants me to come back," she said. "He says he needs help getting his house in order. That maybe it's time to finally throw out some old baggage and start fresh."

"Do you think he's speaking literally or figuratively?" I asked.

"Both, apparently. We talked about it."

"That sounds like a lot of work."

Unexpectedly, Charlotte smiled. "I think I'm ready for it. And besides, I really miss Robin. Who's going to walk her if I'm not there?"

So the two of them are back together again. Father and daughter are working on building a new relationship, one that's founded on truth this time. I think they're both enjoying figuring out what comes next.

The one thing Charlotte hasn't been able to do is convince March to let Julia move back into the cottage. It continues to sit empty. In the meantime, Julia has dropped the idea of a lawsuit and has put some distance between herself and Sherm. That recommendation came from Bonnie Raye. It turns out that now that Bonnie's children are grown and gone, she has some extra room in her house and in her heart. Julia has gratefully left the small apartment in Norwalk and gained a Mother Hen.

As for me, I'm steering clear of Aunt Peg's pet projects for the foreseeable future. Between diapers to change, homework to oversee, and a new puppy to housebreak, I have plenty to keep me busy at home. If that makes my life sound dull, right now that suits me just fine.

Maybe someday Edward March will find another coauthor and *Puppy Love* will be published. If so, I'll put the book on my reading list. Right at the bottom, where it belongs.

Center Point Large Print
600 Brooks Road / PO Box 1
Thorndike ME 04986-0001 USA

(207) 568-3717

US & Canada:
1 800 929-9108
www.centerpointlargeprint.com